Losing Her Fear

Linda Fausnet

Published by Wannabe Pride 2018

Editing by Linda Hill
Cover Design by Chuck DeKett
Formatting by Polgarus Studio

FIRST EDITION.

Library of Congress Control Number: 2018912666
ISBN: 978-1-944043-30-8

This book is for anyone who has ever felt too poor to pursue his/her dream. I understand. I've been there. Your hills may be steeper, but they're not impossible to climb.

Don't give up.

Books by Linda Fausnet

Romance

The Gettysburg Ghost Series

Somebody's Darling
Darling Soldiers
Forever, Darling

The Wall Street to Broadway Series

Losing His Shirt
Losing His Cool
Losing Her Inhibitions
Losing Her Fear

Women's Fiction / Chick Lit

Singles Vs. Bridezillas

LGBT Fiction

Queen Henry (**All proceeds from this book go to the Harvey
Milk Foundation**)

Middle-Grade Fiction

The Joyville Sweat Sox

Chapter 1

I hummed to myself as I mopped the ladies' restroom, but I really wished I could sing at the top of my lungs. I loved to sing; it was such a glorious release for me. Singing was an expression of my deepest emotions. It made me feel alive. But I had nowhere to go to let loose the way I wanted to. I lived in a tiny apartment and I took the subway to work, so I was never really alone. Only the super rich could afford to own a car in New York City, so I took the subway. Oh, how I envied people who commuted by car. They could sing all the way to and from work.

As usual, I hummed "In My Own Little Corner" from the musical, *Rogers and Hammerstein's Cinderella*. It was my little inside joke. Fantasizing I was Cinderella made scrubbing toilets a bit more bearable. I had an active imagination, and picturing a handsome prince sweeping me off my feet and carrying me away from all this was my favorite pastime. I allowed myself to softly sing a few lyrics of the song, then quickly went back to quiet humming. I wasn't supposed to be noticed while doing my job. Instead, I was expected to play the part of the stereotypical Hispanic cleaning lady. Quiet and demure.

Invisible.

I worked in a fifteen-story high-rise in Manhattan full of high-powered executives. People rarely spoke to me here, and I often wondered if they thought I couldn't speak English because I have a bit of an accent. It was annoying, since I was born in the United States and was fluent in both Spanish and English.

Again, I had to force myself to quit singing as I mopped. Cringing, I remembered the time I'd been working late, and thinking I was alone, I actually sang out loud. One of the lady executives caught me when she walked into the restroom. God, that had been embarrassing.

Elyse was her name. She was absolutely beautiful. Tall and blond, with gorgeous blue eyes. She was one of the big-deal executives around here, and I was always kind of intimidated by her. But Elyse turned out to be incredibly sweet. She said I had a great voice, and she told me she had some friends in the musical theater business. Ever since then, she'd been gently prodding me to at least meet with her friends. It was kind of her to take an interest in me, but I had no intention of taking her up on her offer. Sure, I loved to sing, but there was no hope of ever doing it professionally. Most performers started acting and singing when they were kids. At the ripe old age of twenty-five, it was probably too late for me. Besides, I was flat broke. Sometimes I felt like all I ever did was work just to pay the rent and keep food in the fridge. I could never afford the acting and singing lessons I would need to make it onstage anywhere.

Still humming *Cinderella* songs, I opened one of the bathroom stalls so I could mop the floor. I let out a weary sigh when I saw the toilet was clogged. I grabbed the plunger from my cart and worked my magic. You never heard about Cinderella having to unclog toilets. Even my vivid fantasies couldn't make this feel glamorous. I set the plunger back on top of the cart and finished mopping the rest of the floor. After I was done with the ladies' restroom, I grabbed my cart and pushed it hard enough to open the door. The door opened all right, but the second it did, the toilet plunger fell off the cart.

And hit one of the male executives right in the stomach.

I gasped in horror.

Keith Foster. Why did it have to be Keith Foster?

People often exaggerate when saying "Oh, he was the hottest guy I've ever seen," but Keith was literally the most handsome man I had ever laid eyes on. Including movie and television stars. With his jet-black wavy hair and deep-blue eyes, he was a vision of manliness. When I fantasized about my handsome prince, Keith frequently came to mind.

"Oh, I'm so sorry!" My face got hot, and I was grateful my dark skin probably masked some of my humiliation.

Keith laughed good-naturedly. "No harm done."

He flashed me a sexy smile that made me weak in the knees. Keith had smiled at me once before in the hallway, and I got dizzy—actually *dizzy* from the way he looked at me.

I nodded apologetically, having no idea what else to say. He continued down the hall, and I watched him walk away. It took physical effort not to sigh dreamily.

Keith worked with Elyse—she was his boss. Most of the time, I had absolutely no idea what he and Elyse were talking about. They worked for Wicket Pro, a technology company, and they threw around complex computer science lingo like they were talking about the weather.

Closing my eyes, I moaned, inwardly cringing over my embarrassing encounter with Keith. I had hit him with a dirty toilet plunger, for God's sake. I usually looked forward to running into him in the hallway, but right now I wanted to vanish into the floorboards. How could I ever look him in the eye again? I would forever be Toilet Plunger Girl to him.

It was pure insanity to think a guy like Keith could ever go for a girl like me. Even my imagination didn't stretch that far. Elyse was definitely more his type. Sexy, glamorous, and super smart.

Then again, Elyse's boyfriend was Luke Rannells, the head of maintenance of the building. No one could have guessed those two would be a match, but they were madly in love. Luke, my boss, was a terrific guy with a great sense of humor. He also happened to be a professional musical theater actor currently working on an off-Broadway show. Though Luke and I had been friends for years, I never confessed my love of singing to him. Elyse had told him though, and now the two of them frequently ganged up to pester me about pursuing theater seriously.

I knew better than to allow myself the luxury of dreaming. Feeling a familiar tug of sadness and regret in my chest, I pushed my cart down the hall. Still, it helped to know I had friends who cared enough to harass me about it.

*****

I headed back to my office to wrap things up so I could head home for the weekend. The first order of business when I got home would be to change my shirt. It had a small wet spot from the plunger incident. Gross. Not a huge deal, though. The cleaning lady was so apologetic, and I felt bad. I could tell she was embarrassed about what had happened.

Luke Rannells sailed by me down the hall, saluting me as he passed.

"Have a good weekend, Keith my boy," he called cheerfully.

"You too. Take it easy."

"You know I will," he chirped as he headed toward Elyse's office.

I turned and watched him as he stood in Elyse's doorway, grinning at her. Feeling a twinge of sadness, I looked away. I used to have a big thing for Elyse. I even asked her out a few times. For a while, I'd really thought she might be The One. Turned out she was The One for Luke. He loved her so much, and her face lit up every time she saw him. I was glad she was happy, even though it hurt to see them together. Getting over Elyse hadn't been easy, and having her boyfriend work in the same building made it worse.

Especially since I'd had the misfortune of seeing them have sex.

Elyse had been working late—she was a workaholic who loved her job and she'd been killing herself trying to get a promotion—and Luke was worried about her and just wanted to take her home. Things apparently got out of hand, and they'd had a spontaneous romp against the wall in her office. The whole thing ended up on the security camera's video. One of my co-workers, Hunter, gleefully showed me what he called a "juicy" video of Elyse and Luke "gettin' it on," as he put it.

The video was horrifically explicit. Luke had torn off all her clothes, leaving her completely exposed. I'd felt like I'd been stabbed in the heart when I saw it. That wasn't even the worst part: Elyse was devastated when she found out her co-workers had seen the humiliating video. I'd never forget the way she looked during those early days after the scandal hit. She was a strong woman, but her eyes were haggard and she looked utterly broken. God, it had hurt to look at her.

I'd wished there was something, *anything*, I could do to ease her pain. Luke wanted the same—he felt awful about what happened, even though it wasn't his fault. Luke was kind of a nut, in a good way, so he cooked up a scheme. He got me and several men who worked in the building—men who Elyse knew had seen her video— to perform a strip dance for her at a local club. It was the craziest thing I'd ever done.

It was funny. Things should have been weird between us

afterward. She did get the promotion and became my boss, but there was no awkwardness between us anymore. We were friends, and I was grateful.

The sharp pain of losing her to Luke had dulled over time. Now I was more jealous of what they had together. They had what I wanted: a loving, stable relationship. I wanted a woman to look at me the way Elyse looked at Luke.

I quickly packed my stuff in my work bag, unsure why I was in a hurry to leave. I didn't have any real plans this weekend. Going to a bar, either alone or with friends, was something to do, but I didn't really enjoy it. Hanging out with my guy friends always made me feel out of place. It might sound cocky, but I'm a reasonably good-looking man and I have tons of money, so it was always easy for me to find female companionship for the night. My friends all expected me to be a playboy, to throw my money around and chase women. I admitted to doing that sometimes. I had needs after all, and sometimes I couldn't resist a night of great sex. Overall though, it just wasn't my style. Though I loved the sex part, I usually felt lonelier than ever afterward.

It annoyed me that a woman could admit that all she really wanted out of life was a loving spouse and a family, but if a guy said it, he got labeled a pussy.

Feeling empty and at a loss, I slung my work bag over my shoulder and headed toward the elevator.

Chapter 2

The elevator doors slid open, and I pushed my cleaning cart inside.

And nearly mowed Keith down in the process. He gasped in surprise. I gasped in horror.

"Oh my God, I'm so sorry!"

Keith laughed as he glanced at my cart, putting his hands up in mock defense. "You're really trying to kill me today."

"Well, the toilet plunger attack didn't work, so I figured I'd try to take you out with my cart."

"Foiled again," he said with a smile.

I wanted to die. Literally, just die right there so I wouldn't have to endure this humiliation one second longer. Again, I asked myself *Why Keith Foster? Why do I always have to act like such an idiot in front of Keith Foster?*

"Ground floor, I presume?" he said with another smile, reaching for the elevator button.

I nodded. Well, thank God he was at least super sweet about everything. A lot of other executives around here would have yelled at me. It'd happened before.

The elevator doors closed and I stiffened, hyper-aware of his proximity to me. I'd never stood this close to him before. As subtly as possible, I drew in a deep breath so I could inhale his scent. Keith wore a deliciously masculine and probably expensive cologne. He looked dreamy in his sharp navy-blue suit with a striped tie.

I felt so ugly in comparison. Dressed in worn-out clothing and smelling of bathroom cleaner, I was plain and frumpy. He probably thought I was a moron because of my klutzy behavior. As much as I loved being near him, I couldn't wait to get away from this awkward situation.

The elevator suddenly lurched to a screeching halt. I screamed and pressed myself against the wall, terrified.

Keith and I stood, paralyzed, in case any sudden movement would send us plummeting to our deaths. When the elevator didn't budge after a few seconds, I let out a breath, realizing the elevator was only stuck between floors. It had happened a few times before, but not to me. It might take a while for maintenance to show up, but we weren't going to die.

I glanced over at Keith and was shocked.

Deathly pale, he leaned against the wall.

"Hey, it's okay," I said softly. "This elevator breaks all the time. Someone will be along to fix it in no time."

It took a few seconds for Keith's eyes to clearly focus on me. His breathing was shallow, and I could see he was sweating.

"Oh," I said gently. "You're claustrophobic, aren't you?"

Keith nodded rapidly and my heart ached for him. He seemed positively terrorized.

"And here I am crowding you," I said, trying to push my cart away from him.

"It's ... it's okay ..." he managed to say. He didn't look okay. I was afraid he was going to pass out.

"We're going to be fine. I promise. Close your eyes and take a deep breath. I promise, there's plenty of air." He closed his eyes and drew in a deep breath. "That's it. Deep breaths. Why don't you sit down?"

Keith opened his eyes and slowly slid down to a sitting position. I pushed my cart as far against the other wall as I could, then I sat down next to him. His expression held a look of sheer desperation. Instinctively, I reached over and took his hand in mine.

"I—I'm sorry," he said. He seemed embarrassed as well as afraid.

"Don't be sorry. It's all right," I said soothingly.

"Hey! You in the elevator. Can you hear me?" came a male voice from somewhere outside the elevator car.

"Luke?" I called out.

"Yeah. Crista?"

"Yes, it's me."

"We're gonna get you out as soon as possible. I promise. Are you okay?" Luke asked.

"Yes, I'm fine."

"Are you alone?"

"Bet … you wish … you were … alone," Keith managed with an apologetic smile. "Would be … easier."

I smiled and squeezed his hand in support.

"No, Keith Foster is with me," I said.

Keith looked surprised that I knew his full name, and I felt my face get hot.

"Elyse is a friend of mine," I said, hoping my explanation would make me seem like less of a stalker. "I know you work with her."

He nodded.

"Okay, good," Luke said. "Just try to keep calm, and we'll get you out of there in no time."

"See? It won't be long," I reassured Keith.

"I hate taking the elevator," he said between shallow breaths. "I have to take it because I work on the tenth floor. Usually just hold my breath the whole time until it's over. I always take it on the way up, but most of the time I walk down." He let out a weak laugh. "Serves me right for being lazy."

He was sweating profusely now. I wished there was something I could do to help him.

"I'm sorry you're stuck with me. I'm so sorry," Keith moaned.

"You don't need to keep apologizing. I just hate that this is so hard for you," I said softly. He gazed gratefully into my eyes for a moment, and my heart skipped a beat. I had a sudden, vivid fantasy of him, covered in sweat and gazing at me with such tenderness, looking exactly the way he did now while making love to me. I swallowed hard, forcing myself to focus on the task at hand. I would file the visual away for later use.

Keith moaned and closed his eyes. "I think I'm going to pass out."

"Oh God, I don't know what to do!" I said, trying not to panic. I patted his cheek gently to try to keep him alert. "Open your eyes. Try to focus on me."

He opened those lovely blue eyes of his and looked at me. It took him a moment to focus his gaze, but he managed.

I suddenly remembered that I kept a bottle of water in the bottom of my cleaning cart. I reached under the cart and grabbed it. Holding the bottle to his lips, I supported the back of his head with my other hand and helped him drink. A thrill rippled through me. After all my hours of fantasizing about Keith, I could hardly believe I was actually touching him.

He drank a bit, then let out a breath. "Thanks. That helps."

I took a clean cloth from lmy cart, poured some water on it, then held the damp cloth to his forehead. It appeared to help clear his head, and his eyes seemed to focus better. I pressed the cloth to his sweaty neck. He moaned softly and said again, "That helps. That helps."

"Good. You're so hot," I said, then wanted to kick myself. I meant temperature-wise, but it came out sounding wrong. He was too preoccupied with trying to stay conscious to notice. "Here, let's get your jacket off. And let's loosen your tie."

He nodded weakly. I helped him off with his jacket and began struggling with the knot on his tie, so he helped me. Our fingers touched as we worked together to loosen it, and another thrill went through me.

"We should— You should maybe undo a few buttons on your shirt," I said shyly. I would have loved to slowly unbutton every last one and rip the shirt right off him, but I knew it would be wrong to take advantage of him in such a vulnerable state.

He began unbuttoning his shirt. I turned away, feeling modest. When I turned back, a small, sexy smile curled his lips. He clearly found it amusing that I was too shy to look at his chest.

"You're so sweet to take care of me," he said. "I feel so bad. I don't even know your name."

"Crista. Crista Rivera."

"Crista," he repeated in his deep, sexy voice. My heart soared to hear him say my name.

Keith's breathing sounded a bit steadier now. I allowed myself the briefest glance at his smooth, muscled half-exposed chest. With his white shirt hanging open, he looked like the cover of a romance novel. Breathtakingly handsome was the only way to describe him.

I picked up the damp cloth, poured a little more water on it, and handed it back to him.

"Thanks," he said, taking the cloth and pressing it to his forehead.

"Crista?" Luke called out.

"Yeah?"

"The guys are working on the problem, but it might be a while."

Keith moaned and started panting again.

"You okay?" Luke asked.

"Uh, yes," I said. Keith had gone frighteningly pale again. "We're okay. But please hurry if you can."

"We will, Crista," Luke said, sounding worried. "We'll have you out as soon as we can. Hang in there."

"God … it … could … be … hours." Keith's eyes were wide with terror. "What if … what if we're stuck here all night?"

"I'm sure it won't be anywhere near that long," I said, feeling my panic rising and trying not to show it. Keith looked so freaked out, I was getting scared.

He clutched his chest and moaned. "I feel … like I'm having … a heart attack …"

"No, no, God no!" I cried out.

"It's not …" I watched helplessly as Keith tried to speak. "I'm not …" Anger and frustration mixed with his expression of fear as he gasped for breath. He clearly hated feeling out of control. "Panic attack … just a panic … not a heart … attack. Just feels like it."

Keith locked eyes with me, searching my face for understanding. He must have known he was scaring the hell out of me.

"I understand," I said gently, taking his hand and squeezing it. "You're not gonna die, you just feel like it right now."

His expression relaxed a bit. "Yes."

Keith's eyes rolled back and his head slammed into the wall. He still clutched his chest. Even though I understood this was a panic attack and not an actual heart attack, it was still terrifying to witness. I felt like I was watching a man die right in front of me.

So I started singing.

I sang "In My Own Little Corner," watching nervously as Keith's eyes opened wide. I had startled him a bit—probably a good thing. His panic subsided slightly, and his breathing evened out a little.

On the surface it was kind of a silly song. Cinderella sang about how she used her imagination to be anything she wanted to be; fantasizing allowed her to escape her ordinary life. I did exactly that all the time as I cleaned the building, which made me feel a bit exposed as I sang the song in front of Keith.

After only a few lines, I stopped. My stomach fluttered with nervousness.

"Keep going," Keith whispered, still sweating and panting a little.

I continued my song. I laughed shyly when I sang the part about imagining I was a girl who men went crazy for. Keith smiled at me, which gave me the strength to keep singing. Something in his tender gaze made me feel safe. Like it was okay to let myself be vulnerable with him.

"What song was that?" he asked when I reached the end of the song.

"It's called 'In My Own Little Corner' from the *Rogers and Hammerstein's Cinderella* musical. I love musicals, and that one is my favorite. I know it's silly, but I hum that song all the time when I'm working. Pretending I'm Cinderella is what helps me get through the day."

Oh dear God. I cannot believe I actually said it out loud.

In that moment, I wished the elevator floor would open up and swallow me whole. After the toilet plunger and nearly hitting Keith with my cart, I thought I couldn't possibly embarrass myself more in front of him. How wrong I was. Next, I'd be blurting out that he was my fantasy prince in my private Cinderella scenario. What in the hell was wrong with me?

Keith's gaze softened, and he smiled. Incredibly, the warm, safe feeling washed over me again. He didn't think I was stupid or silly.

"That's very clever. Shows you have a wonderful imagination. You're as pretty as Cinderella, too."

I drew in a breath, too overwhelmed to speak. He was only being nice, I was sure. Even so, I was astonished at how I'd gone from feeling utterly humiliated to feeling calm and at peace.

"Will you sing some more? You have a beautiful voice, and it keeps my mind off this death trap."

He was only joking, but his breath hitched a bit when he said it. To him, I was sure this tiny elevator felt like a tomb.

"Of course," I said. I thought about what I *should* sing, versus what I *wanted* to sing. Though I'd always had a silly crush on Keith, right now I felt particularly close to him. We *were* close, both physically and somewhat emotionally, because of the circumstances. I wanted to choose an unabashedly romantic song and sing it while gazing into his eyes.

Instead, I decided on a song from Monty Python's *Spamalot.* Not one of the sillier ones, but a great song about pursuing your dreams, called "Find Your Grail." I launched into it, watching Keith sit back and visibly relax as I sang.

He nodded and smiled when I finished.

"Beautiful," he said, his voice still hardly above a whisper. He looked weak, yet calm.

"Do you want to hear another one?" I asked, suddenly worried. The last thing I wanted to do was have him trapped, hearing me perform against his will.

"Yes, *please,*" he said earnestly. "I mean, if you don't mind. It's helping a lot. Really."

"Of course I don't mind."

The next song I chose was "I'm Not that Girl" from *Wicked.* If ever there was a song that described my situation with Keith, it was that one. A song about wanting a man who was way out of your league, the lyrics involve a handsome man who chooses Glinda, the beautiful blonde, instead of Elphaba in the show. I pictured Elyse when I sang the line about the girl with the golden hair. A classy, gorgeous woman like her was the type Keith would choose. He might already have a girlfriend like that, for all I knew.

"That's a pretty song," Keith said after I'd finished singing. "But sad."

I nodded, swallowing hard. "Yeah. Okay, I need to think of a fun song now. Oh, I know. Have you heard of the show *Bye Bye Birdie*?"

"Yeah, I think so. Don't know anything about it, though."

"Well, there's a song in there called 'Spanish Rose.' The woman's name is Rose and, even though she was born and raised in America, her mother-in-law is super racist and doesn't want her son to marry a so-called Spaniard. So, Rose sings this song about how she's gonna be as Spanish as humanly possible to annoy her mother-in-law."

Keith chuckled.

I launched into the song and gave it everything I had. I'd never considered myself a particularly comic performer, but I thought I did pretty well with the song. I really got into it, using my list of cleaning supplies as a Spanish fan, and narrowing my eyes at him when I sang the word "Americano" with derision.

Keith laughed heartily as I sang, and my body tingled all over. I rarely had the chance to sing in front of anyone, and having his approval was exhilarating. It warmed my heart to see him relax, and I could see my singing really helped him cope with his terrible anxiety.

"That was a good one," he said with a broad smile lighting up his handsome face.

"Thanks."

There was a moment of silence between us, then Keith drew in a shaky breath. I knew I couldn't allow him any time to fixate on being stuck in the elevator, or he would start to panic again. I wracked my brain but couldn't come up with another song to distract him.

"Do you have any requests? Is there anything you want me to sing?"

"Let me think," he said, and his breath slowed again.

That's it. Don't think about where you are. It's okay.

I wanted so much to reach out and take his hand again, but I resisted the urge.

"I don't know much about musicals. I did see *Phantom of the Opera* once. That was pretty good."

"Okay, perfect."

Drawing in a deep breath, I began singing "Think of Me." I had gotten my wish: I finally had the chance to sing a romantic song to Keith without being too obvious, since he had suggested *Phantom of the Opera*. It was cathartic for me to implore Keith through song to *think of me, just think of me once in a while.* The song made me wonder if he would think of me, remember me, once this ordeal was over.

The song had some really high notes at the end, and I was nervous that I wouldn't be able to hit them. To my relief, I thought I sounded pretty good.

Keith's bright-blue eyes opened wide. "Wow. Just *wow.* That was amazing. Your voice is beautiful. *Perfect.*"

"Thanks," I said, shyly looking down. Inside, I was exploding. It wasn't only his kind words, but the way he looked at me: he wasn't just being nice. I knew he was genuinely impressed with my voice, and it sent my heart soaring again.

"Do you sing professionally?" he asked.

"Oh, no. I could never do it."

"Why?"

I lifted my head and met his gaze. "Money, for one thing. I could never afford all the fancy voice lessons and acting coaches you would need to get into a show."

"You know Elyse has all kinds of friends in the music business, right?"

"Yes, I know."

"And Luke. You know Luke Rannells, right?"

"Sure. He's my boss."

Keith laughed. "Oh, right. Duh. You know he's a theater performer, right? You should—"

I laughed. "Yes, I know. Both of them are constantly pestering me to meet all their theater friends. Elyse knows I like to sing. She caught me once. Singing while I was cleaning the ladies' room."

Keith's lips turned upward into a sexy smile. "Were you being Cinderella at the time?"

Heat flooded my cheeks. Why on earth did I tell him my secret?

"Yes," I said, laughing self-consciously.

"That's pretty cool," Keith said softly. His gentle tone melted my heart. "So, you have thought about pursuing singing for a living?"

"I've learned not to think about it."

"But Elyse can—"

"It's too late, Keith." I gazed into his kind eyes. "Most people start when they're very young."

"It isn't too late, Crista. It's never too late for someone with your talent. You say Elyse and Luke keep pestering you about singing? Well buckle up, because I'm going to start pestering you now, too."

I laughed, shaking my head. There was no chance I would even consider it, but I appreciated Keith's thoughtfulness. It meant the world to me.

The elevator suddenly lurched upward. I screamed as my head banged against the elevator wall.

Keith reached over and touched my head, his eyes wide with concern. "Are you all right?"

I nodded, too overwhelmed to speak. Keith's delectable lips were close enough to kiss. I stared at his face for a moment, wanting to memorize it. I could feed off this fantasy for hours, remembering how close his face had been to mine and imagining him dipping his head down to kiss me.

The elevator kept moving, but a bit more slowly now. I snapped back to my senses, realizing we were about to be rescued. I glanced down at his shirt, still hanging open.

"You might want to …" I began.

"Oh, right," Keith said, as he quickly buttoned up his shirt. I picked up his suit jacket and helped him on with it.

Keith stood up, then held out a hand to help me up.

Like the prince holding out his hand to help Cinderella out of the carriage.

In that moment I didn't care if it was silly for a woman of my age to have such childish dreams. I needed the fantasy, and it felt real and romantic and perfect.

Keith stared intensely, hopefully, at the elevator doors, as if willing them to open.

Oh, please, please let the elevator be working. I couldn't bear the look on his face if we found out we're still stuck.

The doors slid open. We'd safely arrived back on the tenth floor, where we'd begun this adventure.

It must have taken every ounce of his willpower not to dash out of the "death trap," but he gallantly gestured for me to exit first. Leaving my cart, I walked briskly out of the elevator with Keith following close on my heels. Relief flooded through me as I heard him take in a huge breath and let it out.

A small group of people were waiting for us. Suddenly, they all burst into applause.

"Brava!" someone shouted.

It took me a moment to realize they had heard me singing in the elevator shaft. I laughed as I surveyed the friendly faces smiling their approval. I was surprised to find, for once, I wasn't embarrassed to be overheard singing: I was proud.

Luke stood, arms crossed, looking angry. The twinkle in his eyes gave him away, though. That, and Luke rarely got mad about anything.

"What's yer problem, bucko?" I asked him.

"I see how it is. You'll sing for him," Luke said, jerking a thumb in Keith's direction, "but you won't sing for me."

"Well, I had to do *something* to—" I stopped myself, realizing I couldn't embarrass Keith by revealing his fear. "To pass the time. Took you long enough to get us out."

Luke unfolded his arms and wrapped one around my shoulder. "I know. I'm so sorry, Crista. Are you okay?" His brown eyes were full of genuine concern.

"I'm fine, Luke. Really."

Elyse rushed over to me, her arms open wide. She engulfed me in a big hug.

"You okay? It must have been so scary," she said after letting me go.

"It was, but it's okay. Keith kept me calm."

Keith caught my eye and smiled. I could see the gratitude on his face. Being claustrophobic was nothing to be ashamed of, but I figured he'd be uncomfortable if anyone else knew about his panic attack. He had nothing to worry about; his secret would always be safe with me. "You kept us all calm with your singing," Elyse said. "Let us know you guys were okay."

"That's good," I said with a smile.

"Go home and get some rest, okay?"

"I will. Thanks."

The crowd dispersed, and Luke and the other maintenance guys went over to inspect the elevator. Keith walked toward me.

"Crista, I can't begin to thank you enough. I never could have gotten through this if it weren't for you."

I allowed myself the indulgence of gazing into his eyes, still trying to capture the way he looked in this moment. I might never get this close to him again, and I wanted to remember every second.

"You don't have to thank me, Keith. It was no trouble at all."

"You're so kind, but I know I've been a handful to say the least."

"I'm happy to help. Really. I'm just grateful you weren't in there alone."

Keith visibly shuddered. "Me too."

"Take care of yourself. Maybe get some cold water and then get outside in the fresh air."

"Yes. Sounds wonderful."

I allowed myself a few more precious seconds of gazing into his eyes, then headed over to my cleaning cart, which Luke had taken out of the elevator for me.

Back to reality.

Chapter 3

After grabbing a bottle of cold water from the vending machine, I headed down the stairs. As soon as I got out of the building, I leaned against the brick wall.

Freedom, sweet freedom.

Being in the elevator had felt like being buried alive. I shuddered just thinking about it. In my mind, the walls were closing in around me, ready to crush me to death at any moment.

Until Crista started to sing. With her beautiful voice, she had managed to get my mind off my situation, which was no easy feat. God bless her lovely soul.

It had been humiliating to lose control. I struggled just to breathe in there. Archaic as it seemed, I couldn't help thinking the man should be in control in those situations. That the woman should be the hysterical one, with the man wrapping his strong arms around her to protect her until the crisis passed.

Nope. Not me. I had to cower in the corner like a frightened rabbit. The more I thought about it, the more embarrassed I felt.

Then I pictured Crista's pretty face. Her beautiful brown eyes filled with worry for me. Not a trace of annoyance or contempt— only concern for my welfare. She'd comforted me as if she really cared. I took another sip of cold water and a deep breath of fresh air. Closing my eyes, I relaxed against the cool brick of the building. Remembering Crista's tender touch as she'd held my hand.

I once dated a woman for a year and a half, and she never once touched me that way.

Crista Rivera is The One. The One I've waited for all my life.

My eyes flew open. That was crazy. *Crazy.* I shook my head, laughing softly at myself.

Remember when you thought Elyse Pippin was The One, dumbass?

Even the mere thought was lunacy. Crista was a sweetheart, and she had been my savior. It was just the extreme circumstances that made my feelings about her so intense.

I headed to my car, still taking deep breaths to clear my head. I rolled all the windows down as soon as I got in. I couldn't bear feeling boxed in again. Thank God I didn't need to take public transportation and have tons of people crowding around me.

Once I got home, I popped open a beer and flopped down in front of the TV. Finally, I was starting to feel better. That was the thing about panic attacks; they don't stop right away once a crisis is over. Sometimes it takes quite a while to feel normal again.

Resting on the couch, my mind wandered back to Crista. My attraction for her was as powerful now as it had been when I left work, but the feeling would probably pass as I decompressed from the fear and adrenaline from being trapped in the elevator. I'd been so wrong about Elyse being the right woman for me. I no longer trusted my own judgment.

But the feeling I had for Crista seemed different somehow. It was more than mere attraction this time. Was I crazy? Or had I met my future wife?

Maybe this odd sensation of euphoria was due to the sheer relief of being free from the awful enclosed space. That, and now my head was spinning from drinking two beers on an empty stomach. I grabbed my cell phone and ordered some Chinese food.

Settling back on the couch, I figured I would just sleep on it tonight. I was hardly thinking clearly right now. Good thing I didn't have Crista's phone number—I might have done something rash and stupid. For all I knew, I would wake up tomorrow and my sudden, intense longing for her would disappear.

I hoped it wouldn't. If I was lucky, maybe I would even dream of her tonight.

*****

I thought about Crista all weekend long, my fantasies of her growing stronger instead of fading with time. I had seen her in the office before, but I'd never realized how beautiful she was. Dressed in her worn cleaning-lady clothes, she still looked lovely. Soft and feminine. I couldn't begin to imagine how gorgeous she would be when she was dressed up. Maybe she couldn't afford fancy clothes.

It got me thinking of all the wonderful ways I could spoil her. Most of the women I dated certainly had a lot of fun spending my money. Crista didn't seem to be the type, though. That appealed to me. She'd sat with me in the elevator, holding my hand and comforting me, without expecting anything in return. She knew what I did for a living— she must have known I was wealthy—but she didn't ask anything of me. The women I picked up in bars were usually in a big hurry to get into my pants, both in the bedroom sense and in the wallet sense.

It made me smile to remember Crista shyly turning away when I unbuttoned my shirt. Her lovely dark brown skin didn't show it, but I wondered if she'd blushed. Thinking of her skin reminded me of her pretty, dark brown hair and gentle brown eyes. Oh yes, Crista Rivera was beautiful, inside and out. And she never looked lovelier than when she was singing to me.

Crista came alive when she sang. Her transformation—from relatively shy and quiet, to bold and confident—had been fascinating to watch. Her voice was loud and strong. She had the "it" quality people talk about. Stage presence. She was incredibly talented, beyond simply having a good singing voice. I looked forward to joining Elyse and Luke in trying to cajole her into singing professionally.

As I went about my weekend business, getting groceries and picking up my dry cleaning, Crista was never far from my mind. My thoughts kept drifting back to my favorite moments with her in the elevator. When she held my hand and spoke softly to comfort me. When she smiled. When she sang. I thought about how charming her Cinderella fantasy was. I found it amusing that I fell for her after I heard her sing. Wasn't that how it always happened in fairy tales?

I imagined how nice it would be to spend time with Crista outside of work. To take her to a fancy restaurant and gaze into her eyes across the table. I envisioned what might happen afterward. How wonderful it would be to take her back to my place. To my bedroom. To see her lovely dark hair spread out over the pillow and have her slender legs wrapped around my back as I made love to her. Lately, my dates had ended with a quick, albeit exciting, tumble in the sheets. Going out with Crista would be nothing like that. With a woman like her, I would want to take my time and enjoy every moment.

Had she thought about me at all this weekend? Or had she forgotten about me? It was impossible to tell if she was interested in me romantically. While we were stuck I'd concentrated mostly on breathing and not passing out. But that one moment when the elevator suddenly jerked upward, she'd banged her head and I reached over and touched her. When I asked if she was all right, something in her eyes gave me hope that maybe she felt something for me.

By Sunday afternoon I declared it official. I was well and truly smitten with Crista Rivera. The question now was, what would I do about it?

25

Chapter 4

As soon as I got to work on Monday, I immersed myself in fantasies about Keith. Since our elevator adventure, Keith had gone from being a hazy image in my imagination to a much more vivid reality. He was no longer just a handsome man who fit my image of Prince Charming. Still a vision of masculine perfection, Keith was also kind and vulnerable. He had said I was as pretty as Cinderella, and I had a beautiful voice. My stomach fluttered and my heart pounded every time I thought about it. Although his claustrophobia had made our elevator experience a nightmare for him, he had been kind and offered me encouragement as I sang for him. If that was Keith Foster at his worst, what was he like at his best?

As I vacuumed the hallway carpet, I found myself thinking about another song from *Cinderella*, called "Ten Minutes Ago." Sung by the prince, it was about the way he felt when he first met Cinderella at the ball. In that moment, he knew he had met the love of his life. I indulged in the fantasy of Keith feeling the same about me. It was ludicrous, of course. I was sure Keith had forgotten me the moment he left work on Friday. For all I knew, he had a hot date that night. He might have taken her back to his place afterward and made passionate love to her.

My chest physically hurt when I thought about Keith being with another woman. I shoved the thought away and returned to my land of make-believe. In my mind, Keith belonged to me. I lost myself in delightful flights of fancy about him as I worked. Remembering how close our faces had been in the elevator, it was easy to imagine him closing his eyes and gently pressing his lips to mine. Sighing, I could practically feel his sweet kiss. My mind wandered further, and I imagined him picking me up and carrying me to his bedroom. He would gaze lovingly at me as he undressed me, taking his time to caress every inch of my body. Masterfully taking control, his blue eyes would bore into my soul, then he would put himself inside me. Keith would be the perfect lover. Gentle, yet masculine and dominant. The two of us would get lost in one another, drowning in passion and pleasure and love.

I had never been with a man, and it was rare for me to have such vivid sexual fantasies about anyone. But Keith would be a tender and gentle lover, exactly the kind of man I wanted to be my first.

Still dreamily humming to myself, I switched off the vacuum cleaner and began wrapping up the cord.

"Hey there, Cinderella," came a voice from behind me. I whirled around to find Keith standing there, looking knee-weakingly handsome and smiling at me. I gasped, feeling my face get hot. For one irrational second, I was afraid he had somehow read my mind and knew I'd been in the midst of a sexual fantasy about him.

Get it together. He has no way of knowing what you were thinking. Act normal.

"H—how are you feeling?" I asked.

"Much better," he said. I thought I saw a hint of embarrassment on his face. He probably felt uncomfortable about our time in the elevator. "A little tired from running up and down the stairs all day."

"I guess you don't want to set foot in an elevator ever again."

"Well, you know, it wasn't all bad," he said with a grin. "At least I got to spend time with you."

I wanted to swoon in his arms. I had to get a grip on myself. Fantasies were one thing, but Keith was way out of my league. Allowing myself to think for one second that a guy like him would ever be interested in a girl like me was dangerous, and it would only end in heartbreak.

I'd made that mistake before. I had learned the truth the hard way. If something seemed too good to be true, it couldn't be trusted.

"Thanks again. For everything you did to help me. I'll never forget it," Keith said, gazing at me. Dear God, the look in his eyes was just like my fantasies.

He's just being nice. Don't be crazy. I guarantee he has some smart, gorgeous woman in his life. Somebody glamorous and high-class like Elyse. He's just humoring the cleaning lady.

"Oh, it was nothing really. Well, I better finish up my work." I grabbed my cleaning cart and rushed off to the ladies' room where I knew Keith couldn't possibly follow me.

*****

I watched, helpless, as Crista disappeared into the women's restroom. She had seemed nervous, but that didn't mean she had any interest in me. Before speaking to her, I quietly watched her work. She'd sung softly to herself and had appeared lost in thought. Then, she'd seemed startled to see me, and I was afraid I might have made her uncomfortable by calling her "Cinderella." Maybe she regretted confessing to me about pretending to be in a fairy tale while she worked.

Like a moron, I stood staring at the restroom door. I was desperate to talk to her again, but I couldn't very well stay here like a creep outside the ladies' room. Sighing, I turned around and headed to my office.

Doubt crept into my thoughts. Crista might have ducked into the restroom to avoid me. For all I knew, she already had a boyfriend. Even if she was single, she might not find me appealing. I wished I had some way to learn more about her situation before I tried to make a move on her.

As I walked toward my office, I heard a phone ring down the hall and a female voice answered.

Elyse!

Maybe she could help. I spun on my heel and paused outside Elyse's office, waiting for her to finish the phone call that ended up being mercifully brief.

She looked up and smiled when I appeared in the doorway.

"Hey," she said cheerfully.

"Hey," I said, suddenly realizing I hadn't thought about how to casually bring up the subject I needed to discuss.

"What's up?" she asked after I'd paused for an uncomfortably long time.

I closed her office door and took a seat across from her. "I wanted to ask you about something. I hope this doesn't cross any personal boundaries."

"I think you crossed that bridge when you stripped for me, Keith," Elyse said bluntly.

We both laughed, and I felt more at ease. Even so, I blushed slightly at the memory. Getting onstage to perform a strip dance was the wildest thing I'd ever done, but I'd never regretted it. To ease Elyse's pain and humiliation, it had been totally worth it.

Elyse leaned back in her chair, giving me her undivided attention. "Now, what did you want to talk to me about?" She smiled encouragingly, probably aware I was nervous.

"Okay. You're friends with Crista, right?"

"Crista who works in this building?"

I nodded.

"Yeah," she said. "I mean, I don't know her really well. We've never hung out outside of work, though not for lack of trying. I've told her a million times I want her to meet all my theater friends."

"I know," I said, nodding. "Did she … Did she tell you what happened while we were stuck in the elevator?"

Elyse raised an eyebrow and smiled slyly. "No. What happened in the elevator?"

With a laugh, I said, "No, no. Nothing like that. I've got pretty bad claustrophobia, and I was a total mess. Full-blown panic attack."

"Oh, Keith. That must have been awful for you," she said, leaning forward to look me in the eye.

"So, she never mentioned it to you?"

"No, I had no idea."

I wasn't surprised. Crista had covered for me when we were rescued, and she was still protecting me.

"Thank God she was in there with me. She was incredibly sweet, and she kept me calm."

Elyse smiled. "That's why she was singing. To keep your mind off everything."

"Yes! And it worked like a charm. She took such good care of me. I mean it when I say I was a total mess. I was all sweaty and gross, and I could hardly breathe. Can't tell you how many times I almost passed out and she pulled me back from the brink. She was wonderful."

Elyse nodded thoughtfully.

"So, do you … Do you know if she's seeing anyone?" I asked.

"Are you saying you're interested in her?"

I swallowed and nodded.

"Oh, Crista is the *sweetest*!" Elyse gushed. Then she reached over and squeezed my hand. "And so are you. You guys would make a *great* couple."

"You really think so?"

"Yes! And to answer your question, I don't think she's seeing anyone. She's never mentioned anyone at least."

"Good, good."

"Do you want me to try to find out for you?"

"You don't mind?"

"Of course not," Elyse said, her eyes lighting up. "She's such a wonderful woman."

I nodded, picturing Crista's soft-brown eyes and dark, cascading hair. "She's amazing. And so talented. I had no idea. When she sings, she looks lit up inside. And her voice … I've never heard anything like it. Did you hear her? Especially on the *Phantom of the Opera* song with all those crazy high notes? I mean, damn. I was completely blown away."

Elyse cackled. "Oh, those performer types. That's how they get ya. You hear them sing and you fall in love."

Now Elyse was the one who looked lit up inside, talking about Luke. I was filled with a renewed sense of gratitude that they'd found each other. He made her so happy.

"So, I have your permission to tell her straight out you're interested in her?"

I thought about it for a moment. It would be incredibly awkward if Elyse told Crista about my feelings for her, if it turned out she didn't feel the same way. Things had been quite awkward between Elyse and me when she found out I had a thing for her. It got even more embarrassing when she got a promotion and became my boss. No, I didn't want to go through that again.

"Yes," I blurted out, surprising even myself. Life was short, and I was crazy about Crista Rivera. Some risks in life were worth taking.

"Great. Just leave everything to me. I'll get the lowdown for you," Elyse said with a sly smile.

*****

Elyse spotted me in the hallway on Tuesday morning and rushed toward me.

"Hey, Crista," she said with a smile. "Can I talk to you for a minute?"

"Sure."

"In here," Elyse said, motioning for me to join her in the conference room. My stomach fluttered with nervousness, hoping I hadn't done anything wrong.

"Am I being fired?" I asked, only half joking.

She laughed and plopped down in a seat at the conference table. "Of course not. If you were, I'd make Luke do it. No, I just want to ask you something."

Elyse looked excited about something, so I calmed down.

"What's up?" I asked.

"Do you have a boyfriend?"

I blinked. "What?"

"A boyfriend. Are you seeing anyone?"

"No. Why?"

"Goody!" she said, clapping her hands with excitement.

I laughed and said, "What are you up to, Elyse Pippin?"

"It seems you made quite an impression on Keith when you were stuck in the elevator with him."

Keith. My mind immediately went to my favorite image of him, when he had reached over and touched my head, asking "Are you okay?"

"He's a good guy," I said noncommittally. It was nice of Elyse to try to set the two of us up, but the mere idea of us together was insane. I hoped she hadn't said anything to Keith about this yet. Just thinking about the look on his face when she floated the idea of him dating the cleaning lady made me cringe.

"Yeah, he is. He told me all about what happened. How he had a really bad panic attack and you took good care of him."

"The poor man. It was awful for him. I'm surprised he told you. He seemed kind of embarrassed about it."

"I think he still is a little. He said he was a total mess. All sweaty and gross."

Now my mind flashed to the image of Keith, hot and sweaty with his shirt hanging open. I bit my lip, then said, "He was sweaty, but he sure wasn't gross. God, he's beautiful."

Elyse laughed.

"He is one good-looking man, that's for sure. With those blue eyes and dark hair, Luke says he looks like Superman."

"He *does* look like Superman!" *He's built like him, too.* I chose not to say that out loud.

"Keith thinks you're a wonderful woman, Crista," Elyse told me.

"I think he's wonderful, too," I said with a sigh.

"Then you'll go out with him?"

"What? No!" I stared at her. She had clearly lost her mind.

"Why not?"

"Guys like Keith don't go for women like me, Elyse."

"Why would you think that?" she asked, looking bewildered.

"He's rich and handsome and he's a high-powered New York executive. I'm the cleaning lady for God's sake."

"So? I'm Keith's *boss*, and my boyfriend is the maintenance guy." I blinked.

"Ha! Don't have an answer for that, do ya?" Elyse said triumphantly.

"No, I guess I don't. Even so, Keith would never be interested in me."

"But he *is*, Crista. He told me."

"He did?" I asked, shocked.

"Yes. He came to talk to me because he knows you and I are friends. He asked if I knew if you were seeing anyone, and I promised him I would find out." Elyse laughed. "I know it sounds so high school. He 'like-likes' you and wanted me to help."

I struggled to keep my emotions in check, wanting with all my heart and soul to believe what Elyse was telling me. But I couldn't. It would destroy me when everything turned out to be a lie. A man of Keith's success and stature couldn't possibly be interested in me. For all I knew, he was the type who slept with a lot of women and simply wanted me to be next on his list. Maybe he found my Mexican-ness "exotic" and wanted to bed a Latina. It wouldn't be the first time a guy had treated me that way. Or perhaps Keith was just sleeping his way through the office.

He didn't seem the type, though. Not at all. It was strange. I barely knew him, but I felt as if I knew him intimately. Something about the way he'd looked into my eyes and responded to my touch—it was more than just the relief of my calming his fears during his panic attack. The connection between us seemed deeper. And then there was the way Keith had gazed at me when I sang.

No. I had to put a stop to this immediately. The notion of being with Keith was a fantasy that should stay buried deep in my heart, where it belonged.

"Well, if he said it, he was only being nice. He's glad I was there to support him through the ordeal, and that's all."

"No, that's not all," Elyse insisted. "Crista, he really cares about you. He thinks you're sweet and kind and pretty."

"Pretty," I scoffed. I dressed in rags at work while surrounded by gorgeous executives.

"You're so beautiful, Crista," Elyse said, and the tenderness in her voice made tears form behind my eyes. "You have no idea. And when you sang for him … Keith told me how lovely he thought your voice was. How talented and special and wonderful you are."

For the briefest of seconds, I allowed myself to believe. Believe

Keith had fallen as hard for me as I had for him. Then I came to my senses.

"Just forget it, okay? Believe me, it isn't possible. Guys like Keith do not go for girls like me. That's just the way it is."

I jumped up and hurried out of the conference room. Elyse had been so kind to me, and I felt terrible about rushing off.

But I had to protect my heart before it got crushed into dust.

Chapter 5

I looked up as Elyse appeared in the doorway of my office on Wednesday afternoon.

"Got a minute?" she asked.

"Sure," I said, suddenly feeling nervous. She rarely visited my office, so I had the feeling she was here to give me a report on Crista.

Elyse shut the door and took a seat across from me. It always felt a bit strange to have her in here. After she was promoted to Senior Vice President of Worldwide Strategy and Operations, she moved to a huge corner office, and I inherited her old one.

The one where she'd had sex with Luke.

At first it had been rather painful for me to have to work in here, but I had eventually gotten over it. I didn't really think about it much anymore, but it was hard not to with her sitting across from me, mere inches from the very wall where Luke had had his way with her.

"So, I talked with Crista," Elyse began cautiously.

My heart sank. If Elyse had good news, she would have excitedly burst into my office.

"Oh," I said, trying not to show my disappointment, to salvage what was left of my pride. "Guess she's not interested, huh? Or she's seeing someone?"

"No, she's not seeing anyone."

"Then she's just not interested," I said, hurt and humiliation flooding through me. Too late, I realized what a mistake it had been to involve Elyse in all this. It was bad enough that *she* had shot me down, but now she knew Crista didn't want me either.

"No, no," Elyse insisted kindly. "That's not it at all. I think she does have feelings for you. I mean, I'm not totally sure."

"Well, what did she say?" I asked. My heart thumped in my chest as my emotions alternated between despair and hope.

"I told her that you were interested in her."

"Yeah, and …" I leaned forward, abandoning any attempt to look cool. This was too important. I needed *answers.*

"And she didn't believe me."

"What?"

"She doesn't believe you have feelings for her," Elyse said. My brow furrowed, so she added, "I know. That's the look I had on my face, too."

"How could she not believe you? Why would she think you'd make up something like that?"

"She thinks you're out of her league, Keith," she said gently. "She said guys like you don't go for women like her."

"But I do. I am," I sputtered. "I mean, I'm crazy about her!"

Elyse smiled. "I know. The trouble is convincing her."

"How do I do that?"

"I'm not sure, but you need to be careful with her. She seemed defensive, and she clearly has trouble trusting people. There's probably a reason."

"You think somebody hurt her?"

Elyse nodded, her expression filled with sympathy. I changed my mind about having gone to Elyse for help. It had been the right thing to do. Sure, she was excited about matching us up, but she genuinely cared about Crista's feelings as well as mine.

"So, you know, take care when you're pursuing her, okay?"

I nodded. The last thing I wanted to do was upset her.

"It's funny, I remember Luke being kind of defensive on our first date. Like he was afraid I thought I was better than him because he was the maintenance guy."

"Really?"

"Yeah." Elyse laughed and shook her head. "I don't consider myself the elitist type, but I have to confess, I nearly said no when he first asked me out. I was afraid the date might be uncomfortable. I wondered what on earth we could possibly have in common."

I smiled as I thought about it. It was hard to imagine; she and Luke were so madly in love.

"Crista said she doesn't believe a rich, handsome executive could ever be interested in the cleaning lady."

"She called me handsome?"

"Yes," Elyse said with a laugh. "Her exact words were, 'God, he's beautiful.'"

"Wow," I said as a surge of adrenaline coursed through me. *Crista found me attractive.*

"I have to admit, before Luke asked me out, I didn't pay much attention to the cleaning and maintenance staff. Did you?"

I shook my head slowly.

"Did you know her name before the elevator incident?"

A wave of guilt crashed over me. "No. No, I guess not."

"It's possible that she noticed you before, but you never noticed her."

"God, I hope not," I said. "I hate to think she might have been hurt because I didn't notice her."

I remembered the one sad song Crista sang for me in the elevator. I couldn't remember what show she had said it was from, but the song was about not being the girl that the guy wanted. In it, he went for some other beautiful girl and left her behind.

Could she have been singing about herself? About how she thought she wasn't beautiful enough for me?

My heart ached at the thought. Crista was the sweetest, most beautiful, most talented woman I had ever known. I would be the lucky one if she chose me.

"I still think this could work out between you two. Just, you know, tread carefully. Be gentle with her." Elyse stood up and smiled at me. "And then be sure to invite me to the wedding."

*****

I forced myself to wait until the following week to approach Crista again, but it wasn't easy. I was nervous, but excited, about asking Crista out. Still, I knew Elyse was probably right when she told me to be gentle. I wouldn't hurt Crista for anything in the world, but she had no way of knowing that.

Throughout the week, I did my best to find her around the office so I could catch her eye and smile at her. She always smiled back, but she seemed uncertain. Finally, I figured I'd waited long enough. This time when I caught her eye and smiled, I gathered up my nerve and walked toward her. Crista smiled and turned away.

And then she walked into the elevator.

I froze, wanting to dash over and join her, but I just couldn't. I hadn't gone near the elevator since we'd gotten stuck. I watched helplessly as the doors closed and she disappeared. It was after 6pm— she was probably heading out for the day. I couldn't bear the thought of having to wait until tomorrow, so I sprinted toward the stairs.

As I ran down, I thought about all the times she'd ducked into the ladies' room when I'd passed her in the hallway over the past few days. Was I being paranoid, or was she avoiding me? If she was avoiding me, was she trying to protect herself from getting hurt, or was she just trying to blow me off because she had no interest in me?

I was making myself crazy with all the speculation. It was time to get some answers once and for all.

Panting, I made it down to the lobby, hoping she hadn't beat me there by too much. I didn't see her anywhere, so I dashed out the glass doors of the building. Looking to my left, she was nowhere in sight. I looked right and saw her heading down the street.

I jogged in that direction. "Crista!"

She whirled around, looking alarmed. Gasping for air, I realized I had not thought this through in any way, shape, or form, despite my days of obsessing over speaking to her. When I went to a bar, I could pick up any woman in a heartbeat. I was smooth, calm, collected. I felt wealthy and powerful and in control.

Now I was panting and out of breath, with the woman I desired more than anything in the world staring at me as if I was an alien from another planet.

"Sorry. Sorry! I wasn't … chasing you … it's just … I had to … stairs …"

Crista's lovely face broke into a soft, sympathetic smile. She understood. At the moment, she didn't seem to think I was crazy. I had plenty of time to screw this up, though. Patiently, she waited until I regained the ability to speak. "Sorry. I just wanted to catch you before you left for the day. I wanted to ask you if you wanted to go out sometime."

Crista smiled sadly, and my heart went out to her. She drew in a breath, and her body tensed with fear. Elyse was right. Someone had hurt her.

"Why?" she asked.

"Why? Because I really like you and I think you're a wonderful woman, Crista."

"That's so nice of you, Keith. But I don't think so," she said, looking down.

"Are you sure? It wouldn't have to be anything big. We could just go for a drink or—"

When she looked up again, I was horrified to see tears in her eyes. "Crista, what's wrong?" I asked.

"I just … I don't understand what you want from me."

Good God, I was an idiot. I clearly did not know how to take a hint. The woman said no, and here I was harassing her on the street. I recalled doing the same stupid thing with Elyse. She had kindly and gently rebuffed my advances, but I persisted because I'd been *so sure* she was The One. Just like I was sure Crista was The One.

"Oh, Crista, I'm so sorry. You said no when Elyse asked you for me, and you're saying no now. I should have respected that. I didn't mean to upset you."

Crista gazed into my eyes, and I was struck with a sudden, irrefutable certainty.

It's different this time. I can feel it. She IS The One.

I didn't want to give up on her, but I knew I had to. It wasn't right to keep hounding her.

"I wanted a chance to get to know you better, but I didn't mean to upset you. I promise I won't bother you anymore. It's a standing offer, though. If you ever want to meet for coffee or something, you let me know, okay?"

Crista glanced up and to her left. We were standing right in front of a small coffee shop. She looked into my eyes for a moment.

"Is that a yes?" I asked.

"Yes," she said with a smile. "I have time right now for a quick cup of coffee if you want."

"I would love that," I said, smiling warmly at her.

This is your one shot. Don't blow it. Don't come on too strong or you'll scare her off.

I walked over to the door and held it open for her.

Scanning the place, I found a small table for two. Crista followed me to it. I pulled out a chair for her, and she seemed surprised. It made me wonder if she had dated jerks in the past who didn't know how to treat a lady. "So, Cin—," I began, then stopped. "Does it bother you when I call you 'Cinderella'?"

"No," she said, looking amused. "I think it's kind of cute."

"I'm not making fun of you when I call you that, you know."

"I know," Crista said with a laugh. "I can tell by the way you say it."

"Good. Now what can I get for you, Cinderella?"

"A coffee with a little cream, sugar, and some cinnamon would be nice."

"You've got it." I headed up to the front. A few minutes later, I returned to the table with our drinks.

"Thank you," she said, accepting the cup from me.

"It's my pleasure." I sat down across from her. "I'm sorry if it seems like I've been stalking you like a crazy person lately. I've just been thinking a lot about you since our misadventure in the elevator. Thanks again for everything you did to keep me from losing it completely."

"I'm glad I could help," she said as she sipped her coffee.

I gazed at her affectionately, wanting to know everything about her but hardly knowing where to start.

"So, where are you from? I mean, are you Puerto Rican, or ..."

Crista laughed. "I'm from here. I was born and raised in New York City."

Oh, dear God. I can't believe how badly I'm already screwing this up. She probably thinks I'm a racist moron.

"Oh, I—I'm so sorry. I—I didn't mean—"

Crista put down her coffee cup and reached across the table, putting her hand in mine. She wore the same gentle, sweet smile she'd had while she took care of me in the elevator. "It's all right, Keith. People ask me that all the time because I have brown skin and a bit of an accent. I don't mind at all. I was born here, but my parents are from Mexico. From a small county called Ticuani. They moved here when my mom was pregnant with me."

"Oh," I said, feeling relieved. Crista had an incredible way of comforting me when she spoke. No matter how dumb I was acting, she never made me feel stupid. Maybe I was crazy for believing she was The One, but all I knew was I felt good all over when I was with her. "So, do you speak Spanish?"

"*Claro que si*," Crista said. "Of course."

She made eye contact with me and smiled encouragingly. She must have known I was nervous and worried about saying the wrong thing. When Crista smiled at me, I felt like it was safe to talk to her about anything. She wouldn't laugh at me, and she wouldn't get angry if I put my foot in my mouth again.

"I'm fluent in Spanish and English. *Soy fluido en espanol y en ingles.*"

I took a risk and told her, "You sound so sexy when you speak Spanish."

Crista laughed. She squeezed my hand once more before letting go so she could sip her coffee. "Do you speak any Spanish?"

"None. I took French in high school, which is pretty useless."

"Hmm," she said thoughtfully. "I can say stuff to you in Spanish that I'm not brave enough to say to you in English. *Tienes un cuerpazo y hermosos ojos.*"

"I have Google Translate, you know," I said, raising an eyebrow. Her eyes opened wide, and I laughed. "Don't worry. I'll never remember what you just said."

Crista said shyly, "I said you have a great body and beautiful eyes."

"Thank you," I said, feeling a tingle of excitement ripple through me. "Do you ever go to Mexico to visit?"

"Yes, my parents and brothers and I try to go at least every other year. We go in January because there is a big celebration in Ticuani for *Padre Jesus*. He's our patron saint. They actually do a celebration here in New York, too. So, we go there if we can't get to Mexico."

"What is it like in Mexico? I've never been."

"It's nice. Quiet, especially compared to New York City. It's a slower pace of life there. Has its pros and cons, I guess. Ticuani is very poor, and it can be sad to visit."

"Yes, I guess so."

"My grandparents still live there, so it's always good to see them. I have some cousins there too. I try to send them money when I can, but it's hard. I work two jobs right now, and it's still hard for me to pay my own expenses sometimes."

I couldn't begin to imagine how hard Crista had to work for so little. My cushy desk job paid me far more than I was worth, that was for damn sure.

"I like visiting Mexico, but ..." She stopped, looking thoughtful for a moment. I wanted so much for her to open up to me, so I didn't dare move a muscle. "But sometimes I feel like I don't really belong anywhere. I'm not Mexican enough to fit in there, and I'm not American enough to fit in here."

"That must be very hard, Crista."

Her soft-brown eyes met my gaze, and I was again overwhelmed with the certainty that I was looking at the woman I would spend the rest of my life with. I ached to ask her if she felt the same way, but she might think I was completely nuts.

"I never talk about this kind of thing to anyone. I don't know what it is, but I feel safe when I'm with you."

"I know exactly what you mean," I reassured her. "I feel the same way about you."

"Nobody sees me as an American when they look at me. They assume I'm from another country, so it's hard to feel like I belong here."

"That's just what I did. I'm so sorry, Crista."

"It's okay. I'm not upset about it. It's just that so many people assume I don't belong here. That I might be here illegally. At work, most of the time people don't even speak to me. I always wonder if it's because they think I don't speak English. Besides, as a member of the cleaning staff, I'm supposed to be invisible. That is, unless there's a mess to clean up."

Although I was grateful Crista was opening up to me, I wasn't sure what to say.

"I hope I never made you feel invisible," I finally said.

"You didn't," she said. "Until the elevator, you never really spoke to me, but you always smiled at me. You never looked through me like so many others."

"I'm sorry I never talked to you before."

"Well, to be fair, I never spoke to you either. I thought about you, though," she said, looking down at her coffee.

"You did?" I asked, astonished.

"Yes," she confessed, still looking down.

"Are you close with your family?" I asked, changing the subject. As much as I was dying to ask her to elaborate, I wanted to make her more comfortable.

"I am," she said, finally looking up and smiling. "I have two bratty younger brothers and I'm very close with my mom and dad. My brothers still live in the city, but my parents are in New Jersey now."

"How old are these bratty brothers?"

"One is eighteen and one is twenty. They're good guys for the most part. Traditionally, Mexican men are supposed to be the ones in charge, you know? That's how it's been for a long time. It's one of the many things that makes it complicated when Mexicans move to America. Women gain more power, which is good, but it can be hard for some of the men to get used to it. When we visit Ticuani, it's perfectly acceptable for my two younger brothers to tell me what to do."

"And do they?"

"Kind of," Crista said, amusement shining in her eyes. "But they're mostly joking." More forcefully, she added, "But I'm very independent. They know better than to try to tell me what to do."

I held my hands up in mock defensiveness. "Good to know."

She giggled, then took another sip of coffee. I watched her for a moment, feeling like I could sit there and admire her for hours.

"Does your dad tell your mom what to do? I mean, they both grew up in Ticuani."

"No, my father has always been more modern thinking, thank goodness. Knowing him, he would get bored with a docile woman who agreed to follow his orders. My parents have a wonderful relationship. They've been married for forty-two years now. I always say they remind me of Morticia and Gomez Addams the way they can't keep their hands off each other."

"That's really sweet."

"It is." Crista's face shone with obvious affection for her family. "That's the kind of relationship I want."

"Do you want to get married and have kids someday?" I asked.

"Someday, yes. But only if the right man comes along."

"Hmmm," I said thoughtfully, making her laugh.

Crista seemed more relaxed than when we'd first sat down, but there still seemed to be a wall of protectiveness around her. I tried to imagine myself in her shoes. What if I had been the building's maintenance man or plumber or something, and suddenly one of the rich female executives had started hitting on me? I would probably wonder what she wanted from me, too.

"Tell me about your family," she said.

"Well, I don't have any brothers or sisters. I guess I'm just the stereotypical spoiled rich kid. Grew up in a fancy suburb in Boston."

"You don't tahk like you're from Bahstan," she quipped.

I laughed and said, "Nope. My parents made sure I spoke properly."

"You're not close with your parents, are you?" she observed.

"Is it that obvious?"

"Kind of."

I was impressed she had picked up on it so quickly. After all, I'd only said a few words about them.

"I know it's ridiculous of me to complain about such things since I grew up so privileged and all, but it was one of those deals where I was raised by a nanny. I didn't see my parents much."

"That's so sad."

Crista was working two jobs just to make ends meet, yet she still seemed to feel genuine empathy for my situation.

"My parents fought a lot, too. So as much as I wanted to have them around, it wasn't all that great when they were there. Still, the one thing I've never had to worry about was money."

"We grew up pretty poor," Crista said. "My father worked in a restaurant, and my mother worked in the garment district. Lots of long hours and little pay."

I nodded.

"But my parents were always around when I needed them. They created a warm, happy, loving home for us." Crista smiled, and the joy on her face made her lovelier than ever before. "So much laughter in my house. I had the most wonderful childhood growing up, and I wouldn't trade it for all the money in the world."

Crista reached over and took my hand. "I'm sorry you had such a hard time growing up. You deserved better."

I stared at her in amazement. It had never really occurred to me that it was okay to complain about my childhood, because I had been rich. I'd had every kind of toy I wanted, never had to worry about going hungry, and I'd had many opportunities in life because of my wealth. But the emotional and physical distance from my family felt like a huge, gaping hole in my heart. In my life. Talking with Crista made me understand that, despite all my privileges, it was okay to mourn the things I didn't have.

"Thanks for understanding. It's not something I ever really talk about. Everybody thinks since I've got money, I must have everything I want in life."

"There's more to life than money, but it sure can make things easier sometimes," Crista said with a weary smile. She glanced down at her coffee cup. "This is delicious. Might not seem like a big deal, but gourmet coffee is a small luxury I can't usually afford."

"I would buy you a whole damn coffee house if you would let me."

She laughed. I did too, but I was serious. I wanted to give her everything she'd ever wanted.

"That won't be necessary. But I appreciate the thought," she said, her eyes twinkling.

My mind wandered back to our time in the elevator.

"I really want to hear you sing again sometime," I told her.

"Well, I can't very well burst into song right here. Or at work."

"But you do sing while you work. I've heard you, Cinderella."

A somber look crossed her face. "I can't help it sometimes. I love to sing, but there's nowhere I can really do it without being a public nuisance. My apartment building is small, with thin walls, so I can't exactly belt out showtunes. Oh, you have no idea how much I envy people who have their own cars and can drive to work. People complain about how awful driving is in New York, but I would just sing the whole way to work." She paused a moment, then smiled. "It felt good to have an excuse to sing when we were in the elevator. I'm sorry you felt so trapped, but for once, I felt free."

"I still think you should try to sing professionally. Have you ever tried auditioning for anything?"

"What, and give up the dream of cleaning toilets and scrubbing floors?"

"Hey, there's nothing wrong with doing that for a living. If you told me it was your dream job, I'd say go for it. But I've heard your amazing voice, and I've seen what you look like when you sing."

"What do I look like?"

"You come alive. You look bright and happy and beautiful. I mean, you're always beautiful, but you're never prettier than when you're singing. It's not only the sound of your voice. It's the passion that radiates from your whole body when you perform. It's called stage presence. Star quality. And you've got it in spades."

"I don't even know what to say." Crista's voice was barely a whisper. "Thank you. And no, I've never auditioned for anything. I've never even set foot on a stage."

"That is a *crime*," I exclaimed, pounding my fist on the table. She laughed and shook her head.

"I used to sing for my family all the time when I was growing up. I was such a ham. Couldn't get enough of it. I never auditioned for plays in school, though I really wanted to."

"Why didn't you? Were you afraid?"

"Yes," she said, absently tracing the coffee shop logo on her cup. "But not of performing."

"Of what then?"

After a long pause, she lifted her gaze to meet mine. "You have to understand, Keith. We were so poor. Sometimes we went hungry because there wasn't enough money to feed all five of us. College was out of the question. Voice lessons weren't possible. Sure, maybe I could have gotten a part in one of my high school's musicals, but it would be the end of the road for me as far as performing. I guess I was afraid if I tried it, then I'd never want to stop. But I would have to, because there was no future in it for me. Being an actor and a singer, those are some of the most competitive fields in the *world*. Doesn't matter if you've got natural talent. It's not enough."

"You know who Johnny Creel is?"

"Yes, I know who Johnny Creel is, and I know where you're going with this," she said wryly.

Ignoring her tone, I pressed on. "He fell for a poor girl, and he loved her so much he built her an entire theater complex."

"And then the two of them became friends with Elyse Pippin and Luke Rannells, who spent the rest of their lives hounding me to go visit The Creel Foundation."

"And then Keith Foster was finally the one to convince Crista to give it a shot and she hobnobbed with those important theater folks and took voice lessons and became a big star and everyone lived happily ever after."

Crista threw her head back and laughed. "That's a nice story."

"Well, I know you're a sucker for fairy tales. I'm not going to let this go, you know. You have too much talent to let it go to waste."

She smiled gratefully at me. "You're very sweet."

Crista drained the last of her coffee. "Well, I guess I better be going. Thank you so much for the coffee and the wonderful company."

"I want to see you again, Crista."

With a doubtful look in her eyes, she asked plaintively, "Why?"

I leaned across the table, took her hand, and kissed it. Looking her in the eye, I asked, "Why don't you think I could be your Prince Charming?"

"Because I think you're too good to be true. Like I told Elyse, life doesn't work that way."

"Except when it does."

"Keith, you're rich and you're handsome. You could have any girl you want."

"You're the one I want. You really think I care that you're the cleaning woman? I'm not that kind of person, Crista."

"You're right," she said softly. "You're not that kind of person, and it's not fair of me to keep accusing you of it. I'm sorry."

"Besides, I think it might be cool to tell our kids someday how their mother once hit me with a toilet plunger."

Crista laughed heartily, and I could see some of her defensiveness slipping away.

I'm not going to hurt you, Crista. I swear.

"Can I take you out this Friday night?"

"I would love it, Keith. Yes."

"Yay!" I exclaimed like an excited kid, making her laugh again. "What do you want to do? Where do you want to go?"

"Honestly, I have no idea. I don't really go out much. I wish I did, I just don't have the time. I feel like all I do is work."

"Okay. Give me a little time, and I'll come up with something cool to do on our first official date."

A flash of excitement lit up her eyes. Some of the cautiousness remained, but she was starting to see I genuinely wanted to get to know her.

"Sounds wonderful. Thank you," she said with a smile.

We walked to the door and I held it open for her before we went our separate ways. I took out my cell phone. After a quick online search, I found the Broadway recording of *Rogers and Hammerstein's Cinderella*. I figured I should listen to it, since it meant so much to Crista.

Hearing the music from her favorite musical as I drove home gave me a terrific idea of what to do on our first date. At least, I thought it was terrific. Maybe it was stupid. I wasn't totally sure, so I decided to talk to Elyse the next morning. Not only did I want her advice, I would need her help to pull off my plan.

Not only did Elyse love my idea, she helped me put the final touches on it so it would be even better than I had anticipated. I knew the date was going to be wonderful, no matter where we went or what we did. Even so, I wanted my first date with Crista to be memorable.

Perhaps something to tell our kids about someday, in addition to the toilet plunger incident.

Chapter 6

So much for protecting my heart. It was far too late for that. Keith was dear and kind and perfect, not to mention impossible to resist. Spending time with him had been wonderful. Talking with Keith felt like being with a close friend. A close friend who happened to be dashingly handsome. I rarely talked to anyone about how it felt to be Mexican-American, especially in today's climate. Not that anyone ever asked me how it felt.

When Keith leaned in to listen to me, I knew it was safe to confide in him. And oh, those eyes. I could get lost in the blue of his eyes.

I was excited about our date on Friday night, but also quite nervous. I kept worrying about what I should wear. What if he took me someplace really fancy? I didn't own any fancy clothes, only a few simple dresses.

Although we didn't get a chance to talk anymore during the week, we exchanged smiles and secret glances whenever we saw each other. It was rather exciting. It did make me wonder, though, if Keith would ever tell anyone here about our relationship if we started dating seriously. Would he be ashamed to admit he was going out with the cleaning lady?

After obsessing all week about my wardrobe, I approached Keith in the hallway on the morning of our date.

"Hey there," he said with a handsome grin. "I'm glad it's finally Friday. Been looking forward to taking you out all week."

It comforted me that Keith spoke in a normal tone of voice. So far, he seemed to have no intention of hiding me.

"Me too," I said. "I just need to know what I should wear."

"Hmmm. Wear something that makes you feel beautiful."

Somehow, he always knew the right thing to say.

"Okay," I said softly as the weight of worry lifted from my shoulders. Keith had this way of making me feel perfect just the way I was. "I can't wait to see you tonight."

Keith's smile broadened. "Six-thirty can't come soon enough, as far as I'm concerned." I watched him walk away, missing him already.

He'd looked so grateful for my words. It made me realize how unfair I'd been to try to keep him at arm's length. He had been nothing but warm and kind to me, and I had no reason to think he had an ulterior motive.

I still had a tiny, niggling doubt that this must be too good to be true. My muscles tensed whenever I thought about how dangerous it might be to trust a man like Keith. My immediate concern was he would expect sex tonight after our date. I knew it was hardly uncommon for people to have sex after the first date, but it was far too fast for me. I needed to be sure a man genuinely cared for me before I would even consider sleeping with him. With Keith, I needed extra reassurance. He was rich and powerful, and I needed to make one-hundred-percent sure he wasn't playing some kind of game with me.

I'd been played before, and it nearly tore me apart. I would not allow that to happen ever again.

I did my best to shake off my concerns and allowed myself to be excited about our date. If Keith made a move, I would simply tell him I wasn't ready. That was all there was to it.

At the end of the day, I rushed through my final office cleaning. I needed time to go home and get ready. Keith had said he would pick me up at my place, so I'd texted him my address.

I breathed in the warm, spring air as I walked from the subway toward my tiny apartment in Jackson Heights in Queens. Shivers of delight ran through me just thinking about being with Keith tonight. Then I got a text from him. My heart nearly stopped for a moment, thinking he might be cancelling our date.

Hey Cinderella. I couldn't find a carriage pulled by horses on short notice, but I am sending a car to come pick you up. Can't wait to see you.

I wondered exactly what "sending a car" meant. Good Lord, he really was wealthy. It was so strange, and such a contrast to my own life.

I felt slightly relieved. Sending a car probably meant a driver would pick me up and Keith wouldn't see my apartment. It was nothing to be ashamed of, I knew. I worked hard to afford my place, and I was proud of my apartment and the neighborhood—one of many "Little Mexicos" in New York—where I lived. I loved it. Delicious food, friendly neighbors, and I could speak Spanish whenever I wanted, without receiving hateful stares.

Proud as I was of my place, I worried the contrast to Keith's life might be overwhelming for him. I was *poor*. Every dime I had went to basic living expenses: food and rent. I didn't have the time or money for much else. It might have been a bit of a shock for him to visit me here, especially on our first date.

I hurried to my apartment to get ready. I knew exactly what I wanted to wear. My favorite dress was a white, off-the-shoulder dress with a blue flowered pattern. Made in Mexico, it flowed down past my knees, light and airy and feminine. Yes, it made me feel beautiful. Although still concerned about being underdressed for wherever

Keith was taking me, I was thrilled for the chance to have him see me in something other than my grungy work clothes.

At precisely 6:30 there was a knock at my door. A handsome gentleman in his late thirties or so, with brown hair and friendly blue eyes smiled at me when I opened the door. He was smartly dressed with a chauffeur's cap, which he tipped by way of greeting.

"Hello. Ms. Rivera?"

"Crista, yes." I looked him up and down and returned his smile. "Wow, Keith really went all out, didn't he?"

"Mr. Foster said only the best for you. My name is Joey, and I'll be your driver this evening. Are you ready to go, or do you need more time?"

"I'm ready," I said, picking up my wrap and my purse.

Joey led me out onto the street where a number of my neighbors had gathered around. A limo was a rare sight in this neighborhood. He opened the door and helped me inside. It wasn't a horse-drawn carriage, yet I certainly felt like a princess with this royal treatment.

"Wow, I've never been in a limo before," I said, not even trying to play it cool. Joey seemed nice and not snooty at all, so I figured it was safe to be myself.

"Well, I hope you enjoy it," Joey said, his eyes crinkling with warmth as he smiled. "There are plenty of cold drinks in the bar there. Wine, beer, soda. Please help yourself."

"Thank you so much. Where are we going?"

Joey smiled apologetically. "I've been instructed to keep it a secret until we get there. I'm sorry."

I laughed. "That's okay. I'll find out soon enough."

"Press this button right here if you need anything, okay?" Joey said, gesturing to the call button.

"I will. Thank you."

Joey shut the door and headed up to the driver's seat.

I couldn't get over the spaciousness of the car. There was more room to spread out in here than in my own living room. Keith must have spent a lot of money to rent this limo for me. It was thoughtful, yet a bit overwhelming. I wondered if I could ever get used to his wealth.

I expected the car to head toward Manhattan, perhaps to a fancy restaurant, but we seemed to be driving to Brooklyn. My stomach tingled with excitement. The mere idea of seeing Keith and having an official date with him was thrilling. We could hang out on a park bench and eat hot dogs for all I cared. As long as I was with him.

After a half hour or so, the limo stopped. Joey gallantly helped me step out of the car and closed the door behind me.

"Right this way," he said, offering me his arm. I took it and giggled happily, and he seemed pleased with my excitement. We walked up to a building that took up an entire city block. Then I saw the name on the building.

The Creel Foundation.

"Oh, the little sneak!" I said with a laugh.

Smiling a tad guiltily, Joey punched in the security code to open the front door. I wondered if Keith had told him I liked to sing.

Joey led me down a long hall filled with pictures. I recognized the beautiful red-haired girl featured in many of the photographs. Rosemary Sutton. She was the girlfriend—fiancée, actually—of the famous Johnny Creel. Heir to a billion-dollar fortune, Johnny had been notorious as a spoiled playboy. I'd heard he was pretty obnoxious until he fell in love with Rosemary and became a changed man. Johnny had used his wealth for a good cause, building this huge theater complex for Rosemary to use as a rehearsal studio and, most importantly, for teaching acting, dancing, and singing lessons for underprivileged kids.

Joey waited patiently as I stopped to look at the photos. I stared, mesmerized, at a photograph of Rosemary, dressed in 1960s garb, onstage in the ensemble of *Hairspray* on Broadway. She was stunningly beautiful in the picture, and oh, how I admired her.

Her story had been on the news and TV after two videos of her singing with Johnny went viral. In the first video, Johnny sang to her by way of apology for acting like a big jerk. Rosemary responded with a fiery song of anger, before gently transitioning into one of forgiveness. It was only a few minutes long, but it was full of passion and drama. More recently, a video of Johnny proposing marriage through song had become famous. Elyse and Luke were in that one, all part of a musical routine staged by Johnny to serenade Rosemary. Moved by his loving gesture, Rosemary sang a love song from *Thoroughly Modern Millie.*

Rosemary Sutton was such an inspiration to me. For years, she'd worked a full-time day job while performing in community theaters at night, before she moved to New York. Johnny had been famous his whole life. Pretty much everything he did was big news. To me, Rosemary was the real star.

I'd lost count of how many times I had watched those videos, not to mention the dozens of other performances Rosemary had posted online. Beautiful, and mesmerizing when she performed, it was no wonder she'd made it to the Broadway stage. She was incredible.

Rosemary had been broke like me once, too. And look at her now.

I laughed when I saw the next photograph: Luke, surrounded by a bunch of adorable kids playing musical instruments. It was from the show *School of Rock*—he must have played the lead.

"I work with him," I explained.

Joey nodded with a smile.

I finished looking at all the pictures, and finally allowed poor Joey to do his job and take me to wherever we were going. As we walked a bit faster, I saw Joey send a quick one-word text. *Now.*

He led me to a set of double doors and opened them for me. I stood, astonished, as I looked upon the biggest and loveliest auditorium I had ever seen. There must have been two thousand seats, and the stage was huge, with a heavy red velvet curtain pulled open. Keith stood in the middle of the stage and music played.

My heart leapt when I recognized the overture to *Cinderella.* I gasped and covered my mouth.

My heart began to beat rapidly as Keith walked down the steps from the stage.

"Mr. Foster will take care of you from here," Joey said, gesturing for me to go join him.

"Yes, thank you. Thank you so much!"

"It's been my pleasure, I assure you," he said with another tip of his cap.

I walked—more like floated—toward Keith. His blue eyes sparkled, and he was a vision in his dark-blue suit and tie. It was a different suit than he had worn at work today, and I felt honored that he had clearly spent time and effort to look his most dashing tonight.

Keith greeted me at the bottom of the stage steps and reached for my hands and held them. He let his gaze travel leisurely up and down my body.

"My God, you look beautiful," he said, admiring my dress.

"And you look so handsome," I said, wishing I could come up with a better word to describe how gorgeous he was.

He gently kissed my hand, then led me up to the stage. My legs felt a bit shaky as I gazed around in wonder. Keith let go of my hand.

"Go on. Explore."

I drew in a deep breath and walked to the center of the stage and looked out at all the empty seats. I stood there for several minutes lost in the fantasy of what it might be like to actually perform here.

Keith came up behind me and leaned in to murmur in my ear. "Stay right there," he instructed.

"Okay," I said with a small laugh. I was so mesmerized by this place that I could hardly think straight. Keith walked over to the sound system at the side of the stage. He turned off the overture, then I heard the first few notes of "In My Own Little Corner."

I turned to see Keith with a huge grin on his face. "Go on. I know you know the words to this one, because I heard it in the elevator. Sing!"

Reflexively, as if I had been preparing for this moment my whole life, I turned toward my imaginary audience and launched into the song. The sound of my own voice stunned me. I *never* had the chance to belt out a song the way I longed to. Even in the elevator I had toned it down because of the people working on the elevator who would think I was nuts.

Here, at long last, I had permission to sing my heart out. In that moment, I *became* Cinderella. And what a perfect song. I sang loudly and proudly about using my imagination to pretend I was any number of things rather than a poor, overworked woman. I sang about being in my own little corner, being anything I wanted to be. Fantasizing I was a princess, a prima donna in Milan, an heiress, a huntress on an African safari, and a girl that men went crazy over. Surprising even myself, I swept across the stage, utterly lost in my performance.

I felt free and happy and energized in a way I'd never felt; so wrapped up in my song, I nearly forgot Keith was there.

When the song ended, I stood onstage for a moment, panting with exhilaration. I wanted this moment to never end.

"My God, Crista," he whispered. He appeared to be genuinely stunned at my performance. He wasn't the only one. I'd had no idea I could perform like that. I had always wildly fantasized that someday

I could get up onstage and sing, but until now, I never knew if I was actually capable of it.

I walked over to Keith, not taking my eyes off his. Those beautiful blue eyes were filled with joy at seeing my happiness. I was struck with a sudden realization, a certainty.

This is not a man who is using me for anything. I don't have to be afraid. His heart is pure. I can feel it.

Keith pulled me into his arms and embraced me. After a little while, he let go of me and said, "That was incredible. You're such a gifted performer."

I didn't know what to say. All I knew was, for the first time I *felt* like a gifted performer.

He stroked my face and said, "Listen, I'm not the greatest at this, but I'm going to do my best, okay?"

I frowned, having no idea what he meant. He walked over to the sound system again and selected another song.

My heart caught in my throat as I recognized the song. "Ten Minutes Ago." The song in which the prince falls for Cinderella and realizes his entire life has changed in a matter of minutes. I'd lost count of how many times I had thought about the song as I worked, imagining Keith as the prince in this scenario.

He walked over to me, put his hand around my waist, and began to dance with me. And *sing*. He actually sang the words to "Ten Minutes Ago" as he led me across the stage floor. His voice wasn't fancy, but he hit the notes perfectly.

We gazed deeply into each other's eyes as we danced. It was as if Keith could see right into my soul as he made my fantasy become a reality. I wasn't sure what was more exciting—being in Keith's arms, or being on the stage. Both experiences were magical.

He finished singing the prince's part, and I found it easy to sing Cinderella's part, fearlessly serenading him as we danced across the stage. Keith was right. I *did* come alive when I sang.

When the song ended, I took a step back and curtsied to him as if he were actually royalty. He laughed softly, looking charmed.

Feeling bold, I drew in a deep breath and serenaded Keith with "He Was Tall," the song from the show where Cinderella reflects on how dreamy and wonderful the prince was. I was a bit nervous about singing anything without the music behind me, but I did pretty well. I smiled broadly at him as I got to the line about the prince having blue eyes. Lowering my head, I sang the part about how all the ladies turned their heads to see him, and how I did the same. I lifted my head shyly to look at him as Cinderella had done.

I'd always had a deep passion for singing, but I hadn't realized how much fun acting could be. Of course, I was falling hard for Keith, so this was hardly just for show. Even so, standing on this stage, singing and acting, made me feel transported to an enchanted land of make-believe.

"That was beautiful," Keith said when I finished my song. Wordlessly, he went back over to the sound system. Soon, the strains of "Cinderella's Waltz" began to play. He bowed to me, then put one hand around my waist and took my hand in his, leading me in another dance across the floor.

This song was entirely instrumental, and we danced together in perfect harmony, never taking our eyes off each other. When the song began to wind down, Keith slowed his dancing.

Kiss me, I implored him with my eyes. There would never be a more perfect moment for a first kiss.

Keith cupped my face in his strong, masculine hands, gazed into my eyes, then closed them and lowered his lips to mine. I wrapped my arms around his neck and let out a soft, dreamy moan as he kissed me.

It was the most magical moment of so many others this evening.

The raw power and passion in his kiss was like nothing I'd ever experienced. My entire body tingled with affection and desire, and I was struck with another sudden realization. I knew it as surely as I knew my own name.

Keith is the man I will spend the rest of my life with. Someday, I will hear the words "You may now kiss the bride," and Keith will be standing across from me. Kissing me passionately just like he is right now.

After our long and perfect kiss, our lips eventually parted. Keith ran his fingers tenderly through my hair.

"Thanks for taking a chance on me," he said.

"Thanks for not giving up on me," I said, feeling tears form in my eyes. How could I have thought this man's intentions were anything but honorable?

"Will you do something for me?" Keith asked.

"Of course. Anything."

"Will you sing for me again?"

I smiled wryly. "You're sneaky, tricking me into coming here after Elyse and Luke have been trying for months."

He shot me the sexiest, most mischievous smile I'd ever seen.

"What do you want me to sing?"

"I loved the song you did from *Phantom of the Opera*. Will you do that one?"

"Of course," I said, adrenaline already pumping at the idea of taking center stage again.

"I'll see if I can find the music," he said, walking across the stage. "Okay, got it," he said after a brief search.

The strains of "Think of Me" began to play. And I began to sing.

It was a rich and powerful song with a terrific build. As I sang, I alternated between looking over at Keith and gazing out at the invisible audience. Once again, I was floored by the sound of my own voice. I truly hadn't known I was capable of projecting so well.

I brought the song to its intense conclusion, grateful I managed to nail the final high notes. Keith applauded loudly, and I bowed to the imaginary audience. I went over to where he stood, and he pulled me into his arms.

"Thank you for making me do this. This whole thing," I said as I glanced over at the stage, out at the auditorium, then back to him. "It's been so wonderful. The limo must have cost you a fortune."

Keith wrinkled his nose in the cutest way. "Honestly? It didn't cost a dime. The limo belongs to a friend of Elyse's, and the driver works for him."

"Well, it's the thought that counts." My throat tightened and tears sprang to my eyes. "And this was the most thoughtful thing anyone's ever done for me."

He smiled and ran his fingers through my hair, gazing at me fondly. "You're so incredibly talented. You have so much to offer, and I want to do everything I can to help share your gift with the world. I was afraid you wouldn't come if I told you where we were going."

"I don't know. It would have been pretty hard to say no to you."

He leaned in and kissed me again, sending shivers of delight all through me.

"You must be starving by now. May I take you to dinner?"

"That would be lovely. Thank you."

Keith put his hand on my back and led me to the double doors of the auditorium. I took one last look at the majestic theater space before he turned off the lights.

Chapter 7

Joey and the limousine were waiting for us when we came out of The Creel Foundation. Crista's eyes lit up when she saw it, and she shook her head in wonder.

"This was my first ride in a limousine," she said with a lovely smile. "It's so much fun!"

Her enthusiasm was infectious. She appreciated every gesture I made for her, no matter how simple. It was quite a difference from the jaded women I usually dated.

Joey tipped his cap to her before opening the limo door. I knew he was getting paid by David Groff, his employer, but I still had every intention of giving him a generous tip at the end of the night. He certainly deserved it.

I followed Crista into the limo and sat beside her on the back seat, watching as she surveyed the luxurious interior of the car as if she was seeing it for the first time.

"Incredible," she said. "The only time I've ever seen the inside of a limo is on TV and in the movies."

"Well, I'll be sure to hire one when you open your first show on Broadway."

Crista laughed heartily, like it was the craziest thing she'd ever heard. She still didn't seem to grasp how talented she really was. If I could convince her to seriously pursue theater work, there was no doubt in my mind that she had a good shot of making it big.

She snuggled up next to me, and I put my arm around her and pulled her in close. So far, I'd been very careful about not coming on too strong. She'd seemed so wary of me ever since we'd first met, and I knew I needed to take things slowly. I'd done my best to stay tuned to her signals this evening, not kissing her until I was pretty sure it was what she wanted.

I'd been nervous she might be angry about me tricking her into visiting The Creel Foundation, since she'd said no to me, Elyse, and Luke so many times. To my relief, the evening could not have been more perfect. Crista seemed overjoyed to be there, and my God, she was beautiful when she sang. I knew she'd be a natural onstage.

Dancing with her in my arms had been glorious. Admittedly, I was a complete sap when it came to old-fashioned romance. I loved that kind of thing, and I wanted nothing more than to shower Crista with attention and affection. I'd never dated anyone who would have appreciated the kind of evening I had prepared for her tonight. Most of the women I'd been out with would probably have laughed in my face, thinking the whole thing was cheesy and stupid.

Not Crista. She was enthralled, and I relished the dreamy look in her eyes when we'd danced across the stage floor. She deserved to be treated like a princess. It also felt good to feel in control for once. Finally, I'd had a chance to show her I was a man and not a wimp like I'd been in the elevator.

Crista sighed softly as she settled comfortably in my arms. I felt her body relax against mine, and once again, I was overwhelmed with the certainty that we belonged together. Being with her felt right, like she was what I'd been missing my whole life. My parents never showed any affection toward each other or to me, so I wasn't sure how I ended up being such a touchy-feely kind of guy, but I was. It was nice having Crista around, so I could have someone to take care of. It was dumb to get too far ahead of myself, but I couldn't shake the image of us with a bunch of kids. A family to care for. Something to come home to after a hard day's work.

We didn't talk much on the ride to Manhattan, but the silence was comfortable. It was enough for us just to be together. As I held her in my arms, I absently traced the pattern on her delicate dress. It suited her perfectly; she looked so pretty.

Joey double-parked right outside the entrance to Cicero's Restaurant. He took Crista's hand and helped her out of the limo, and then I got out.

"Just give me a holler when you're ready for me again," Joey said. "Enjoy your meal."

"Thanks, Joey," I said.

I put my hand on Crista's back and led her into the restaurant. I'd made a reservation, so we were seated right away. She seemed a little nervous as she scanned the room.

"You all right?"

"I feel underdressed," she said. It was a fancy restaurant, so all the men wore suits and the women mostly wore darker-colored dresses, perhaps more suited for evening wear than Crista's lighter one. Not that it really mattered. My only concern was Crista's comfort.

"I think your dress is perfect. Elegant and pretty, like you. You're easily the most beautiful woman here."

"I'm sure that's not true," Crista said with a shy smile. Then she added softly, "But you make me feel like it is."

We gazed into each other's eyes for a moment, and that familiar sense of peace and comfort settled over me. I wondered if she felt the same way.

The sommelier, a young woman in her thirties or so, with her blond hair tied back, arrived at our table. "Good evening."

"Good evening," I replied.

"May I start you off with some wine tonight?"

"Gosh, I haven't even looked at the list," I said, picking it up from the table. I scanned it for a moment. "Yes, I'll have a glass of Sauvignon blanc."

The wine steward turned to Crista, who looked anxious and unsure of how to answer.

"Do you like wine, Crista?" I asked gently.

"I, well, I like sangria."

"We have an excellent mango strawberry sangria," the sommelier offered.

"Oh, that sounds delicious. Thank you," Crista said.

"Wonderful. Your server will be with you shortly."

"Thanks," I said. I flipped open my menu, and Crista did the same. Discreetly, I lifted my eyes to watch her, still trying to read her signals to make sure she was all right. I remembered what Elyse had told me about Luke's defensiveness on their first date. I certainly didn't care if she was poor, but I didn't want her to think for a moment that I thought less of her for it. I wasn't better than her because I was rich. I was simply lucky.

Crista scanned her menu and let out a small gasp. "Everything is so expensive," she whispered.

"Don't you worry about that," I told her.

The crease in her forehead told me she was very much worried.

"Hey," I said, reaching across the table and taking her hand. "I work a lot of overtime, and sometimes I feel like my whole life is my work. That's not the way I want my life to be. The truth is ..."

I paused for a moment, not sure how much I wanted to confess to her. The gentle expression of concern in her soft-brown eyes told me I had nothing to fear by confiding in her.

"The truth is I'm pretty lonely most of the time. Sounds dumb, but I work all the time and have all this money piling up and nothing to do with it. I love taking you out and doing things with you. I mean, the limo and the theater thing tonight, that didn't cost me anything because I've got connections and all, but I would have spent thousands to make that happen if I had to. It would all be worth it to see you smile and just to be able to spend time with you."

The tension in her brow relaxed a bit, and she nodded. I got the feeling my confession about being lonely helped to even things out between us. I remembered her saying she wouldn't have traded her loving family for anything in the world. Yes. She understood what I was trying to say.

"So please. Let me spoil you, Cinderella."

That got a big beautiful smile from her.

We placed our orders and chatted for a while, sipping our wine and enjoying each other's company. At the same time our meals were brought out, a pianist arrived and began to play a lovely grand piano in the center of the restaurant.

"Oh, that is so pretty," Crista said, and I could see how much she loved music. Her eyes danced with joy as she listened.

"Well, what are you waiting for? Get up and sing for us."

She giggled. "Can you imagine getting up and belting out showtunes in a place like this?"

I chuckled too. She wasn't wrong. It would be hilarious to see how people would react.

"Yeah, I can just see me going …" And with that, she leaned in toward me and quietly sang a line from "Everything is Coming Up Roses" in an exaggerated Ethel Merman voice. I had to cover my mouth to keep from laughing out loud.

"That would be priceless," I told her.

We ate in silence for a short while, enjoying the beautiful piano music and the ambiance of the restaurant. Crista seemed much more relaxed now. I could understand why she felt out of her element, just as I would if—or hopefully, when—I had a chance to visit her neighborhood in Queens.

We finished our meals. Rather, I finished my meal and Crista had half of hers boxed up because she couldn't eat it all. As we waited for the check, Crista gazed across the table at me.

"This whole night has been incredible," she said. "I'm sorry I kept running away from you at first. It wasn't that I wasn't interested. I've *always* been interested. Even before the elevator."

"Really?" She'd alluded to it before, but I wanted to hear more.

"You were always my fantasy prince, Keith. You know, while I was working." She closed her eyes and let out a breath, then opened her eyes and looked at me. "I was utterly horrified when I hit my prince with a toilet plunger."

We shared a laugh.

"I thought it was cute!"

"I know," she said with a grateful smile. "That's one of the things that makes you so wonderful. At first, I was overwhelmed. I couldn't let myself believe you were actually interested in me."

"I know on the surface we're very different people. I understand why you might have trouble trusting my intentions, but when two people are meant to be together, there doesn't have to be a logical reason."

"It does feel like we're meant to be together, doesn't it?" she said.

I swallowed against the lump in my throat.

She feels it, too.

The server brought the check before I could answer, but I believed the look in my eyes told her all she needed to know.

Joey was waiting outside for us when we left the restaurant.

"You look tired," I said to Crista. "Are you ready to go home?"

"Yes, I think so."

"We're ready to head back," I told Joey. "Thanks for everything."

"My pleasure," Joey said. I slipped him a hundred-dollar bill. "Thank you, sir. Very much appreciated."

I clapped him on the back and followed Crista into the limo. We settled in close together, her head resting on my shoulder. After a little while, she lifted her head to look at me.

"This was the most wonderful night of my life," she told me.

"Mine too."

She shot me a wry look, but I was serious. Sure, I had the means to go to fancy restaurants every night of the week, but what good was that without someone to share it with? I couldn't ever remember being happier than I was right now.

Gently lifting her chin, I kissed her. She put her arms around my neck and eagerly kissed me back. My cock grew hard, and I wanted nothing more than to take Crista back to my place and make love to her all night long.

I had no intention of making a move, though. Not tonight. I had to take things slow with Crista. She'd been wary enough about going out with me tonight, and I didn't want her to think for a second that I had any ulterior motives.

Sure enough, Crista began to pull away when our kissing became more passionate. She broke off the kiss and settled back down next to me, her head on my shoulder again.

"I like when you lay on me like this." I played with her hair and kissed her forehead. There were plenty of ways besides sex to show my affection for her, and I knew that was what Crista needed. Lots of reassurance that I wasn't playing games with her.

"I like it too," she said with a happy sigh.

When we got to Jackson Heights, Joey helped Crista out of the limo, and I walked her to the front door of her apartment. She seemed nervous. I was fairly certain she wasn't ready to invite me in to see her apartment yet. My heart ached to see that she lived in such a poor neighborhood, but I tried not to show my concern. If I had my way, someday she would live with me in my Manhattan apartment.

Smiling at her and gently stroking her hair, I said, "I had a wonderful time tonight. And I look forward to many more wonderful dates with you. If you want, that is."

"Of course, that's what I want," Crista said, looking up at me with those sweet brown eyes.

"Before I go, I just want to say …" I cupped her face with my hands. "There are two things I know for sure, and I hope sometime soon you'll realize them too."

Crista regarded me with fascination, waiting.

"You belong on the stage. And you belong with *me*."

I kissed her tenderly, yet firmly, one more time before turning to go.

Chapter 8

When I woke up on Saturday morning I thought I had dreamed everything. For a moment, I lay in bed relishing the dream of Keith dancing with me across the stage floor.

Then it dawned on me that it really had happened. All of it. Keith sending a fancy limousine for me. Him standing on the stage of The Creel Foundation, looking more handsome than he'd been in my wildest fantasies. Keith dancing with me, holding me in his arms, kissing me.

It was all real.

I never stopped smiling the entire weekend, even though I worked through most of it. I cleaned several private homes on Saturdays to supplement my income from my regular job, and my employers probably thought I was high or something. I certainly felt like I was floating on air.

Not only was spending time with Keith exhilarating, but singing onstage was an experience I knew I'd never forget. It made me a tad wistful, though. I was beginning to regret not trying out for the theater shows in high school. That had probably been my only real chance. No use fretting about it now. My life was full of regrets, stupid mistakes, and missed opportunities. I should be used to it.

I shoved those negative thoughts away and allowed myself to indulge in the sweet memories of my magical date with Keith. He could not have been more generous, more thoughtful.

And such a perfect gentleman.

Though I was grateful he hadn't made any sexual advances yet, I couldn't help but fantasize about Keith making love to me. I just knew he would be a tender, passionate, terrific lover. He was always so attentive to my needs. Oh, yes. He would know exactly how to satisfy me.

I wished I could do the same for him. Good-looking, wealthy, and charming, Keith had probably been with lots of women. *Experienced* women who knew how to please a man in bed. As much as I wanted to have sex with Keith, the thought made me incredibly nervous.

But in my fantasies, everything was perfect. In my imagination, our lovemaking was sensual, emotional, and intensely pleasurable. Vividly, I pictured Keith on top of me, pounding me hard and moaning my name over and over. It was easy for me to imagine what Keith looked like covered in a sexy film of sweat, because I had seen him like that in the elevator. In my fantasy, it was the physical exertion of fantastic sex that made him sweat, his face filled with passion and desire instead of fear.

I could spend hours dreaming about all the ways Keith and I could physically exhaust each other. I did just that all weekend. He was all I could think about.

Keith might not know I was a virgin, but he probably knew I wasn't the type to have sex on the first date. As much as I desired him, I was tremendously relieved when he kissed me goodnight and left it at that. I truly did trust him, but I still couldn't shake the last vestiges of doubt that he was using me for some reason. His gentlemanly manner helped put some of those doubts to rest.

I could hardly wait to see him on Monday. I wondered how he would treat me at work. Would he acknowledge our personal relationship, or were we supposed to keep it secret?

To my disappointment, I didn't even see Keith for most of the day on Monday. I hadn't seen Elyse either, so I suspected they'd been tied up in meetings all day. It was after 4pm when I walked past Elyse's office and heard her call my name. I backtracked and went in.

"So, how was your weekend?" Elyse asked with a knowing smile.

"Perfect," I said, dropping into the seat across from her.

"Was it wonderful and awesome and super romantic?"

"Yes, yes, and yes. Was the Creel Foundation thing all your idea?"

"No, not at all. The limo was my idea, but the rest was all Keith. I mean, I helped coordinate with Johnny and Rosemary about using the theater space, but that was it." She leaned in toward me. "Did you sing for him?"

"Yes," I said.

And I also sang for me.

I remembered how, for a brief moment, I had gotten lost in performing and had nearly forgotten Keith was there watching me.

"It was amazing," I said.

"Hey, Romeo!" Elyse yelled suddenly, looking out her office door.

Keith chuckled and ducked his head into her office. "You bellowed?"

"I sure did," Elyse said with a grin.

"Hey," Keith said to me with a tender, affectionate look in his eye. Only in my fantasies had any man looked at me like that.

"Hey," I said back. It was a simple one-word exchange, but I knew our eyes said so much more to each other.

I missed seeing you today. I had a wonderful time over the weekend. I love being with you.

"If you guys are done undressing each other with your eyes, I have a question for you," Elyse said bluntly.

I laughed and looked down shyly. I could feel Keith's eyes still on me, and it was kind of a turn-on. As if he was aware I had frequent sexual fantasies about him. I wondered if he'd thought about me that way. I certainly hoped so.

"I don't know if you two have plans for this Friday night yet, but Luke's off-Broadway show is opening. Do you guys want to come?"

"What do you think?" Keith asked. "Do you want to go?"

"Sure, I would love it! I would be honored to be there to support him on his special night. I've never been to an off-Broadway show. I've never been to a Broadway show either."

"Really?" Keith asked, eyes wide.

I shook my head.

He turned to Elyse and smiled. "I'm sure Luke's show will be awesome. With him in it, I'm sure it will be hilarious."

Elyse smiled proudly. "I know. He's been working so hard on it for so long. I can't wait to see it."

"Great. Count us in, then," Keith said. "Well, I better get back to work. My boss'll kill me if I don't finish this presentation on time."

"Yes. Yes, she will," Elyse said firmly.

Keith grinned at me, then headed out into the hallway.

"I better get back to work, too," I said, standing up. "Thanks so much for all your matchmaking help with me and Keith."

"Happy to help," she said, smiling.

I went out into the hallway and, within seconds, I heard footsteps. I turned to glance behind me, and there was Keith. He grinned mischievously, then he cupped my face and kissed me. Oh, how I had ached for another kiss since he left me at my doorstep on Friday night. His touch quenched my deep thirst.

When he lifted his lips from mine, I let out a slightly nervous laugh. I looked down the hallway. A few people were standing around, but nobody was paying any attention to us.

Keith smiled at me. "Don't worry. There's no rule against dating a co-worker here. I checked with HR." He kissed me once more, then said, "Okay. I'm really going back to work now."

With that, he turned on his heel and headed toward his office.

My heart overflowed with joy as I watched Keith walk briskly away. He clearly had no intention of hiding our relationship at work. In a daze, I walked down the hall to pick up my cleaning cart.

This time, I wouldn't have to turn to my fantasies to get me through the work day. All I had to do was think about my real life.

*****

Keith came to pick me up at my apartment on Friday night. I considered trying to meet him at the front door of the building so he wouldn't have to see the inside of my tiny, 500-square-foot studio apartment, but I decided against it. He'd have to see my place sometime; there was no point in putting it off.

I opened the door to greet him, and he took a full step back to look me up and down. "Wow, you look beautiful!"

I smiled and twirled around so Keith could see all of my dress. Since this was an evening event, I figured none of my light-colored dresses would be appropriate. I'd bought a dark-blue knee-length dress for tonight. Thank God for Goodwill stores.

Keith planted a kiss on my lips before taking a look at my apartment. I saw a flicker of sadness in his eyes. I didn't mind living in such a small space. I'd lived in cramped apartments with my family for most of my life, and now I lived in a cramped apartment all by myself. It may not have been much to look at, but it was all mine.

"Your place is nice," Keith said with a smile.

"Thanks," I said, glancing at my tiny living room, trying to see it from his perspective. I turned back and watched as Keith surveyed my living room; the hardwood floor; my somewhat worn-out blue couch; and my wooden entertainment center with a small television in the center. His eyes opened wide as he took in the ornate floral tapestry I had hanging on the wall. He walked over to inspect it more closely.

"This is really beautiful," he said.

"My grandmother made it," I said proudly.

"Really?" Keith asked, looking impressed. "Your grandmother who still lives in Ticuani?"

My heart swelled. I couldn't believe he remembered. He was the first man in a long time who had paid that much attention to me, and I was constantly amazed by his thoughtfulness. I hadn't known men like him existed outside of fairy tales.

"Yes, that's the one."

Keith scanned the rest of my apartment. I had various pieces of art displayed on the walls—cheap prints, mostly. Even so, they brightened up the place.

"You did a nice job decorating in here. Very nice. Everything is pretty, but it feels homey, too."

I smiled at him. "Yes. That's exactly how I feel about living here. I'm guessing you could fit about five of my apartments into your place, huh?"

Keith shrugged as if it was no big deal. "Maybe. I don't know. Are you ready to go?"

"Yes."

He slipped his arm around my waist, and we headed out to his car.

Though the limo ride had been fun, I enjoyed being in Keith's car even more. The car itself was nice—a comfortable BMW sedan of some sort—but I really loved being next to him in the passenger seat. It felt as if we were a real couple, out on a date. I was happy being by his side wherever we were.

We parked the car and walked hand in hand to the New York City Center—the theater where Luke's show would debut tonight. Elyse spotted us the moment we walked into the lobby and waved us over.

I gasped when I saw who was with her.

Keith chuckled. "Oh, yeah. Everybody's here. Well, you knew she was a personal friend of Johnny Creel's."

I nodded. Though it was a bit surreal to see Johnny Creel up close, he wasn't the one who had me starstruck.

"Good to see you again," Keith said, offering Johnny a firm handshake. "I can't thank you enough for letting us use your gorgeous theater the other night."

"My pleasure," Johnny said, his warm gray eyes full of kindness and humor. "I know how it is. You gotta go all out when you have a classy girl you want to impress."

Johnny turned to me and shook my hand. "Nice to meet you, Crista."

"You too," I said. I drew in a shaky breath and turned to Rosemary. It was like I was meeting my idol, and I had absolutely no idea what to say to her.

"Crista, it's so nice to finally meet you," Rosemary said, her lovely green eyes shining with warmth. She was even prettier in person.

"You too." It was a woeful understatement. I held out my trembling hand, and she shook it with enthusiasm. "I'm a huge fan of yours. I just love your work. I've seen all your videos, and I just think you're great."

I knew I must have sounded like a babbling idiot. As always, Keith was clued into my emotions, and he stepped in to help.

"I've told Rosemary all about your amazing singing voice," Keith offered.

"Yes, *everybody* has been telling me about how well you sing,

Crista. I know Keith might be a tad biased, seeing as he's crazy about you," Rosemary said, offering him a playful wink. "But Elyse and Luke are around professional performers all the time, and they know talent when they see it. They're both quite impressed with you."

Elyse grinned at me, and I wanted to kiss her for talking me up in front of my hero.

"I would love to hear you sing sometime," Rosemary said.

"Oh, I would be so nervous to sing in front of you!"

Rosemary placed a gentle hand on my shoulder. "Don't be. We were all new at this once. Any time you want to meet with me at the foundation, you just say the word."

"Thank you. Thank you so much!"

Keith locked eyes with me and smiled. I loved that I didn't have to explain to him how much Rosemary's words meant to me. He knew.

Elyse drew in a deep breath and let it out. She looked a bit pale.

"Are you all right?" I asked her.

"I'm a nervous wreck. I can't help it. Tonight is so important to Luke. He has such high hopes for this show. He thinks it might even have a chance of making it to Broadway. I just hope everything goes well tonight."

"I know exactly how you feel," Johnny said with great sympathy. He glanced over at Rosemary and chuckled. "I never told you this, but I threw up the night you made your Broadway debut."

Rosemary's eyes grew wide. "You didn't!"

Johnny laughed. "Oh God, I was a mess. I mean, I knew you'd do great, but it's like Elyse said. There's so much riding on one night, and you're terrified something might go wrong."

Elyse's face fell. "Exactly," she whispered.

A man in a very expensive suit walked up to us. He pointed to Elyse. "You see that face? That's going to be me in a few months, when you make your off-Broadway debut."

The woman on his arm—a gorgeous lady with bright-blue eyes and brown hair—laughed happily. "Luke's gonna be fine," the woman said, letting go of the man's arm and rushing over to hug Elyse.

"Thanks, sweetie," Elyse said, hugging her friend tight. "Susie, I want you to meet Crista."

"Crista," Susie chirped brightly. "I'm so glad to meet you finally. I've heard so much about you."

"Nice to meet you, too," I said to Susie, shaking her hand.

"Good to see you again, Keith," Susie said. She looked over at Elyse and back at Keith. "He really *does* look like Superman, or maybe Clark Kent in this snappy suit."

Keith laughed and actually blushed a little. It was the cutest thing I'd ever seen.

The sharply dressed man extended his hand to Keith. "Nice to see you."

The two men shook hands, then Keith slipped his arm around my waist. "And this is Crista."

The pride in his voice and the way he put his arm around me, made me know he was happy to be there with me. Keith always made me feel special and cherished. I couldn't believe I'd been worried he would try to hide our relationship.

"Nice to meet you, Crista. I'm David Groff," he said, shaking my hand firmly. I wasn't sure what to think of him. He seemed rather stern and gruff.

"David's the one who lent us the limo," Keith explained.

"Oh, thank you so much!" I gushed. "It was so beautiful!"

David's face softened; he had a gentler side after all. "My pleasure."

"I feel like I'm gonna throw up," Elyse said so abruptly, it made us all laugh.

Rosemary and Susie were at her side. "He's gonna be fine, Elyse. Really," Rosemary assured her.

"The show is gonna be great," Susie said. "I used to rehearse it with him all the time."

"Yeah, I remember," Elyse said in a wry voice, and she, Rosemary, and Susie all shared a laugh.

"I'm Luke's scene partner at the foundation," Susie explained to me. It felt good the way she made an effort to include me in the conversation. "And there are a fair amount of love scenes in the show."

"Oh, I see," I said with a laugh. "I can think of worse things than kissing Luke."

"Right?" Rosemary said.

"Hey!" protested Keith and Johnny, and we all laughed again.

"Luke's gonna be terrific tonight," I told Elyse as I put an arm around her. "He's super excited about the show, and he keeps telling me how funny it is. You know how Luke is—he's hysterical. If anything does go wrong, he's great at improv. He'll know how to cover, and nobody will even know."

"That's true," Elyse said, her worried expression relaxing a bit.

"He'll have the time of his life tonight. You'll see," I said.

Rosemary nodded. "Come on. Let's go cheer him on."

Rosemary put one arm around Elyse and the other arm around me as if we were already old friends. I wanted to squeal with delight.

Rosemary Sutton is treating me like I'm one of her friends.

I saw Keith and Johnny exchange amused smiles as we all headed to our seats.

Walking into the theater was like stepping into a fairy land. Maybe I should have played it cool, but I couldn't. I gasped when I saw the ornate ceiling and the huge stage.

Susie smiled warmly. "You've never been here before?"

"I've never been in any real theater before. The only shows I've ever seen were in high school. That, and I've seen every movie version of every musical ever made."

Her blue eyes softened as she looked at me, then around at the theater. "Doesn't matter how many different theaters I've been in. Still gets me, you know?" Susie put a hand over her heart and I heard the hitch in her voice.

I nodded, overcome with a strange emotion that was somehow familiar and unfamiliar at the same time. I felt drawn to this place, like it was home. Staring at the stage, I remembered how it felt when I stood onstage at The Creel Foundation and sung my heart out. What would it feel like to perform onstage with a live audience?

"It's beautiful, isn't it?" Keith said softly. I gazed up at him and nodded, not knowing what else to say. He smiled at me, and it was as if he could read my mind. He could see how being in the theater affected me.

"Over here, guys," Elyse called, showing us to our seats. "I wanted to make sure we sat where he could see us. So he knows we're all here to support him."

"He knows, Elyse," I assured her, and she smiled gratefully.

We took our seats, and Keith put a protective arm around me. Finally, the lights dimmed, and I heard Elyse draw in a shaky breath.

We settled in to watch the show. The musical, called *Pirated*, was a hilarious show about three pirates who always tried to act tough and one-up each other. One by one, each pirate falls in love with one of his captives and decides he wants to give up his marauding ways to live happily ever after. None of them want to admit to each other that they've gone soft, so they alternate between being sweet with their women and tough with each other. One scene had Luke running back and forth between his girl and his pirate friends, and his character kept getting confused as to how he was supposed to behave. I laughed so hard, I had tears running down my face.

I was filled with so many conflicting emotions, it nearly made me dizzy. Happy to be close with Keith, his arm wrapped lovingly around me. Relieved Luke was doing well, and that his future as a performer looked bright. Energized by the laugher and enthusiasm of the crowd. Envious of all the actors onstage, giving incredible performances and clearly feeding off the energy of the audience. And finally, the aching emptiness of knowing it would never be me on a stage like this.

Rosemary, Luke, and Susie had been performing since they were children. They had all spent years and years learning their craft, going to auditions, and paying their dues. It was probably already too late to make my dream of performing come true.

And that really is my dream, isn't it? To be a performer.

As much as I tried to deny it, this heavy ache in my heart confirmed it. That was what I wanted most in life. To sing, to dance, to be onstage where I belonged. Being here in this theater and watching other people experience my dream, live and in color onstage, made it starkly clear. There was something missing in my life. There was a deep, empty hole in my heart that not even Keith's devotion could fill. Keith could probably give me the money for singing or acting lessons, but nothing could ever make up for all the lost time.

It was simply too late.

As the cast took their final bow and we gave them a standing ovation, Keith whispered in my ear, "That could be you someday."

My eyes filled with tears, knowing it couldn't possibly be true.

We met up with Luke backstage, where we descended on him and poured out our love and congratulations. Elyse wept with relief and joy as she held onto him. I was proud to be a part of such a beautiful moment.

Rosemary walked over to me and looked me sternly in the eye. I was taken aback. Was she angry with me for some reason?

"I know that look, Crista," Rosemary said firmly. "You want this. The theater is as important to you as it is to me and Susie and Luke. I can see it in your eyes."

I swallowed hard, not knowing what to say. I didn't know how to express my doubts, my fears, my certainty that I had already missed my chance to pursue the theater life.

As if reading my mind, Rosemary said, "It's not too late, Crista. It's never too late. You just say the word, and I will do everything in my power to help you."

Rosemary reached out and squeezed my hand. Then she looked over at Keith as if to say *I need you to convince her to accept my help.*

She went over to join Johnny and the rest of the group, and I turned to Keith.

Wordlessly, he pulled me into his arms and held me for a long time. I rested my head on his shoulder and he stroked my back tenderly. Once again, I felt that powerful connection between us. He'd watched me as I watched the show, and he knew I was experiencing pain and doubt and fear.

Keith let go of me and looked me in the eye.

"Everybody else believes in you, Crista. Now it's time for you to believe in yourself."

Chapter 9

Keith hesitated at my doorstep, allowing me to take the lead. I was a tad nervous about inviting him in, but I wasn't ready to say goodnight yet. I opened the front door with my key and gestured for him to go inside.

I sat down on the couch, and Keith sat beside me.

"This was a wonderful night," I said.

"Yes, it certainly was. But then it always is when I'm with you."

He leaned in close, brushed the hair out of my face, and kissed me. I moaned softly, melting at his touch. No one had ever kissed me with such sensuality and passion. I found myself getting lost in his kisses; they grew more passionate with each second.

A deep, masculine groan escaped from Keith's throat, and he pushed me ever so slightly back onto the couch. I suddenly realized this wasn't simply a make-out session.

It was foreplay.

As much as I ached to have Keith make love to me, it was simply too soon.

And I had no idea how to tell him.

I was such an idiot for getting myself into this situation. We had shared a beautiful evening, and then I had invited him in and started kissing him on the couch. What did I think would happen? I adored Keith, but I wasn't ready to give myself to him yet.

Keith's kisses deepened, his tongue exploring my mouth. It was sensual, erotic. We were both getting more aroused by the moment, and I started to panic. He was probably used to having sex with women by the second or third date. I felt so out of my element, and I felt awful for turning him on with no intention of satisfying his needs yet.

How could I tell him no when I'd already let things go this far?

As it turned out, I didn't have to.

Keith broke off his kiss and gazed at me with concern. "Hey, are you okay? You seem a little tense."

He gently massaged my right shoulder, and I realized my entire body had stiffened up.

"Y—yes. I'm okay. It's just that …"

His blue eyes opened wide as he searched my face.

"I just … I don't want to move too fast," I said, dreading his look of disappointment.

Keith's handsome face softened. "Oh."

I loved the way he said the simple word. "Oh," as if to say *Oh, is that all?*

"Well, I can understand that." He massaged both my shoulders to help my muscles relax. "Crista, we'll go at any pace you're comfortable with, okay?" he said, gazing deeply into my eyes as if to make sure I understood how much he meant those words.

Fighting back tears of emotion, I nodded. As usual, I had underestimated him. I should have known he would understand. He always did.

"I'm so sorry. I'm just not ready yet."

"Hey, don't be *sorry*. There's nothing to be sorry about. I'm just glad you told me," Keith said, his brow furrowing with worry.

"There's absolutely no pressure, no timetable for anything physical, you understand? I'm just happy to be here with you."

"Thank you," I said with relief.

"Is it okay if I kiss you again?" he asked.

"Of course."

Slowly, tenderly, he placed his right hand on my cheek. Gazing into my eyes for a long time, he finally spoke. "You're so beautiful, Crista."

Keith leaned in and pressed his lips on mine, kissing me softly. His kiss felt completely different, yet every bit as wonderful, as it had a moment ago. It was still sensual and arousing, but much gentler this time. I knew it was his way of reassuring me that he wasn't angry or disappointed.

"You're so wonderful," I whispered when our lips finally parted. "There's no one else in the world I'd rather be with."

Keith smiled, his eyes dancing with joy. "That's more than enough for me."

He sat back a little, resting his elbow on the couch and looking at me. "So, what did you think of your first real theater experience?"

"I don't think I even have the words to describe it," I said, recalling the jumbled mess of emotions I'd experienced all night.

Keith nodded, waiting patiently for me to continue.

"It was amazing and a bit overwhelming."

"It made you think more about giving performing a try, didn't it?"

"I guess so. It seems so impossible, though. I'm sure everybody on that stage started acting and singing when they were little kids, you know?"

"Maybe. And you're so ancient at the age of what, twenty-four?"

"Twenty-five."

Keith's eyes grew wide with exaggerated shock. "Oooh, twenty-five. You'd better take it easy before you break a hip."

I laughed, which made Keith smile. My heart fluttered in my chest. He was never more handsome than when he smiled.

"You heard Rosemary. She said it's never too late."

"Oh, isn't she the sweetest? She's my *hero*. It was such a shock to see her there. It was so unexpected. I hope I didn't make a complete blubbering fool of myself in front of her."

"Of course not. I think she was quite taken with you. Elyse says Rosemary loves helping performers, and she seems to want to take you under her wing."

"Can you imagine?" I asked. *The* Rosemary Sutton helping me learn to sing and perform.

"Yes. Can you?"

"Maybe," I said softly. Keith grinned and nodded.

"There's so much lost time to make up for. So much to learn." I let out a breath, feeling tired and hopeless just thinking about it. "And it's not like Rosemary could teach me everything I need to learn to even attempt this whole crazy thing. There's so many different classes I would need to take."

"Would you be willing to go through all that? Take all of those classes and learn everything, if you could?"

"In a heartbeat," I said, surprising even myself with my sudden answer. It would be a lot of work, but I really wanted to learn proper singing and acting techniques. To push myself to be the best performer I could possibly be, so I could have even a remote shot of making it onto the stage someday. "Oh, what I wouldn't give to be able to get a theater degree!"

"Crista," Keith said, his eyes focused intently on me. "You know I could pay for you to go to school."

I laughed at the idea.

"What?" he asked, looking offended and a bit hurt.

"Oh, Keith," I said, running my fingers through his jet-black hair. "I'm not laughing at your incredibly generous offer. I could never let you do that, though."

"Why not?"

"It just … It wouldn't be right."

"I have more money than I know what to do with, and you're flat broke, despite working yourself to death. It makes sense, doesn't it?"

"No. It doesn't. We've only been out on two dates, you crazy man. And now you want to put me through school?"

"Yes," he said, and I could tell by his expression that he was serious.

"You're a dear man. But you're also *muy loco*."

"Probably," he said with a laugh. "But I really want to take care of you."

Something about that made me uncomfortable, but I wasn't sure why.

"I mean it. You should let me pay for your schooling."

"Keith," I began. He must have heard the weariness in my voice, so he put his hand up in surrender.

"Okay, okay. We'll table this for now, but I'm not done with this."

"Fine."

"Will you at least talk to Rosemary and let her help you?"

I fell silent for a moment, contemplating. Keith watched me intently, waiting for my answer.

"I'm scared," I said at last.

He nodded and patiently waited for me to continue.

"Being at the theater tonight … It hit me hard. How much I want this. To give it a shot. To try performing somewhere—anywhere— just to see what it feels like." Keith nodded again. I couldn't remember the last time anyone just listened to me talk. It was such a relief to get these things off my chest. To unburden myself to someone who cared.

"I felt empty tonight. Sitting in the audience and watching all those actors up onstage. It was like something was missing in my life. Deep down, I think I always knew I would feel that way if I went to the theater. I would go and get a glimpse of everything I ever wanted, and then I'd have to trudge back to my ordinary life with no hope of making my dreams come true."

"There's hope now," Keith said.

I nodded. "Maybe."

"You said you're scared. Why?" He asked the question with concern but without judgment.

"My whole life I've known there was no possible way I could afford to go to school, to become a singer and actor. So I could fantasize about being onstage while knowing it couldn't possibly happen. In some way, it was an excuse not to try."

"You're running out of excuses now, aren't you?"

"Easy for you to say, isn't it? You're awfully pushy, you know."

Keith took his elbow off the couch and sat up straighter, leaning close to look me intensely in the eye.

"You're right. I am pushy. Because I've seen the way you look when you're onstage. It's as if you were born to be there. You told me yourself, you feel like you've been set free when you sing. You've kept this incredible talent and energy and drive all bottled up your whole life, and now it's time to let it all loose. You *are* a performer. It's in your blood. There's no limit to what you can do if you could somehow put aside your doubts and fears and go for it. You're at the crossroads of your life right now. Your choice is to either reach for your dreams, or live a life full of regrets."

I stared at him in astonishment, touched to my very core at his words and the passion with which he'd said them. We'd known each other for such a short time, and yet it was like he understood me more deeply than people I'd known all my life.

"I know you're scared. And you're right—it's easy for me to say this because I'm not the one putting myself out there. I've seen what you're capable of, and I truly believe you can do this. That you can and will succeed. But even if you don't, you'll live a life with no regrets, no wondering 'what if?'"

I reached out and Keith pulled me close and held me.

"I believe in you," he said simply. He released me and said, "Look. You don't have to do anything drastic like quit your job and join a traveling improv circus."

I laughed, and Keith smiled.

"But you've got options now. I've made my offer—"

"Keith."

"Which we're not gonna talk about right now," he said, holding up his hands in mock defense as if I was about to hit him. "Your other immediate option is to talk with Rosemary and figure out where to start. She wasn't born a Broadway star, you know. She grew up poor just like you."

"I know. That's one of the reasons I admire her so much."

"She made her dreams come true, and so can you. All you have to do is decide you're going to give this a good, honest shot. What do you say?"

Keith's blue eyes bored into me, demanding an answer.

"Yes. I'll do it." The moment I said the words, I felt the aching emptiness start to drift away. For the first time in my life, I had a real purpose. A dream. A goal. A reason to get up in the morning that, for once, was more than simply surviving and working to pay my bills.

I had a mission.

"That's my *girl!*"

"Am I really your girl?" I asked.

He cupped my face. "God, I hope so."

I nodded, and he grinned and dipped his head for a kiss. Then he got up.

"I'd better let you get some rest. You've got a lot of work to do. You've got your whole life ahead of you now."

An unfamiliar and utterly delightful sensation of exhilaration rippled through me. I already couldn't wait to wake up in the morning to start my new life.

"You're right," I said happily.

"I'm going to be right by your side through all of it, Crista."

I nodded, knowing deep in my heart it was true. Keith would be at my side. Always.

To have and to hold. For richer or poorer. In sickness and in health.

I walked him to the door and we lingered there for a moment.

"Someday soon, I promise, you won't have to go home after our date."

Keith smiled tenderly at me and said, "When you're ready. And not one moment before."

He bent down and kissed me goodnight.

"Sweet dreams, Cinderella."

Chapter 10

It was a rather uncomfortable ride home, seeing as my cock was harder than the gearshift. I'd had one hell of a hard-on the whole time Crista and I were making out on the couch. Spending time talking with her about her dreams had been wonderful too, though; it had distracted me a bit from my raging libido. I was already so proud of her, and I couldn't wait for the day when she finally got up onstage and performed for a live audience. I'd be right there, front and center, cheering her on.

Now that I was alone in my car, with plenty of time to reflect on Crista's beauty and how exciting it had been to make out with her, my horniness was back with a vengeance. As badly as I wanted to have sex with her, I'd meant every word about taking our time. Her expression when she'd told me she needed to slow down had just about broken my heart. She'd seemed so afraid of disappointing me. I *was* a little disappointed: the way we'd been going at it on the couch made me think tonight would be the night.

Looking back, I realized *I* was the one going at it hot and heavy. I hadn't meant to pressure her. Thank God I picked up on her distress and stopped before we went farther than she was comfortable with. I didn't know why she still had such a tough time trusting me.

I needed her to understand how much I cared for her, and that I was in this for the long haul. She didn't need to be afraid to be honest with me.

Elyse had said Crista was hesitant, as if she'd been hurt before. Crista was clearly protective of her body, and I worried that some asshole had taken advantage of her in the past. Maybe some jerk had slept with her and never called her again. It hurt just thinking about it. She deserved so much better. All the more reason to take my time with her and make sure she never, ever felt pressured into being intimate before she was ready.

Her trust in me was also important in regards to letting me help her with her theater stuff.

I didn't think she quite realized how wealthy I was. I could pay for all four years of her college—at a *good* college, too—and not even miss the money. It was crazy not to let me do it. She'd seemed pretty defensive about the whole thing—yet another wall I would need to break down. Seeing the light in her eyes when she performed at The Creel Foundation, not to mention the pain in them when she watched Luke's show tonight, let me know she'd never be complete unless she gave theater a try.

Since I knew in my heart that we were meant to be together, all the time and patience it might take to get her to trust me would be worthwhile. I'd never hurt her, and someday she'd come to understand that. Lovely and gentle and kind Crista, with her soulful, deep brown eyes and perfect breasts. So far, the closest I came to touching them was when she'd pressed against me on the couch.

Groaning deep in my throat, I stepped on the gas. I'd have only my right hand to relieve my needs for the foreseeable future, but it was okay. Crista's feelings were a hell of a lot more important than my horniness. She seemed so surprised every time I opened the door for her, pulled out her chair, or did any number of things a gentleman should do for a lady. She clearly wasn't used to being pampered, and I had a feeling she'd never had a man take care of her needs in bed, either. When we finally made love, I would be sure to take my time with her. Get to know her body, and make sure I satisfied her completely. I found myself getting lost in a vivid fantasy of her brown eyes opening wide as I gave her pleasure beyond anything she'd ever experienced.

Yes. Crista would be well worth waiting for.

Chapter 11

I woke up the next morning and practically sprinted out of bed. I had a house to clean, but for once I didn't mind. A little part of me had been afraid I wouldn't feel as enthusiastic today as I had last night. After all, some things that seem like a good idea at the time kind of lose their shininess in the bright light of day.

Not today. I was still excited. Right now, my only real goal was to work toward getting into a show. Any show. I didn't care if it was in a dingy dinner theater or some run-down community center. It was time to give this a shot, if for no other reason than to prevent myself from wondering "what if"?

I never would have found the courage to try if it weren't for Keith. I had no idea how he managed to stay so patient with me. He seemed happy that I was finally going to give performing a shot, so at least he could feel like he was making some progress with me.

As I got dressed to go to my cleaning job, my mind whirled with thoughts of my dizzying array of emotions last night. But I knew I really had no choice anymore. If I ever wanted to feel complete, theater needed to be a part of my life.

Rosemary was even more amazing in person than in all those performance videos I'd seen. I hoped she'd been sincere in her offer to help me and wasn't simply being polite. She'd given me her phone number, and I was dying to call her. I told myself it was far too soon—I didn't want to come off as pathetic by calling her right away.

But I couldn't stop myself. It was only 9:30am and I didn't want to wake her on a Saturday, in case she was a late sleeper, so I texted her instead.

It was so amazing meeting you last night!

So much for playing it cool. I didn't really regret sending the gushing text, though. Rosemary *was* amazing.

I've been thinking a lot about what you said last night, and I really would like to try my hand at this. I'm scared to death, but I think it's time I quit stalling and went for it.

Nerves on edge, I grabbed my purse and headed out to the subway. I hoped Rosemary wouldn't regret offering to help me. My phone buzzed in my pocket a few minutes later.

It was great meeting you too, Crista. Would love to meet with you so we can talk more. I don't suppose you're free for lunch today?

I stared at my phone, hardly believing my eyes. Rosemary Sutton wanted to meet me for lunch. Everything was happening so fast, and I couldn't have been more excited. I returned her text right away to tell her I would be available in a few hours right after work.

Great. Let's meet at Sardi's. My treat!

I gasped. Sardi's. Rosemary Sutton was going to meet me at Sardi's Restaurant. Good God, things didn't get much more Broadway than that. Sardi's was an institution—the famous restaurant featuring the caricatures of Broadway and Hollywood celebrities. I'd seen the outside of the place lots of times, but I'd only seen the inside in movies and on television.

I headed onto the subway in a daze. I bit my lip to keep from grinning in public like an idiot. I knew somebody with the connections to get a last-minute lunch reservation at *Sardi's*. Rushing through my cleaning job, I got my work done in half the time it usually took. If I was going to lunch at Sardi's, I needed time to race back home and change my clothes.

My legs shook as I walked down the street toward the restaurant. I was a nervous wreck by the time I got to the place. I wasn't sure what made me more nervous—the fact that I was going to Sardi's, or that I was meeting Rosemary.

She was waiting outside when I got there, and she immediately put me at ease. Rosemary was dressed nicely, but not so fancy as to make me feel underdressed. She wore dressy slacks and a pretty, white blouse. I had on a simple knee-length pink dress which I hoped was appropriate for the occasion. It was yet another Goodwill find.

Rosemary smiled warmly, her pretty, green eyes sparkling with friendliness. Maybe she had felt nervous about going to fancy places like this when she'd first started dating a billionaire.

"I'm so glad you could make it," she said, offering another comforting smile.

"I can't believe I'm really at Sardi's."

"Right?" Rosemary said, her enthusiasm matching mine. "It's a Broadway institution. Not gonna lie. I cried when Johnny took me here the first time. Actually *cried*."

I laughed, and she did too.

"I get super emotional about anything theater-related. I can't help it," she told me.

"I understand." I thought about how deeply moved I'd been in the theater last night.

Rosemary opened the door and I followed her inside.

"Ms. Sutton! Good to see you," the man at the host stand said. "Right this way. Your table's waiting."

The guy made a big show of ushering us to our table, and heads throughout the restaurant turned to watch us.

"Your server will be right with you," he said before leaving.

I tried not to gape at my surroundings, but it was a struggle. I stared at all the famous pictures on the walls, then turned back to Rosemary.

"Wow, I feel like I'm here with royalty," I told her.

She smiled, but there was a weariness in her eyes. "I'm always treated like royalty in New York, but it's because I'm Johnny Creel's girl. It has nothing to do with me."

"But you're famous. You've been on Broadway."

"In one show. In the ensemble. I mean, don't get me wrong, I'm insanely grateful for the opportunity. Believe me, it's farther than I ever really thought I would get. But right now, that's not what I'm known for. I'm Johnny's fiancée and, soon enough, I'll be Mrs. Johnny Creel."

A soft smile played on her lips when she said it, and I could see that marrying a famous billionaire was a double-edged sword. I could see the love in her eyes, and I could tell how much she wanted to marry Johnny. At the same time, she wanted her own identity.

The server arrived to take our order.

"Do you want to share the appetizer plate? It's got prosciutto and melon, asparagus in smoked salmon, with capers and shrimp," Rosemary said.

"Oh, that sounds amazing."

"Great, we'll have that."

"Very good, Ms. Sutton," the server said.

"Wow. Everybody knows you around here," I said.

Rosemary shrugged modestly.

I smiled at her and said, "Just think. Maybe someday your picture will be up on the wall after you've played some amazing leading role on Broadway."

"Can you imagine?" Rosemary said softly. Then she laughed, "Because I sure have."

I laughed with her, feeling a little more relaxed. It was overwhelming to be here, but in a good way.

"So, let's talk about you. What are your goals? What exactly are you looking to do?" Rosemary asked me.

"Well, that's what I'm trying to figure out."

Rosemary nodded, pausing to smile at the server who brought our diet sodas.

"I guess the first step is to start learning the ropes. Learn how to sing properly. My first goal would be to get good enough to perform on the stage somewhere, anywhere, to see how it goes."

"Have you always wanted to do this?" Rosemary asked.

"Yes. Ever since I was a little girl, I was always singing and dancing around the house. I just never had the opportunity to try it for real. It's not like we had the money when I was growing up. It was tough just to survive sometimes."

"Believe me, I understand. It was the same way for me growing up. We never had extra money for anything. We got evicted from our house when I was eleven years old," Rosemary said sadly. "I'll never forget that day. When I got home from school, all our stuff had been thrown out onto the front lawn in the rain."

"That's awful. I'm so sorry that happened to you."

"Thanks. It was really hard on my parents," she continued, and I heard the catch in her voice as she spoke. "They worked constantly, but somehow it was never enough."

I nodded, understanding completely. My parents had worked incredibly hard to support me and my brothers. They tried to hide their exhaustion, but I could see it in their eyes.

Rosemary went on. "I was determined not to let it stop me, though. In high school, I auditioned for everything I could. Then I went on to community theater after graduation."

"I guess that's what I should have done," I said, feeling a familiar sensation of regret. "At the time, I was afraid it was pointless, you know? I knew there would never be any money left over for theater classes, and I thought it would be useless to dream."

"I can understand that," Rosemary said empathetically.

I began to feel like I had found a kindred spirit in Rosemary.

"But is it too late?" I asked suddenly. "Doesn't everybody in this business start when they're really young?"

"Many of them do, yes, and—"

She stopped talking when the server arrived with our food. It was excruciating to have to wait for the answer to the question that had haunted me my whole life.

Was it too late for me?

"Like I was saying, a lot of performers do start out very young, and, of course, some of them even make it to Broadway as children. I won't lie to you, Crista," Rosemary said, her tone firm yet gentle. "Starting later does put you somewhat at a disadvantage."

I nodded, feeling physical pain in my chest.

"Casting directors will look at your resume to see what else you've done before, but at the end of the day, it's what's onstage that matters. If you show them what you've got, and they feel you're right for the role, your past doesn't matter as much."

"I understand," I said quietly.

"You just have to make up your mind you're going to give this an honest shot and do the best you can."

I smiled. "That's exactly what Keith said."

"Keith's right," Rosemary said, digging into her food. "He's also insanely hot. I don't know how you can look into those gorgeous blue eyes of his and not fall into a trance."

I laughed. "You're not kidding. He is tough to say no to." I let out a sigh. "Sometimes I feel like that's all I do, though. Say no to him."

"What do you mean?"

Talking with Rosemary felt good. Like we were already old friends. I felt I could confide in her. Even so, I was too embarrassed to admit that I was a twenty-five-year-old virgin, so I stopped short of confessing the whole truth.

"I just need to take things slow with him, you know what I mean? I need time before I'm ready to, you know, be intimate."

Rosemary narrowed her eyes. "And how is Keith handling that?"

"Great! Oh, he's been wonderful. He never pressures me. He told me we'll be together when I'm ready and not a moment before."

Rosemary's face lit up with a pretty smile. "Good. He sounds like a keeper."

"Yes, he really is."

We ate our food for a few minutes.

"Okay," Rosemary said thoughtfully. "So, here's what I recommend you do. I would start with taking voice lessons. You don't want to overwhelm yourself by taking on too much at once, and your singing is the most important thing to focus on. Acting can come a bit later, and then maybe some dancing work. I have a close friend, Susie—you met her the other night. Susie is a professional dancer, so she can provide you with advice on that, if you find you're interested in learning more."

"Okay, sounds great."

"I'll email you a list of voice teachers."

"Wonderful. Thank you so much! Are they, umm, well, are these lessons expensive?"

"Kind of," Rosemary said gently.

I nodded.

"Maybe, you know, Keith could help you with that."

"Oh, he would help in a heartbeat if I let him. Can I ask you a personal question?"

"Sure."

"I—I don't want to offend you," I ventured cautiously.

"It's okay, Crista. You can ask me anything," she told me with an encouraging smile.

"Does it bother you that Johnny and his family paid for your theater degree? I'm sorry. It must be awful having everybody know all your personal business, but I read in the entertainment news and stuff that Walter Creel paid for you to go to NYU."

I looked down at the table, hoping I hadn't already ruined our new friendship.

Rosemary laughed. "Now that's a fair question."

I looked up at her and she smiled at me. "Really?"

"Of course." Rosemary glanced down at her left hand where Johnny's shiny engagement ring sparkled on her finger. Stunningly beautiful, it had a huge diamond in the center, surrounded by lots of smaller ones. It must have cost a fortune. As I watched Rosemary look fondly at the ring, I knew she didn't care how much it was worth. She was thinking about the man who gave it to her.

"The answer is a resounding 'yes.' I did struggle with taking the Creel's money for my education. At least at first. It all seemed too much. I felt like, how could I possibly accept such a generous gift?"

I nodded, carefully taking in Rosemary's words.

"In the end, it was just too much to resist. I'd wanted to go to college my whole life, and to have them dangle my dream right in front of me … I just couldn't say no. Besides, the Creels are drowning in money. Hard to imagine, but a four-year college degree from NYU was a financial drop in the bucket for them."

Shaking my head, I tried to imagine what it must be like to have that kind of money.

Rosemary laughed. "I know. Makes your head spin, doesn't it?"

"Yes. Keith already offered to pay for college for me."

Rosemary's eyes opened wide. "He did?"

"I know. It's insane. We've only been together a short time. I know it sounds crazy, but I feel like I already know I'm going to marry him someday."

"Oh, that's wonderful Crista. And it doesn't sound crazy at all. Sometimes you just know right away."

I laughed. "And sometimes you don't!"

Rosemary chuckled. "Right. If somebody had told me I was gonna marry my boss, Johnny Creep …" She shook her head with disbelief.

"Johnny Creep? Is that what you used to call him?"

"Oh, yeah. We all did at work."

Rosemary and I had a good giggle over that.

I gazed over at the caricatures of celebrities on the wall, sincerely hoping Rosemary's picture would be up there someday. Picturing my own seemed too far-fetched, even for a fantasy.

Then again, I'd never dreamed Keith Foster would actually look my way.

"It was incredibly sweet of Keith to offer to pay for my theater degree, but it seems so weird to me. I'm uncomfortable with it, and I don't know why."

"It's understandable. Makes you feel unequal. At least, that's how I felt."

"Yes! Exactly. Like I would always owe him something, even though I know he'd never make me feel that way."

"Yeah. It's funny, I remember when I agreed to move to New York with Johnny, I swore up and down I was gonna get a job once I got here." Rosemary shook her head. "It seems kind of crazy now. I mean, Johnny's a billionaire. We live in this super fancy apartment in Chelsea. We have *servants*. That's still weird to me, I don't mind telling you."

"I bet. I can't imagine."

I wondered if Keith had a housekeeper. A cleaning woman who came to his house like I did for others. It was such a bizarre notion to me.

"I'm not comfortable with being waited on hand and foot, and I thought it wouldn't feel right to come to New York and just live in luxury and not pull my own weight. Then when we got here and were surrounded by the Creel's wealth, it seemed preposterous for me to go get some stupid job to contribute a pittance to our living expenses."

"Yeah, I guess so."

"As it turns out, I work all the time. I busted my ass at NYU. It's been tough, but I loved it. And I went on auditions all the time, and then was incredibly lucky to land the role in the *Hairspray* revival."

"You weren't lucky. You earned it."

"I hope so," she said softly. In all the interviews I'd seen, Rosemary had made it clear that when it came to her career, she wanted no interference from Johnny and his influential family. Though they paid for it, she wanted to get accepted on her own merit. When it came to auditioning, they were not to use their power and influence to help her. Elyse had told me Rosemary trusted Johnny and his family to respect her wishes, but she still feared their fame had helped her get the part.

"But the point is, I'm always busy. When I'm not in school, at an audition, or in a show, I teach the kids at The Creel Foundation. I never feel restless or bored. And that makes me happy."

I was pleased to see the joy in her eyes as she spoke. Yes, she had accepted the Creel's money, but she still wasn't exactly a member of the idle rich.

"That's good," I said.

"But the bottom line is, you do what makes you comfortable. I understand exactly where you're coming from. If you don't feel good about taking Keith's money, you don't have to. But it is okay to accept it, if it's what you want."

"Thank you so much, Rosemary. It helps so much to talk with somebody who really gets it, you know?"

The server came back to check on us. "Can I get you anything else?"

Rosemary looked over at me.

"Not for me, thanks."

"Just the check then," she said with a smile.

"I even feel weird about having you pay."

"Oh, please don't. It's my pleasure, believe me," she said. "Okay, so we have a plan for you. I'll send you a list of good voice teachers, and you'll pick one and get started, right?"

"Yes." One way or another, I would get those lessons. I either had to figure out a way to pay for them, or agree to accept Keith's help. It would make him happy to help me, that much I knew. Because he was a dear, thoughtful man.

"Then I think the next step will be working on your audition songs."

"What? Really? Already?" It was impossible to imagine actually going on an audition. I had absolutely no idea what I was doing.

"Yes," Rosemary said firmly. "It's never too early. Don't worry. When the time comes to go to an audition, you'll be ready. It's never too early to start preparing your audition book."

She took one look at my expression, then burst out laughing. "Don't look so panicked. I didn't know anything about this kind of stuff at first either, but you've got lots of friends now to help you. Me, Luke, and Susie—we've all been there, and we'll be with you every step of the way. An audition book is a list of songs you've prepared, ones you really know cold, and can show off your range.

You want to pick a good variety of different songs, mostly showtunes but with some pop songs in there, too. Get started with your voice lessons, and then we'll get started on your audition book. You can do this, Crista. I know you can."

"I don't know how to thank you, Rosemary. I really don't."

"Don't you worry about that. I had lots of people help me along the way, and I'm thrilled to be able to help you." She smiled and squeezed my hand. "And when you get really good, someday you'll get the chance to help somebody else."

"Can you imagine?" I shook my head.

"Yes," she said with such confidence, it made me feel confident too.

Rosemary paid the bill and we headed out.

"This was so much fun, Crista. There's nothing I enjoy more than talking theater shop with another performer."

Another performer. Rosemary Sutton had called me a performer. Tears formed in my eyes.

Rosemary laughed. "Stop it! You'll get me started."

She grabbed me and hugged me tight, which made my tears spill openly.

"I'm so proud of you for going after your dreams, Crista."

"Thank you," I whispered. "I'm starting to be proud of me, too."

Chapter 12

Crista greeted me at the door of her apartment on Saturday wearing a pretty dress and a prettier smile.

"Hey," she said, putting her arms around my neck and kissing me.

"Mmm …" I eagerly returned her kiss. "Now that's what I call a greeting. You look nice."

I took a step back to admire her delicate, knee-length blue cotton dress.

"Thanks. And you look very handsome."

I had on black trousers and a dark-blue button-down shirt, which was more casual than I usually wore at work. Crista eyed me up and down. I was pleased to see her gaze linger on my chest where I had the first few buttons undone. Then she looked into my eyes.

"Wow. This blue shirt really makes your eyes stand out."

No kidding. My blue eyes were probably my best feature, and I loved wearing blue clothing to match. She smiled and pressed her lips to mine again, like she couldn't resist. Crista always knew how to make me feel desired.

She broke off the kiss and said, "I have so much to tell you!"

I grinned at her. "Great. Let's get going, then. We can talk in the car."

Crista squealed like an excited little girl as she grabbed her wrap and headed out the door with me. The moment we got settled in the car, she turned to me with her sweet brown eyes open wide.

"You won't believe what happened today. Rosemary took me to Sardi's. Sardi's! For lunch. Oh my God, it was incredible."

Damn, I wished I'd thought to take her to Sardi's. I should have realized how much it would mean to her. In the end, it didn't matter who took her. She was happy for the opportunity to go, which was what mattered the most. Besides, I knew how much Crista admired Rosemary.

"That's great," I said. "Did you guys talk about theater stuff?"

"Yes, and it was wonderful. She's the nicest person ever, and I swear it felt like we were old friends already. She made me feel a lot better about everything. Especially about starting to learn singing and acting so late. She was honest with me, though. I have a lot to catch up on. Everything is easier if you got started earlier, but she said it's not too late."

"What did I tell you?"

"You were right," Crista said with a smile.

"So, what did she suggest?"

"She said the best thing to do is start with voice lessons, and she told me I should start preparing a bunch of audition songs."

"Really? Audition songs already? That sounds exciting."

"It is exciting! Oh, but I wouldn't be using the songs for a while. Rosemary said it's a good idea to get started right away, though. That way I have plenty of time to practice and get really good before I actually try auditioning."

"That makes sense."

I tried to glance over at Crista as much as I could while I drove. She looked so damned cute when she was all excited.

"Did Rosemary tell you where to go for voice lessons?"

"Yeah, she's gonna email me a list of her recommendations, and I'll pick somebody from there."

I knew I had to approach the second part of my question carefully. "So, do you know how much these lessons cost?"

Her face fell. I hated to see her smile disappear. "I'm not sure, but I know they're not cheap."

"Crista, you know I would be more than happy to pay for the lessons. That, and anything else you might need."

"I know you would," she said quietly.

"Will you let me pay for it?"

"I don't know. I just don't know. It's so sweet of you to offer, Keith. I hope you know how much I appreciate it." She reached over and put her hand on my shoulder, squeezing it with affection. "It just doesn't feel right."

"I would do anything for you. Even if I was broke, I'd figure out a way to pay for those lessons. I'd go pick up cans on the side of the road and sell the aluminum. I'd sell my blood! And … maybe … other bodily fluids."

That got a laugh out of her. I was grateful to see her smile again.

"I'd sell a kidney. I'd hock my own mother's jewelry! I would, baby. But I don't have to do any of that. All I have to do is write a check. But you have to let me."

Crista fell silent.

"I mean, you're going to let me pay for dinner, right?"

Crista sighed. "Might as well. Rosemary paid for lunch."

"I enjoy spending money on you."

"I know. And it's very generous of you. It just takes some getting used to, I guess."

"I've never had a woman fight me on spending money on her, that's for sure," I said, shaking my head. The last woman I dated, Regina, practically made a career out of shopping with my money. She'd hinted at marriage, but I hadn't been able to shake the feeling that all she'd wanted was a sugar daddy. That was why I'd ended things with her.

"I'm sorry," Crista said sadly, still rubbing my shoulder. "I'm being difficult."

"You're not difficult. You're a challenge." I flashed her what I hoped was a sexy grin, and added, "I *like* a challenge."

Crista laughed softly, then met my gaze and held it for a moment. Unless I was mistaken, there was desire behind those brown eyes of hers. The more time I spent with Crista, the more attractive she became to me, and the more I wanted her. From the look in her eyes, the feeling was mutual.

I started to hope she might be ready to have sex soon.

Once we got settled into our seats at Norbert's, my favorite Italian restaurant, Crista asked to hear more about my life.

"Here I've been chattering the whole way over about all my theater stuff."

I relished the unmistakable light of excitement when she said "my theater stuff."

"I want to hear about what you've been up to. I know you've been busy at work. You seem so tired sometimes." She reached across the table to take my hand.

Her expression and her touch were soft and filled with gentle concern. It reminded me of the way she'd taken care of me in the elevator. I wasn't used to being fussed over and having somebody actually care about me. I found I really enjoyed it.

"What have you been working on?" she asked.

"Oh, you know. The same old boring technology stuff."

"Is it boring to you?"

"Well, no."

"Then it won't be boring to me," Crista said with a smile. "Tell me about it."

She kept ahold of my hand and gazed at me intently, as if she really wanted to know.

"Okay, well I had this idea a while back that WicketPro should try to branch out into the healthcare sector. I mean, it's already a successful international company with offices in several countries, but the main focus has been on network security and software development for large companies."

I scanned Crista's face, expecting her eyes to glaze over. On the contrary, she was alert and attentive. She nodded at me to go on.

"So, a while back, I floated the idea of us getting into software development and other information technology for hospitals and healthcare facilities. After all, those places are always trying to keep pace with the latest technological advancements. Anyway, I put together a proposal for Elyse. She's the Senior Vice President of Worldwide Sales Strategy and Operations." I laughed. "She actually got the promotion I wanted."

"Oh, I'm sorry."

"Eh, it's okay. She's great at what she does, you know? She deserved it. Elyse really liked the proposal I put together, and she presented it to some of the higher-ups during one of their meetings. After that, I got the green light to run with the idea."

"That sounds exciting!"

"Yes, it is. I've been working with some start-up tech companies who develop that kind of software. Technology to maximize efficiency of EHR—that's electronic health records. Things are moving forward pretty well, and we might even end up acquiring one or more of the start-ups for WicketPro."

Crista smiled, looking amused.

"What?"

"I like seeing you get all excited about your work."

A ripple of warmth spread through me as I realized Crista felt the same way I did when she got excited about her theater plans. She thoroughly enjoyed seeing me happy. I doubted Regina even understood what I did for a living. She certainly never asked me about it. All she knew was how much money I made.

"You're so smart, Keith. I think it's sexy."

I laughed. "Thanks."

We chatted animatedly throughout the meal, never running out of things to say. It was funny—I'd thought Elyse and I would be perfect for each other because we did the same thing for a living and had so much in common. But Crista made me realize how much fun it was to be with someone with completely different interests. She didn't know the first thing about technology and I knew very little about theater, but we were excited for each other. Telling her about my work made it seem fresh and exciting, and I loved hearing about all the new things she was learning about singing and performing.

After dinner, I slipped my arm around her waist as we waited for the valet to bring my car.

"Do you want to come over and see my place? It's not far from here."

"Sure," she said with a smile. Her lack of hesitation was encouraging. I was aching to take her to bed, but I knew whatever trust issues she had were making it difficult for her to take the next step in our relationship. I would let her take the lead. If I was lucky, she would lead me to the bedroom.

I drove to my high-rise apartment building on Central Park West.

"I can't believe you actually live here," Crista said as she looked up at the sixteen-floor building. "The only time I see places like this is when I go to clean them."

I nodded. It made me sad to think of her working so hard all the time—and such physical work—both on weekends and at the office building in Manhattan. And yet, she struggled to pay for her rent and food. It was unfair. I worked hard at my job, too, but her circumstances made me realize how grossly overpaid I was.

Crista glanced at the elevator and then looked at me questioningly.

"I know," I said with a slight grimace. "I'm on the twelfth floor, so I don't have much of a choice."

Crista gave me a sympathetic smile.

Once we were alone together in the elevator on the way up to the twelfth floor, I took the opportunity to kiss her. She eagerly kissed back. I was trying to walk the delicate line between showing her I desired her without pressuring her. I'd learned to look for signs of tension in her body. Most of the time she seemed torn about spending the night with me. We'd be making out like crazy, then her muscles would tense up and she'd pull back. I knew she felt bad about saying no to me.

"Mmmm," she moaned as we kissed. So far, so good.

Crista pulled away abruptly when the elevator stopped, but only because she didn't want to get caught fooling around. She looked out into the hallway when the doors opened, but the coast was clear.

"I can't wait to see your place!" she said happily.

I led her to my door and gestured for her to go in first. Her eyes opened wide as she surveyed my place. She did a full scan of the living room, her eyes growing ever wider.

"This place is enormous!"

Crista walked over to my fluffy cream-colored couch and matching chair. Running her hand over the soft material, she looked down at the polished wooden floor. She walked across the room to the kitchen area where I had a bar and three tall chairs, as well as a kitchen table with a U-shaped leather booth area. She stood in the kitchen and gazed out across my vast living space. Crista's entire apartment could fit in this one room. I wondered if she was thinking the same thing.

"There's an upstairs, too."

"There is?"

I nodded.

"Keith, this place is beautiful," Crista marveled as her gaze traveled across the walls filled with framed art. I looked around, too, and thought how nice her grandmother's tapestry would look displayed on the wall. My place was nice—very sleek and modern. If Crista moved in, I knew she would add her personal touch, with splashes of color everywhere. I loved the idea of her bringing all her Mexican crafty stuff here. It was easy to imagine being cozied up to her at the breakfast table in the morning.

"Do you have a cleaning lady to take care of all this?" Crista asked.

I frowned. I hated to have her thinking about cleaning this place when I'd been fantasizing about her as the lady of the house.

"Well, yes. I do."

"That's so weird," she said, shaking her head.

"Why?"

Crista crossed the room and put her arm around me. "I didn't mean it in a bad way. You have a huge apartment and you work all the time, so it makes sense. I'd do the same thing if I had the money. It just takes some getting used to … dating somebody so wealthy. People like you are usually my boss."

"The only place I want to boss you around is in the bedroom," I blurted before I could stop myself.

Fortunately, she burst out laughing. "*Estas loco.*"

She punched me playfully on the shoulder, but I saw the glint of interest in her eye, like the idea intrigued her.

"Come on, I'll show you the rest of the place."

"I feel like I need to pack a lunch for the journey," she joked.

"I promise I won't let you get lost." I led her down a narrow hallway, just off the kitchen, and up the stairs. I took her into one of my favorite rooms—the smallest in the apartment.

"Look at this!" Crista exclaimed when she saw the little library. There was a large, comfortable red velvet chair and foot stool in the middle of the room, flanked by two tall bookshelves. The shelves were stocked with tons of books, including literary classics, history books, mysteries, and general fiction.

"I spend hours in here. I love to read."

"I didn't know that," Crista said with a smile.

If she only knew how many times I'd settled in here with a brandy and a book on a Friday night after telling my friends I had plans. I had always preferred this to the bar scene. Not that I would admit it to my guy friends.

Crista slipped her hands around my neck. "Have I ever told you how sexy it is that you're so smart?"

"Yes. But I never get tired of hearing it."

"This is lovely, Keith. Just lovely," she said with reverence as she surveyed my library.

Her words were simple, but they meant a great deal to me. Regina had given the room only a cursory glance when I first showed it to her and told her I liked to read. Then she'd called me a nerd.

That really stung. Showing off my library was showing off a part of myself, and she'd mocked it. It was funny. Luke called Elyse "nerd," and she called him "geek," but it was cute. Playful. I knew Luke found Elyse's intelligence sexy, and she loved that he was a theater geek. Regina had just been mean.

Crista followed me back out into the hallway.

"That's just the laundry room," I said, gesturing to a tiny room.

"You do your own laundry?"

"Well, no. My housekeeper does it."

Crista nodded, looking amused. I walked a little farther down the hall and opened the door to my bedroom. I pulled most of the women I'd dated into the bedroom, where we'd tear each other's clothes off and fuck like rabbits. I couldn't imagine doing that with Crista.

Not that I couldn't imagine having sex with her. I did imagine it. Quite frequently. My cock stiffened, and my balls felt tight. My fantasies of taking Crista to bed seemed so much closer to reality with her standing right next to me. As badly as I wanted her, there was something sweet about us taking our time. I was a romantic at heart, and I knew our first time together would be wonderful. Sexually satisfying, no doubt, but also quite emotional. There would be plenty of time for more sexual exploration later when Crista fully trusted me.

I stifled a moan and forced myself to quit torturing myself with fantasies that might or might not come true tonight.

"So, this is my bedroom," I said, watching Crista lean in to look. Her gaze swept across the room, which was simple and elegant. A smiled crossed her lips when she saw my night table with a fancy reading lamp and a book resting next to it. Soon she was looking at my queen-sized bed, covered with a black and white bedspread. She paused for a moment; I'd have given anything in the world to know what she was thinking.

Maybe she, too, was fantasizing about making love. I wanted to push her down on it, with equal urgency yet much more tenderness than I had with other women. We would start out slow, gently rocking the bed with the gentle rhythm of finally joining our bodies together. God, I needed to stop. I was making myself crazy.

"It's very nice," Crista said softly. "So, you like to read in here, too?"

Yes, when I'm not jerking off, thinking about you.

"Uh, yeah. Yeah I do."

I needed to watch what I said out loud—my bad case of blue balls was clouding my judgment. I drew in a deep breath, reminding myself not to let my out-of-control libido take precedence over Crista's feelings. If she'd wanted to make love tonight, she probably would have made it clear by now.

"So, that's about it for my place."

"Well, I think it's absolutely beautiful," she said, stepping out into the hallway. Away from the bedroom. And the bed.

Stifling a groan of horny frustration, I slipped my arm around her waist. She snuggled closer, resting her head on my shoulder as we walked down the hall and back downstairs. A sense of peace settled over me. Being near my lovely Crista was enough for now.

We returned to the kitchen area.

"I can't believe the size of your fridge," Crista marveled.

"Yeah, it's pretty cool. No pun intended."

She giggled. Crista touched the stainless-steel doors.

"You can open it if you like."

She did, and peered inside at my selection of microbrews, plus the usual milk and eggs and such. She opened the freezer and scanned the bags and Tupperware containers of food.

"You gotta lot of stuff in here," she said, leaning in to read the labels on the Tupperware containers. I had pre-cooked chicken, pasta, fish, and other meals in there. "Did you make all this stuff?"

"Um, well, no. I have somebody who makes a bunch of meals for me to eat during the week."

Crista shut the freezer door and turned to me. Her eyes danced with amusement.

"What?"

"So, you don't do any of your own cleaning, laundry, or cooking."

"You think I'm helpless, don't you?" I sniffed, more amused than offended.

"No, I don't think you're helpless, Keith."

"Yes, you do. You think I'm totally helpless and incompetent. That I can't do a thing on my own. That if I got lost in a forest, I'd never survive." My eyes suddenly grew wide. "Oh my God, I'd be killed!"

Crista let out a long, delicious laugh. She'd never looked sexier. She walked over to me and put her arms around my neck.

"Don't worry," she purred sexily. "I would come rescue you with all my street-smart savvy."

"Maybe I don't wanna be rescued. Maybe I like the idea of being lost in the forest all alone with you."

"Hmm, it does sound rather nice," Crista said, standing on her tiptoes to kiss me. I bent to meet her lips, and she rested her feet back on the floor. She moaned as our kiss deepened.

My cock grew rigid, and delicious fantasies of having the lovely Crista Rivera in my bed ran through my head. I cupped her face, kissing her passionately. Her soft body melted into mine as if we fit together like pieces of a puzzle. Our kiss was deeply erotic, yet full of tender affection.

And then I felt it. Her body tensed again.

I closed my eyes with my lips still on hers. Disappointment and frustration flooded through me, and it took a few seconds of concentrated effort to compose my expression before I broke off the kiss. Crista still wasn't ready, and there was nothing I could do about it. Making her feel guilty about it would only hurt her. I swallowed hard, then pulled back.

At first, she wouldn't look at me. She looked down at the floor instead. "I—I'm sorry you have to drive me all the way home."

"Hey." I lifted her chin so she would look at me. "Taking you back to Queens just means I get to spend more time with you."

"I'm being challenging again, aren't I?" Her voice shook as she spoke, and I was afraid she might cry. It was heartbreaking.

"No. Of course not. Crista, baby, I hope you know how much I desire you and want to be with you, but only when the time is right."

"I desire you too, Keith," she said, tenderly stroking my cheek. "I hope you know that."

I knew she must have her reasons for wanting to wait. I just wished she trusted me enough to share them with me.

"You can tell me anything, you know," I ventured carefully.

A flicker of deep sadness—fear, even—crossed her face for an instant. Yes, there was definitely a specific reason she was holding back. My sexual frustration had vanished, replaced by fear and worry for her. What if something really terrible had happened to her? My God, what if she'd been raped or something? I *really* needed to take it easy until I knew the whole story.

"I know I can," she said, offering no more information. I wasn't about to push her on it.

"Will you do me a favor on the way back to your place?"

"What?" Crista asked a bit uncertainly.

I ran my fingers through her hair, and asked, "Will you sing for me?"

That made her smile.

"Of course I will."

Chapter 13

Rosemary had invited Crista and me to her graduation ceremony at Radio City Music Hall. Normally, students were only allowed a few tickets for the ceremony, but these were hardly normal circumstances. Walter Creel—Rosemary's future father-in-law and famous attorney—had a ton of influence and had undoubtedly made generous donations to NYU over the years, so he could get as many tickets as he wanted.

I had a soft spot in my heart for Rosemary. She had become a dear friend of Crista's over the last few weeks and she had been so supportive of her. Rosemary didn't get enough credit for how hard she worked in her theater career. Mr. Creel might have donated a ton of money, but not until after Rosemary had applied to the school and been admitted to the program on her own merit. It angered me to read gossip stories about how Rosemary was riding on the coattails of the Creel family, when nothing could be further from the truth. She had studied hard and stood in long lines for auditions, just like anybody else. Never asking for special treatment, she'd remained down-to-earth and humble, despite being engaged to a billionaire.

Crista admired Rosemary, which was a good thing. After all, someone else had paid for Rosemary's education. Maybe she could somehow convince Crista to let me pay her way. I wasn't about to broach the topic again any time soon, but I was hopeful seeing Rosemary walk across the graduation stage today might inspire Crista to someday do the same. I could pay her way like Walter Creel did, but the rest of the work would be up to her. I knew Crista would rise to the challenge, if only she would let me provide her with the opportunity to try.

Crista looked stunningly beautiful as she gazed around in wonder at the landmark venue in the heart of New York City. She was wearing one of her flowing Mexican dresses; the white and blue patterned one she'd worn on our first official date. With her face alight with excitement, she was a vision of feminine loveliness.

We took our seats, located a few rows from the front.

"I'm so proud of Rosemary," Crista said with a beautiful smile. "She's worked hard for this and she's wanted it for so long."

So have you, my darling.

"Yes, she certainly has."

I surveyed the concert hall filled with throngs of people. There were news cameras in the back and off to the side, and I was pretty sure they were there for Rosemary. As far as I knew, she was the only celebrity graduating today. Besides, I'd seen Walter Creel in the lobby earlier, giving interviews. He loved the limelight and was seen as a hero for providing a poor girl like Rosemary a chance at an education. I hoped the media circus didn't bother Rosemary too much. This was supposed to be her moment. Johnny would be there of course, but he had said he would arrive at the last minute. He knew his presence would be a huge distraction, and he wanted to keep the focus on Rosemary.

Johnny slipped into the empty seat beside me as soon as the ceremony began.

"Hey man," I said, shaking his hand. Johnny grinned. He was as excited as a little kid. Pride radiated from him, and I could see how much he loved his fiancée.

"Heyyy, glad you guys made it," he said, ignoring the murmurs and heads craning to see him. "She did it, man. She did it! Graduated with honors, thank you very much, all while working at the foundation and even performing on Broadway."

"She sure did. Rosemary's a wonder," I said.

"Yes, she really is," Crista said, tremendous admiration in her voice.

That could be you on the graduation stage, baby. Just say the word.

The ceremony began, and Crista flipped through the program to find Rosemary's name. I watched as she smiled down at the paper.

The audience cheered as each graduate crossed the stage to get his or her diploma, but the place got really loud when it was Rosemary's turn. I glanced over to my right to see Johnny cheering and whistling, his face full of joy. Half of the television cameras were on Rosemary, and the other half were on him.

I turned to my left and was horrified to see Crista crying.

Her expression held a depth of sadness I had never seen in her before. She quickly wiped her tears, but there was no hiding it from me.

"Crista, what's wrong?" I asked.

"Nothing. I'm just really happy for Rosemary," she said, forcing a smile.

I wasn't stupid. I knew the difference between happy and sad tears, especially when it came to Crista. I was attuned to her emotions more than I had ever been with anybody else.

She dabbed her eyes, turning away from me and toward the stage.

Frustration began to build up in me. Once again, she'd refused to trust me and tell me what was wrong. I couldn't understand it. I was willing to go to any lengths to make her happy, but I couldn't do it if I didn't know what was wrong. It was maddening.

After the ceremony, Rosemary greeted us all in the lobby. Holding a bouquet of pink roses given to her by Johnny, she was glowing with excitement. I'd never seen her look lovelier.

Yes. I definitely needed to talk with Rosemary, to figure out how to help Crista.

Luke took the flowers from Rosemary so she could hug her friends with her hands free. We all laughed as Luke preened like a Miss America contestant with the roses in his arms.

Susie squealed and hugged Rosemary tight. "I am so, so proud of you!"

Rosemary teared up as she hugged her best friend. I loved how Rosemary always cried when she was happy. She had practically sobbed when Johnny proposed to her, as was evident by the viral video of the event. I let out a sigh as I watched her. *Those* were happy tears.

Rosemary went on to hug Elyse, then she kissed Luke on the cheek. Next, she came over to Crista.

"Hey, are you okay?" Rosemary asked her. Crista had dried her tears and had more or less composed herself, but her sad expression remained.

"Yes. Yes, of course. I'm just so happy for you. Congratulations!"

Rosemary glanced at me questioningly. I held out my hands, and mouthed, "I don't know." She nodded slightly and reached over to hug Crista, who closed her eyes and hugged her new friend tightly. Rosemary held onto Crista for a little bit.

"Thank you so much for being here, Crista."

"I wouldn't have missed this for anything," she replied when she finally pulled away. "I know how hard you've worked for this. Elyse said it's always been your dream to get your theater degree."

"Yes. Yes, it really has," Rosemary said with a smile. She surveyed

Crista with concern, obviously still trying to figure out what was wrong.

Walter Creel walked into the lobby, and soon there were reporters pestering Johnny and Rosemary to go over with him for photos and to answer a few questions.

"Sorry. Duty calls," she told us. She seemed a little weary at the idea of having to deal with reporters, but the glow of excitement remained in her eyes.

I turned to Crista and she smiled at me. I slipped my arm around her waist and pulled her close. She let out a deep sigh and rested her head on my shoulder.

At least she was allowing me to comfort her physically.

It was better than nothing.

Chapter 14

It had been an emotionally draining day. Watching Rosemary's graduation ceremony had hit me hard. I didn't even know myself how badly it was going to hurt until I watched her cross the stage. Some friend I was. Rosemary had been nothing but kind and gracious to me, and here I was turning her graduation ceremony into a pity party. I had no one but myself to blame for my failures in life, and I felt awful about not being happier for her. I really was proud of her. I hoped she knew that.

Keith seemed irritable by the time we got back to his apartment. It was a little scary. I wondered if he was getting tired of me already. My insecurities that our relationship was too good to be true started to bubble up again. Lately, I'd been feeling optimistic about my chances of a career in theater, and I'd been deliriously happy with Keith. Everything felt upside down today. Seeing Rosemary graduate reminded me of how far behind I was in my so-called career, and now Keith seemed annoyed with me. Tears threatened to spill from my eyes again; it was getting harder and harder to fight them.

"Do you want something to drink?" Keith asked. In his eyes I saw worry instead of annoyance, which was a bit of a relief.

"I would love a sangria," I said.

"You got it." Keith opened the fridge and took out the bottle of wine he always had chilling for me. As he handed me a glass, he gazed into my eyes like he was searching for something. Finally, he said, "I'm worried about you."

"Why?"

"Because you're upset about something, and you won't tell me what it is."

The pain in his voice hurt me to the core. He was hurting because I wasn't confiding in him. Who could blame him? I was being a stubborn idiot. A *scared*, stubborn idiot.

"I'm okay, Keith. Really," I said, looking down at my sangria glass. I swirled the wine a little before I drank, stalling for time. I was dangerously close to spilling my guts to him. My mind was completely at war with itself. Half of me wanted to tell Keith everything, and the other half was blaring out warning signals about getting hurt again if I did.

Keith sighed heavily. He took a beer out of the fridge, popped open the top, and downed half the bottle in one gulp.

"You were really upset today," he said flatly, sounding annoyed again.

I knew it was useless to argue about it, so I said nothing.

"Baby, if you're upset about not being able to go to school, you know there's an easy solution to that."

"It's not easy. Not at all."

"Because you're making it difficult."

"I am not!" I insisted, though I wasn't sure if I was right. I wasn't sure about anything.

"Yes, you are. You're being a challenge again, Crista."

"Why can't you just let this go?"

"It's too important for me to let go. Something is wrong, and I just want to make it better. All I want to do is pay for you to go to school."

"Why do you keep saying you want to do that for me?" I asked, my voice rising.

"Because I love you, don't you understand that?" Keith shouted.

My eyes opened wide. I just stared at him.

Keith laughed suddenly. Shaking his head and putting his beer down on the counter, his expression returned to its usual warmth and gentleness. He walked over and put his hands on my shoulders.

"I'm sorry. I didn't mean to yell that at you. But I did mean it. You frustrate me and make me crazy because I'm in love with you. I love you and you're hurting, and you won't let me help."

I drew in a deep breath and looked into his eyes. His hands still on my shoulders, he waited patiently for me to make the next move.

As I searched those deep-blue eyes of his, I was amazed at what I saw. Truth. The doubtful part of my mind finally started to cave in, allowing my heart to take over. In that moment, I saw in Keith's eyes everything I needed. Honesty. Affection. Desire. I was suddenly overwhelmed with a sense of certainty I had never experienced before.

Keith's love was real. It was okay to trust him.

"I think I need to tell you something," I said softly.

He nodded. His annoyance with me had utterly vanished, replaced by a look of serious concern.

"You can tell me anything," he said, gently lifting my chin.

I walked over to the couch and sat down. Keith took a seat next to me, a little ways away. He seemed to want to give me as much space as I needed. I smiled at him and reached over to take his hand in mine. He smiled back, looking relieved that I wanted to touch him. He must have been worried about what I might have to tell him.

"I just want to tell you why … I feel like I need to explain …" I faltered, having trouble expressing myself. Keith nodded, endlessly patient as always. "Okay. I just need to tell you about something that happened to me."

Keith's expression darkened, and I could tell he was thinking about the worst possible things.

"It's okay. It's not that terrible. It's just … Okay." I drew in a deep breath, hoping that confiding in Keith would unburden me somehow. "Well, a few years ago I worked at a small private college in New Jersey. As part of the cleaning staff."

He nodded, squeezing my hand in support.

"And while I was there, this college guy started talking to me and flirting with me while I worked. Brad was his name." His name tasted like poison in my mouth. I hated even saying it out loud. "At first, I figured he was just being friendly. A lot of the college kids were. I mean, lots of them ignored me and treated me as if I was invisible, but there were a few who would say hello now and again. He was one of them."

Keith nodded, looking quite tense. Though I didn't want to upset him, it felt good to know he cared. His expression was the sweetest mix of love and support and concern.

"One day he asked me out. I thought he was joking!" I said with a laugh. "He was one of the most popular guys on the whole campus. He played football for the college and was probably the most gorgeous man I'd ever seen in my life. So naturally, I thought he was kidding when he asked me out. I'd dated a few guys here and there before then, but nothing really serious. And as I said, I was used to people ignoring me."

Keith sighed softly, looking sad.

"Brad told me he was going to show up every day and ask me out until I said yes. And he did! By the third day, I finally gave in. I really liked him. He seemed nice and funny and smart. Friendly. Everybody on campus loved him. So anyway, we went out to dinner and the movies and had a great time. For the next few weeks, we went out every weekend, and it was wonderful. I really fell for him, you know?" My voice shook. It would be a struggle to get the rest of the story out without crying. I forged on.

"In case you hadn't noticed, I'm not exactly the type to sleep with a guy right away," I said with a laugh.

Keith laughed, too. It was a gentle sound filled with affection, without a trace of mocking. "Yes, I noticed. And that's okay, Crista."

I let out a soft sigh as I gazed at Keith. He was so unlike other men, the way he considered my feelings more important than his own sexual frustration.

"So, after a few weeks of dating Brad, I felt like the time was right to be intimate with him. We talked about it and decided we were ready. He took me out to a romantic candlelit dinner. It was wonderful. We went to an expensive restaurant and we sat near the window."

I stopped for a moment, swallowing hard. I could feel Keith's body tensing up. I wanted to reach out and comfort *him*, to reassure him I was okay.

"During dinner, Brad kept glancing out the window behind me. It was weird. Unsettling. I felt like something strange was going on, but I wasn't sure what it was. Whenever I turned to look outside, there was nothing there. Finally, I turned around quickly enough to see three of Brad's frat brothers out there on the street. Laughing."

I closed my eyes for a moment, then opened them. "Long and painful story short … It was a joke. They had a bet to see if Brad could sleep with the college cleaning lady."

Keith drew in a sharp gasp. "Crista. Oh Crista, honey, I'm so sorry."

Tears filled my eyes, caused not only by the painful memory, but also by Keith's tenderness. His reaction to my confession made me feel safe and cherished. I knew I'd done the right thing by telling him.

I let go of Keith's hand, but only so I could touch his face. "So when I had this dashingly handsome man pursuing me at work," I said as I stroked his cheek. "I was terrified it might be happening all over again. I couldn't let myself believe that a man like you—"

I couldn't fight the tears anymore. I started to cry.

"Crista, Crista," Keith said in a soothing voice, pulling me into his arms and holding me close. "It's okay, honey. It's okay."

He held me in his arms and let me sob onto his shoulder for as long as it took to release all my pent-up emotions. The pain, the humiliation, the devastation I'd endured when I realized Brad had been using me all that time came flooding back. Reliving the experience was awful, but it also felt good to get it off my chest. I'd never told another living soul about what had happened, and it did feel as if a burden had been lifted. I knew my painful secret was safe with Keith. *I* was safe with Keith.

My sobs began to subside, and I finally let go of him. I laughed softly when I saw what a wet mess I had made of his light-blue shirt with my tears. He smiled fondly at me as I tried to straighten out his shirt. I grabbed a tissue from the box on the coffee table and dabbed at my eyes.

"I'm so glad you told me, Crista."

His face was filled with both sadness and understanding. He probably felt better knowing there was a reason I had so much trouble trusting him—that it had nothing to do with him personally.

"I just couldn't believe anybody would do something like that. I thought he was my boyfriend. I was falling in love with him. I thought he loved me, because that's what he told me."

Keith tensed up again, fury blazing in his eyes. He would probably beat the hell out of Brad if he ever got the chance. I was not one to encourage violence, but I doubt I would stop him if the opportunity ever came up.

"So, the next day I quit my job," I said, my emotions rapidly switching from humiliation to anger. At Brad, but even more so at myself. "God, how could I *do* that? It was so *stupid!*"

"It wasn't stupid. Of course you quit. You never wanted to see any of those assholes again," Keith said angrily. I could see his mind whirring, probably trying to figure out how he could hunt Brad down and give him a thrashing. I loved him for it, but a guy like Brad wasn't worth the effort.

"You don't understand," I said wearily. "That was my *chance.* When you work at a college, they have tuition remission. Meaning you get to go for free. Those jobs are incredibly hard to get. And I threw it all away! And for what? A stupid *man.* I think of myself as a strong woman, but letting a man beat me like that was weak of me. It really was."

"Ohhh," Keith said, his eyes full of sorrow. "That's why you cried at Rosemary's graduation."

"Yes," I whispered. "I was happy for her. Really, I was. I just … well, I didn't expect it to hit me so hard."

"Crista, you know I can …" He hesitated, knowing I tended to flip out any time he mentioned paying for school.

"I know, I know. You can afford to pay for my school. I can't tell you how much I appreciate the offer. I really, really do. It's just …"

As always, he waited patiently for me to continue.

"It's funny. I always dreamed of being like Cinderella and having a handsome prince come along and save me. But now that it's happening, it doesn't feel the way I thought it would."

Keith looked so sad when I said that. I could hardly bear it.

"Keith," I said, gazing into his eyes, "the romance part of our relationship is everything I dreamed of and more. I hope you know that. I guess I just feel like I let a bad man get the best of me, and then having another man come along and solve all my problems just doesn't sit right with me."

He nodded, and I truly hoped he understood what I was trying to say. I drew in a deep breath.

"I have to tell you something else."

"Okay," he said, his brow furrowing with concern.

I smiled softly at him, and said, "I love you too."

"Oh," Keith said, laughing and letting out a deep breath. I laughed too. I understood he wasn't laughing at me; he'd just been preparing for me to tell him another awful story.

His handsome face lit up with the most beautiful smile. "Really?"

"Yes. I love you, Keith. I love you so much." I leaned in close and kissed him. "I'm so happy I've found my handsome prince. And you're even more handsome and dreamy and perfect than in my fantasies. And that's saying a lot."

I pressed my lips to his again, and he eagerly kissed me back. Delicious tingles of desire stirred between my legs, reminding me of my long-ignored sexual needs.

Keith wrapped his strong arms around me as we kissed. He stopped for a moment to tell me, "Crista, you're everything I've been searching for my whole life, so I can't help but want to give you everything. I'm sorry I keep pressuring you about school. You have so much potential, so much passion. I just want to help you shine the way you were meant to."

My eyes filled with tears, and Keith seemed a little alarmed. I had been an emotional wreck all day, and he was probably worried about saying the wrong thing and setting me off again.

"See, that's exactly what makes you so dreamy," I said, wiping my eyes and laughing softly.

He smiled, understanding these were happy tears this time. He cupped my face and kissed me again, gently at first, then growing more passionate, forceful, and erotic.

"Keith," I managed to say.

He stopped kissing me so he could look at me, his sweet blue eyes filled with tortured frustration. I was sure he thought I would, once again, get him aroused and leave him unsatisfied.

Not this time.

I'd always felt a powerful connection to Keith, but our bond had never felt stronger than it did at this moment. Even now, when Keith was rock-hard and filled with sexual desperation, he wouldn't pressure me to have sex if I wasn't ready.

Keith was my darling love; my soulmate. The man I was going to spend the rest of my life with. There was no reason to wait one second longer to express my love for him physically.

"I'm ready to be, you know, *with* you now."

He let out a short breath. "Really?"

He looked so hopeful, I nearly laughed. It was adorable.

I smiled at him, and said, "Yes. I think I just needed to know you loved me."

Keith ran his fingers through my hair and gazed into my eyes. "I do love you, Crista. With or without sex. You know that, right?"

Tears of emotion threatened to spill again. Keith Foster was too wonderful to be real. But he *was* real.

"I know, Keith. I know. But I want to be with you more than I've ever wanted anything in my life."

That was all he needed to know. He cupped my face and kissed me with greater urgency than ever before. Our hands were all over each other, our bodies already tangled up together. He kissed down my neck, and I let out a soft cry of pleasure. I felt his long, hard cock pressing against my leg.

It was kind of intimidating.

Though he must have figured I didn't have much sexual experience, I doubt he knew I was a virgin. I wanted to keep it that way. I had no idea what I was doing, but hopefully, I'd be able to fake it.

Keith broke off his kiss and stood up. I was about to get up to follow him to the bedroom, but he had other ideas. He slid his arms underneath me and scooped me up from the couch. It was the most romantic moment of my life.

"Keith," I said, throwing my arms around his neck.

He grinned at me and said in a deep, husky voice, "Now we find out what happens when the prince gets Cinderella back to his palace."

I drew in a breath of anticipation, my panties getting wetter with every word that came out of Keith's luscious mouth. He had never looked sexier, nor more deliciously masculine than he did right now. The feel of his arm muscles bulging as he carried me, the wild look of lust in his bright-blue eyes, the deep timber of his voice, filled with desire. I was nervous yet excited, and I could hardly wait to feel him inside me.

He gazed down at me as he held me close. "Are you on birth control, or do we need something?"

Okay, he *definitely* had no idea I was a virgin. Good.

"Uh, we need something."

"Okay. I'll take care of it." He dipped his head down and kissed me, taking my breath away.

Keith carried me into his bedroom, and gently lay me on the bed. It was like something out of a fairy tale. Every day with this man seemed to be out of a fairy tale.

My God, how I loved him.

He straddled me for a moment, kissing my mouth and down my neck again, driving me wild. Then he climbed off me so he could rifle through his night stand for a condom. I was excited, lying on the bed, waiting for my lover to ravish me. I glanced down at the huge bulge in his pants. It was hard to believe Keith would fit inside me. I started to tremble nervously, but I was determined not to show it.

Keith found a condom and held it up triumphantly.

"Thank God," I said, and he laughed. It would have been awful if we'd gotten all hot and heavy only to have to stop because of lack of protection.

Keith got off the bed and extended his hand to me. "Come here, my love. I want you to undress me."

I eagerly accepted his hand and allowed him to pull me to my feet.

"I've waited so long to see you naked, my prince."

His eyes flashed with excitement. Happiness. I was really into it now, and he knew it.

Keith had taken off his suit jacket when we'd first arrived, so I went straight for his tie. After a moment of struggling, I realized I couldn't get it off.

"Help me!" I said with a giggle.

Keith laughed. He managed to whip off his tie in seconds. He tossed it aside like it was part of a striptease. It was so, so sexy.

"Okay," I purred. "Buttons I can handle."

I unbuttoned his shirt slowly. I waited until I had them all undone before I opened his shirt to look at his chest.

"Mmmm," I said admiringly as I ran my hands over his beautiful broad chest. It was manly and muscular, with a little hair. Jet-black, like the gorgeous crop on his head.

Keith grinned his sexy grin. I pulled his shirt off and started unbuckling his pants.

No matter how big it is, don't look shocked or afraid.

I'd only seen pictures of naked men, sneaking a few looks at an art book in the library, just out of curiosity.

I pulled his pants down, then his underwear.

It. Was. Huge.

I looked up at Keith and said in the sexiest voice I could muster, "Impressive."

"I'm glad you approve," he said. He grabbed the hem of my dress and pulled it up over my head. Keith drew in a deep breath as I stood there in my bra and panties. "Beautiful. So, so beautiful."

I was slightly self-conscious about my plain white lace bra and underwear. I hadn't planned on having sex tonight, so I wasn't exactly prepared. If I'd known, I would have bought a black or red bra and panty set.

Keith unclasped my bra and slid down my panties. He made such quick work of my underwear, it wouldn't have been worth the money for a fancy set anyway. He took a step back to admire me, his eyes filled with a hunger I'd never seen in him before.

Pulling me close, he kissed me, his hard cock pressed between my legs and his gorgeous chest pressed against my breasts. We kissed for mere seconds before he pushed me down. Lying crosswise on the bed with Keith's incredible naked body on top of me made my heart thump wildly. I didn't think I could wait another second for him to take me.

"Lie down on the pillow, darling," Keith said, panting. "I want you to be comfortable."

Keith slid off me so I could reposition myself. He slipped on the condom and straddled me for a moment, looking down at my naked body.

"My God, you're a vision, Crista."

He positioned himself between my legs and kissed me. I swallowed nervously, knowing this was the moment of truth.

"I love you, Crista," he murmured into my ear, and then he plunged inside me.

The pain stunned me. I had expected it to hurt, but not this much. Tears pricked my eyes, and I knew I'd never be able to hide my nervousness and discomfort from him. I had to tell him.

No. I *wanted* to tell him.

"Keith," I said, and he gazed down at me. "I don't want there to be any more secrets between us." I drew in a deep breath and whispered, "This is my first time."

Keith's eyes flew open wide. "Oh!"

I watched as he struggled to hide his shock for my sake.

"W—well I'm glad you told me." I could see his mind spinning, wrapping his head around what I had said. His shock quickly turned to concern. "Oh, sweetheart, I would have been gentler if I'd known. Did I hurt you?"

"A little." *No more lies.* "A lot."

I wiped the tears of pain out of my eyes. The soreness was beginning to subside, easing to a dull throb.

"I'm so sorry, Crista. Do you want me to stop?"

"Of course I don't want you to stop. I wanted you to be my first," I said as I ran my fingers through his black hair.

Keith looked lovingly into my eyes and whispered, "What an honor."

He began to move again, very gently. I let out the breath I hadn't even realized I'd been holding. His beautiful blue eyes stayed locked on mine as he gently, sweetly, made love to me. He began to slide in and out of me slightly faster, all the while gazing at me to make sure I was all right. I began to feel the first ripples of pleasure as he hit the right spot between my legs. I let out a soft cry.

"You okay? Does it hurt?"

"No. No, Keith. It feels good," I reassured him.

He smiled with relief. "Good."

He moved a little faster still, eliciting another soft cry from me. I closed my eyes, wanting to drink in every moment. I could hardly believe I was actually having sex, and *Keith Foster*—the man of my limitless fantasies—was the man making love to me.

"Oh, Keith," I moaned. My cries of passion encouraged him to move faster still, which made me moan louder. I was still slightly sore; how wonderful it would feel next time when he could pound me harder. His gentle thrusts were intensely pleasurable. What he'd do to me when he wasn't holding back!

I opened my eyes to find Keith really *was* holding back. He was sweating, his damp hair hung in his face. Just as I had imagined—sexy, manly, and panting with effort. Though my own pleasure grew with every thrust, I wasn't anywhere near orgasm yet. It obviously tortured Keith to keep himself from finishing.

"Don't hold back, darling. This is only our first of many times together. It's okay, Keith." I smiled affectionately at him. "Let go."

Keith let out a breath, and sheer relief shone in his eyes.

"Crista, Crista, oh God," he moaned as he thrust faster. I let out a sharp cry, and his eyes opened wide with concern.

"It's good, Keith. Oh, it's so *good*," I cried out, to assure him my cries were of pleasure and not pain. I gripped his shoulders as he pounded harder. "Keith!"

The pleasurable sensation between my legs was so strong, I began to wonder if I might reach orgasm after all. Then Keith let out a deep, manly groan as his whole body shook. I loved watching his pleasure as he came. I resented needing the condom. I wished I could have felt the warmth of his seed inside me.

He kissed me gently and pushed back my hair from my face. Still inside me, he said softly, "I love you so much."

Once again, I was overwhelmed with the powerful connection we shared. I knew deep in my heart that Keith was not only my first lover. He was my last, my one, my only. The only one I would ever need.

Carefully, he eased out of me. He disposed of the condom and pulled me into his strong arms. His physical needs satisfied, he was caring for my emotions. I'd never needed closeness more in my life, and he knew it.

Being with Keith was so perfect. He had treated my virginity like a precious gift.

Being close to Keith felt wonderful, but I still felt sexually frustrated. It wasn't his fault I'd been too sore to enjoy sex to the fullest. My pent-up arousal was made worse by resting on Keith's rock-hard chest. I supposed I'd have to take care of my own needs later.

Keith glanced down between my legs. "Oh honey, you're bleeding a little."

"Oh no. Your beautiful sheets," I said, starting to sit up.

Keith put a hand on my chest and gently pushed me back down on the bed. "I'm not worried about my beautiful sheets. I'm worried about my beautiful *girl*. Lie down and rest."

He rooted through his nightstand drawer for some tissues. Taking a handful, he carefully wiped between my legs. In the process, he swept across my clit, still swollen with arousal. I let out a soft cry, just as I had while we were having sex.

Keith raised an eyebrow, obviously noticing the state I was in. He lay back down beside me and slid his right arm under my neck, pulling me close to his naked body. He slipped his left hand between my legs, his fingers gently sliding across my opening, but not going inside. My vagina still throbbed from the invasion of his cock, and I was grateful he was allowing me some time to heal.

I was even more grateful when he began to gently stroke my clit. It was the most delightful way to discover Keith was left-handed.

"Oh," I cried out softly.

"Do you like that?" he asked in a husky voice, his eyes lighting up was he watched what he was doing to me.

"Yes. Oh, Keith, that feels so good."

He shifted his body up slightly so he could reach better, giving me a fuller view of his muscular chest in the process. I ran my eyes down the length of his body, at his bulging arm muscles, his masculine chest, his still partially erect manhood between his legs. Out of the corner of my eye, I saw him smile slightly. He knew his nakedness turned me on, and he loved it.

"Oh, oh, oh," I kept repeating as he stroked faster, driving me insane with pleasure.

"No one's ever done this to me before," I told him, gazing into his eyes. Now that I'd spilled all my secrets and shared my body with him, it was easier to be honest about everything.

Keith grinned his sexy grin, which only intensified the blissful sensations between my legs. I was so close to orgasm, I could hardly take it anymore.

"Faster, Keith. Oh God, go faster," I said, my boldness surprising me.

"Anything, baby. I'll do anything you want," he responded in his deep, manly voice. He circled my clit faster and faster and faster until I completely lost my mind.

I threw my head back and cried out when I came. The explosion of pleasure was intense and all-encompassing. The thrilling sensation seemed to go on forever, wave after wave of utter bliss. When it was over, I closed my eyes and let out a deep breath of sheer satisfaction and complete sexual relief.

I opened my eyes to find Keith gazing down at me with love and tender affection. Feeling the familiar deep connection with him again, I was overwhelmed with love for him.

"That was amazing, Keith. All of it."

He leaned down and kissed me, his love surrounding me like a warm blanket.

Stroking my cheek, he said, "Thank you for trusting me with your body. And with your heart."

I teared up. "This was everything I always wanted it to be."

"I'm so glad," Keith said with a smile. He lay back down, and I snuggled up close to him. The skin-to-skin contact and his heart beating against mine comforted and calmed me.

We lay together until I fell into a deep, comfortable sleep.

143

Chapter 15

Good Christ, I could be thick sometimes. I couldn't believe it had never once occurred to me that Crista was a virgin. Perhaps it was a good thing that she didn't tell me until the latest possible moment. I would have been a nervous wreck about making sure everything was perfect. Then again, had I known, I could have sprinkled a bunch of rose petals on the bed or something. Lit some candles. Stuff other girls would probably think was corny, but that Crista would love.

In the end, it didn't matter. We'd finally made love, and I'd done the best I could on the fly to make sure the experience was special for her.

I'd meant it when I said it was an honor to be her first. Crista clearly didn't take sex lightly and, given her trust issues, letting me make love to her was a huge deal. It was horrifying to think how close she'd come to losing her virginity to that frat boy prick.

My God, she would have been devastated.

That punk had hurt her badly enough just by dating her under false pretenses. She would have felt so violated if she'd had sex with him and then learned the truth of his intentions. Crista deserved so much better than that. She deserved to be with a man who loved her as much as I did. I was grateful her first time had been with me, warm and safe in my bed where I could hold her close afterward.

I'd never forget the way Crista's body felt last night as she lay naked, pressed against my chest. For once, her muscles were relaxed. Part of it was due to the relief of her sexual tension, but it was more than that. Holding her close, I could physically feel her love. Her trust.

I glanced over at her, asleep next to me. Her hair spread out on the pillow, she was still naked, wrapped only in the sheet. My God, she was beautiful. Her dark skin, her dark hair, and delicate facial features—she was a vision of female perfection. I smiled just watching her. Waking up next to her brought me a sense of peace and happiness I'd never known before.

Crista stirred a little. I lay back down on my pillow so she wouldn't think I was a creep for watching her sleep. She was lovely and sweet and perfect. And she was *mine*. For the first time, I had a woman in my life who loved me the way I'd always dreamed of. Women weren't the only ones who craved love and romance. A lot of guys did, too. We just weren't allowed to admit it.

I reached over and pulled a half-awake Crista over to my side. She let out a happy, yet sleepy, moan of approval and eagerly cuddled up next to me. After resting together for a while, she opened her eyes and smiled.

"Do I look different now that I'm a woman?"

"You were always a woman, Crista. You're just a sexually active woman now."

"Hmmm. I look forward to being *very* sexually active with you, Keith."

I grinned at her. "I like your enthusiasm. How are you feeling?"

I was ready to take her again right then and there, but I figured she needed more time to heal.

"Okay. Just a little sore, but good otherwise."

I nodded, then kissed her. "You want to take a shower first?"

Crista yawned and said, "No, you can go first. Hate to break it to you, but I'm not exactly a morning person."

"I am!" I said brightly.

"Oh Lord," she said wryly, making me laugh.

"Go back to sleep if you want, babe. We have nowhere to be any time soon. It's probably for the best that you're not a morning person, you know."

"Why?"

"Theater stars work late on Broadway. Then they sleep in."

Crista's face broke into the loveliest smile.

"Get some rest, my little starlet." I kissed her on the forehead as she giggled. "I'll put a new toothbrush in the bathroom for you. I have a whole pack, I'm pretty sure."

Crista muffled her thanks, then rolled over to go back to sleep.

She was still in bed when I got out of the shower. While she slept, I headed down to the kitchen. I'd been hard at work the last few weeks to learn how to cook a few things. Especially breakfast items. Though I hadn't been sure how long it would be before Crista spent the night with me, I'd wanted to be fully prepared for the event.

We'd been out to dinner lots of times, but we'd never shared breakfast, so I wasn't sure what she liked. I made some scrambled eggs, bacon, sausage, and toast, just to have the bases covered. I still hadn't mastered the art of making pancakes—they always turned out all runny or burned—so I didn't attempt them this morning. The last thing I wanted to do was embarrass myself by setting off the smoke alarm while making her breakfast.

Crista appeared in the doorway, freshly showered and wearing her dress from the night before.

"Is that Cinderella or Sleeping Beauty?"

She laughed and walked over to me. "Sorry I kept you waiting."

"No problem. You needed your rest."

Crista put her arms around my neck. Her muscles were still relaxed and she sighed softly, so I could tell she was feeling emotional.

"You okay?" I asked.

"Yes. More than okay." She nuzzled my neck and cuddled up close to me. "Perfect."

I held her. Yes, she was feeling emotional, but in a good way. I closed my eyes, relishing the way she felt in my arms. Her body relaxed, as it did last night. She clearly had no regrets about having sex with me.

Crista lifted her head and said, "What smells so good in here?"

"I made you breakfast."

"You what?" she asked, her brown eyes dancing with amusement.

"That's right. Your spoiled, helpless boyfriend made you breakfast."

"I never actually *said* you were spoiled and helpless, Keith," she said with a laugh.

"No, but I bet you thought it pretty hard."

Crista looked guilty, which made us both laugh.

"Sausage or bacon?" I asked.

"Bacon."

"Eggs? Toast?"

"Eggs would be great."

"Okay, bacon and eggs, coming right up!"

Crista smiled, looking utterly charmed. It took so little to make her happy. What a change from the high-maintenance women I usually dated.

"I made coffee, too," I said, setting a cup in front of her. I put a small shaker of cinnamon next to her cup.

"You remembered," she said with a smile.

"Yeah, I remembered. Do you know how hard I worked to get that first coffee date with you?"

Crista laughed. "I really have been a challenge. And yet, you conquered me."

She gazed at me seductively, making my cock twitch. Hopefully, she'd be ready to have sex again soon.

"Thanks," she said as I gave her a plate of bacon and eggs. "You got any hot sauce?"

"I think so. Let me check."

I rifled through my cabinets until I found some.

Crista raised an eyebrow.

"What?"

"Kid stuff. Remind me to pick you up some real Mexican hot sauce."

I laughed.

"Come sit with me," she said.

I took my plate and coffee and sat next to her in the kitchen booth. I watched nervously as she took a bite of the scrambled eggs.

"Mmmm, Keith, this is great. What did you put in it?"

"Cheddar and asiago cheese."

"Fancy. I like it!" Crista sampled the bacon. "Crisp and perfect. You cooked it just right. Good job."

She leaned over and kissed me.

"You really like it?"

"I really do. Yes," she said. She gave me a sweet kiss on the lips, before going back to eagerly eating her breakfast.

"Cool."

"Even the coffee is perfect," she said, taking a sip of her coffee with cinnamon.

"Coffee, I know how to make. Everything else wasn't so easy. It took me a million tries to figure out how to cook the bacon without burning it to dust."

"When did you learn how to cook?"

"I've been practicing ever since the first time I brought you over."

Crista's expression softened. "You mean ever since I made fun of you for not doing things for yourself. I'm sorry. I hope I didn't hurt your feelings."

"You weren't wrong. I mean, I'm busy, and I can afford to have people do stuff for me, but I really should learn how to do some things for myself."

"Well, I'm proud of you," she said.

"Thanks." I felt grateful to seem a little less helpless in her eyes.

"I'm doing the dishes," Crista announced after she'd finished eating.

"You don't have to—"

"It's only fair. You made breakfast, I clean up," she said, punctuating her words with a kiss on my nose. I loved how natural it felt having her here, like this was her apartment, too. As if we were a happily married couple.

I sat back in the breakfast booth, watching Crista put the dishes in the dishwasher. She softly sang in Spanish as she worked. I recalled her telling me she couldn't sing much at her place because the walls were so thin.

"You know, the walls are pretty thick here, and I don't have neighbors close by. You can sing louder here."

She glanced over her shoulder and graced me with a beautiful smile. She took my advice. I closed my eyes and listened to her sing. I had no idea what the words meant because it was all in Spanish, but it was lovely nonetheless. After she finished the song, she sang "Think of Me," which made me smile.

I lay back in the booth, eyes closed, drinking in the melodious sound of Crista's voice. It was soothing and sensual, and by far the prettiest sound I'd ever heard.

When she finished the song, I opened my eyes. She'd finished the dishes and had been standing there in the kitchen, singing just for me, watching my reaction. I was glad of it. I hoped she understood how talented I thought she was, and not just because she was my girlfriend.

"That was beautiful, Crista," I said, which made her pretty face light up. I got up and wrapped my arms around her. "You are incredibly amazing in every possible way. I hope you know that."

"You're sweet to say that," she said, sounding as if she didn't believe me.

"I mean it. I'm proud of you. Everything you've done, working hard at two jobs. Being brave enough to go forward with your theater career. Not to mention being brave enough to trust a guy like me after everything you've been through."

Crista gazed up at me fondly as I held her in my arms. "I should have trusted you long ago with my secrets. I should have known you would understand."

"I hated seeing you so upset at Rosemary's graduation," I said, segueing into what I knew was a dangerous topic as skillfully as I could.

"I know. I'm okay now."

"Are you?"

"Of course," she said, looking surprised at my question.

"I can't stand seeing you cry, Crista. Not when we both know there's something I can do to help."

She let out a deep, weary sigh when she caught on to what I was leading up to.

"Can we at least talk about this? Now I have you finally confiding in me?"

"Yes. That's fair I guess."

"I don't understand why you get so angry with me when I say I want to pay for you to fulfill your dream of going to school."

"Oh, Keith," she said, her voice filled with sorrow and regret. "I don't mean to sound mad at you when you're only being kind and generous with your offer."

"Then why won't you let me help you?"

Crista drew in a deep breath and let it out. "It's hard to explain."

"Try. Please, Crista. I want to understand."

She nodded. "It's a lot of things, I guess. For one, my parents worked very hard when they came to this country, and that's where I got my work ethic from. My mother worked horrible hours in the garment district, and my father was a busboy in a Greek restaurant. A *busboy*, can you imagine?"

A twinge of anger crept into her voice. "My parents owned a store in Ticuani. It was successful for a while, but then the economy tanked, and they had to close up shop. When I was growing up, it seemed they worked all the time. They were always there for me and my brothers, though. Always."

I smiled and stroked her hair. I could see how much she adored her family, and it was hard to imagine what it was like. My parents had been little more than a source of money and food for me. Her parents sounded amazing.

"They taught me to always work hard and pay my own way. To not take charity."

"Sweetheart, this would hardly be *charity*. I love you. It's different."

She didn't look convinced. Pausing, she looked contemplative for a moment. "I don't know how to explain ..." She faltered, then smiled. "It's like I said last night; I love how romantic you are. I love all the wonderful, thoughtful things you do. I know you're wealthy, and I think it's sweet how you spend money on me and treat me, well, like a princess."

"I enjoy treating you like a princess," I said, meaning every word.

Crista was a down-to-earth, gracious, classy woman, always appreciative of my every romantic gesture. That was what made it so much fun to do things for her. I'd do anything to see her lovely smile.

"I know," she said adoringly. Yep, that was the one. That smile. "When you do things like that … like what you did for me at The Creel Foundation?" She put her hand over her heart. "Learning the words to the Cinderella musical so you could sing and dance with me? I mean, who *does* that kind of thing in the real world? You, Keith. Only you could be so sweet and thoughtful. It makes me feel like, I don't know, like …"

"Like?"

"Like I'm the woman you love," she finished softly. "And you do romantic things because you love and cherish me."

"I do love and cherish you."

She stood on her tiptoes to kiss me before continuing. "But when you talk about paying for my school and taking care of me financially, it doesn't feel that way. It's not that you did anything wrong. I know you would never lord it over me or treat me like I owed you or anything."

"Of course I wouldn't!"

"I know," she said in a soothing voice. "But even so, it just feels like, I don't know, more like a parent-child relationship."

"It shouldn't feel like that."

"But it does," she said sharply. "That's what it feels like to me. Like I have some kind of sugar daddy who's going to pay for everything so I don't have to worry my pretty little head over such things."

"Crista, it's not like that at all!"

"For you it isn't. I know that, Keith. I understand it's not the way you see it, but it's how I feel. It's okay if you don't understand what I'm saying, but I do ask that you respect my feelings on this."

I let out a deep, frustrated breath. It was hard to argue with her when she put it that way.

"I need to pay my own way. That's just how it is."

She seemed so unhappy when she said that, which only confused me further. "So you are one-hundred-percent sure you do not want me to pay for your college."

"Yes."

"Then what do you want?"

"I don't know."

"Well, I'll be right here by your side when you figure it out," I said, pulling her close. Her body was tense at first, but soon she began to relax.

"Can I just suggest one teeny tiny compromise?" I asked.

"What?"

"Those voice lessons you want …"

Crista opened her mouth to argue but I cut her off.

"Just listen, you stubborn woman!" She laughed, which gave me a glimmer of hope. "I know how excited you are about moving forward in your theater career and how eager you are to get started already. Baby, it might take you months to scrape together the money for the class. Please, please, please just let me pay for those lessons to get you started so you don't have to waste any more time."

I could see she was thinking about it. I froze, as if any sudden move might scare her away like a frightened animal.

"Well," she began, then stopped.

"Just one class. Get the list of teachers from Rosemary if you haven't already, pick the one you want, and then send me the info. That way you can get started on lessons ASAP. We'll figure out the rest later."

Crista didn't look entirely convinced.

I held up my right hand. "Crista Rivera, if you let me pay for your voice lessons, I hereby solemnly swear never to bring up the subject of paying for your college ever again."

Crista smiled broadly. "That's more than fair. Thank you, Keith," she said, throwing her arms around me. I hugged her so hard, I lifted her off the ground.

After I set her back down, I added, "The offer is always, always open, baby. All you have to do is say, 'I want to go to college,' and it's done. But I swear, I won't mention it again until you do."

Crista nodded and quietly said, "Okay."

Chapter 16

I was so excited about my first voice lesson, I could barely sleep the night before. Keith drove me over to the studio on 46th Street in the evening after work, giving me a sweet good-luck kiss before I got out of the car.

"Knock 'em dead, baby," he told me with a sexy grin. I still wasn't crazy about him paying my way, but these lessons cost over a thousand dollars. I couldn't begin to imagine how long it would have taken for me to save up that kind of money.

It really made me think about all the poor people out there in the world. They had dreams, too, but when they were struggling to pay for food and shelter, what chance did they have to follow their heart's desire? That was what made The Creel Foundation so great. Poor kids got a chance to take lessons for free. Maybe when I got good enough, I would be able to teach there. I smiled just thinking about it.

I walked down a hallway to Room 246, where my lesson would take place. I had expected my instructor to be some older, schoolmarm type of lady, but the woman who greeted me was young. In her early thirties, I would guess, she had blond hair and pretty, blue eyes. She reminded me a bit of Elyse.

"Hi, I'm Crista Rivera."

"Nice to meet you," the woman said crisply, shaking my hand forcefully. "I'm Nina Morable."

"Pleased to meet you, Ms. Morable."

"Call me Nina." It sounded like an order.

"Okay."

"Sing something," she commanded.

"What?" I suddenly felt completely unprepared. As if I'd failed to do a homework assignment.

"Sing … something," Nina said, speaking slowly as if I were an idiot. I suddenly felt afraid. I'd always been a good student in high school, and I wasn't used to having a teacher be angry with me.

I cleared my throat.

"Don't clear your throat!" Nina practically shouted. "You're slamming your vocal chords together."

"Okay," I said meekly, which seemed to annoy her further. She flared her nostrils, waiting for me to do as she had commanded. I wanted to ask for clarification. What did she want me to sing? I was too scared to ask her anything. My throat went dry, which I knew was not good for a singer. I thought about asking for water, but what if she yelled at me for being unprepared? Wouldn't a real singer have already thought about drinking water before arriving at a voice lesson?

I somehow found the courage to open my mouth and start singing. I sang "Think of Me," because it showed off some of the high notes I could hit, and because it made me think of Keith. Thinking of him brought me tremendous comfort and eased my fears a bit.

Nina narrowed her eyes, scrutinizing every note I sang. It was impossible to tell what she was thinking. She was silent for a full thirty seconds after I finished. It was the longest thirty seconds of my life.

"I get it. You can sing high notes. You're not trying to be an opera singer. You want to sing on Broadway, right?"

There was something mocking in the way she said it. For the first time since I walked in, I felt angry instead of scared. Who the hell was she to make fun of me?

"Yes," I said firmly. "I want to sing on Broadway."

Though the look vanished as quickly as it came, I could swear Nina appeared impressed with me for a half a second.

"Do you have any idea of how many starry-eyed girls I see come through here wanting to be Broadway stars?"

"I'm guessing a lot."

Nina snorted. "Yes. A lot. Very, very few have what it takes to make it."

She gave me a look of haughty derision, as if she'd already decided I wasn't one of those very few. Her instant rejection hurt me to the core, but I swallowed hard and tried not to take it personally. She'd heard me sing one song, and I'd never had a singing lesson in my life. Of course I was nowhere near ready for Broadway yet.

That's why I'm here.

My teacher studied me for a moment, perhaps waiting for me to have a nervous breakdown. The silence felt incredibly uncomfortable, but I bided my time and waited for her to speak again.

"We shall see," Nina said at last, looking pessimistic. "Okay. Let's get down to business here. Stand up straighter. You can't sing if you're all hunched over."

I obeyed, straightening my spine and standing taller.

"To be a musical theater singer, you don't sing toward the back of your throat. That's for classical singing. Broadway singing is more nasal."

Nodding, I did my best to commit every word to memory. I was eager to learn as much as I could, and I knew she would yell at me if I forgot anything.

"Sing something else," she barked.

My mind spun. It was far more terrifying to sing for Nina, now that I knew what I was up against. I considered something from *Cinderella* but quickly rejected the idea. I was not about to allow this nasty woman to poison my favorite musical by allowing her to tear down my singing of it.

"Sing!" Nina ordered, her piercing blue eyes flashing with annoyance.

Almost clearing my throat out of nervous habit, I stopped myself just in time. I began to sing "Many a New Day" from *Oklahoma*, which was another song that allowed me to show off the high notes.

"Stop!" she ordered after I'd sung the first line. "Didn't anyone ever tell you to sing from your diaphragm? That's Singing 101."

I'd heard the rule, but I'd never really understood what it meant. I couldn't answer her question without looking like an idiot, so I said nothing.

Nina threw up her hands in frustration. Then she started talking to me like I was a toddler, her tone slow and condescending.

"The diaphragm is your breathing muscle. Now, breathe in as deeply as you can, and push out your stomach muscle. Like this."

Nina demonstrated how to breathe through her diaphragm. "Now. Do it."

Would it kill her to say please?

I found myself so scared of her, it was hard to concentrate on the lesson. I drew in a shaky breath and pushed out my stomach muscles as she instructed.

"No! Push *out*. Here," she said, roughly pressing her hand on my midsection and making me jump in fear. She let out a short, annoyed breath. My fear angered her. "Put your hands on your lower ribcage. If you're doing it right, you'll feel this part expand."

I nodded, drawing in a deep breath.

"If your shoulders are pulling up, you're doing it wrong. If the ribcage is expanding but your upper body is still, you're doing it right."

I practiced a few times and finally got the hang of it.

She gave a sharp nod, which was probably as close to praise as I would ever get from her.

"Sing the same song but do it right this time."

Don't clear your throat, don't breathe wrong, don't let your voice shake. And don't cry.

That last part was getting harder by the moment. Nina had me so frazzled, I felt I could break any moment. I'd never been so scared to sing in my life. It was hard, because singing brought me such joy.

I breathed properly this time, and I got through three lines before Nina stopped to yell at me.

"Don't sing at the back of your throat! Sing like this." Nina sang the first five lines of the song, and I was blown away. Her voice was loud and strong, and it was easy to imagine the sound carrying through a Broadway theater. And that was without a microphone. *Wow.* Her voice was amazing and highly intimidating. No wonder she looked at me with such derision. I'd never be able to sing like that. And we both knew it.

"A Broadway sound is more brassy, sharp, edgy when compared to classical singing. Again," she ordered.

I began singing, and again, she told me to stop and yelled that I was doing it all wrong. The lesson went on this way for the rest of the hour. It was excruciating. I felt like her prisoner. As if there was no escape, and I would never see Keith or my friends or family ever again. Tears of terror and humiliation constantly welled up behind my eyes, threatening to explode at any moment.

"All right. Time's up," Nina said at last. "Next time be better prepared. Take care of your voice. Drink a lot of water. All the time.

Professional singers *always* carry water with them."

She shot me another derisive glance, belittling me with her eyes for being a terrible person for not having water with me.

"Avoid alcohol. Drink tea with no caffeine. Gargle with hydrogen peroxide."

"Okay. Got it." I hated the shaky sound of my voice. And I hated Nina Morable.

I picked up my purse, fighting the urge to run out of there.

"Crista," she said sharply as I turned to go.

"If you can see yourself doing *anything* but being a singer, you should."

Chapter 17

Keith had texted me that he'd found a parking spot a few blocks away from the studio. I walked there on shaky legs after my voice lesson had finally come to an end. I kept my head down, fighting tears as I rushed to the safety of his arms.

I opened the door and collapsed in the seat beside him. I must have looked every bit as awful as I felt, because Keith gasped.

"Crista! What the hell hap—"

"I think," I said as I struggled to catch my breath. "I think I just need to cry for a minute."

Throwing my arms around him, I let loose all the emotions I'd been holding in for the last hour. I sobbed quietly into his shoulder, and he held me close and stroked my back. Without a word, he held me and comforted me, which was exactly what I needed.

Eventually, I pulled away from him and grabbed some tissues from my purse. After a moment to compose myself, I felt ready to tell him what had happened.

"My teacher is really mean," I said. It was an understatement. "She was super harsh. Basically, everything I've been doing my whole life is wrong. I've been singing wrong, not taking care of my voice. Apparently, I don't even know how to *breathe* right."

I glanced up at Keith's steely glare. He looked about ready to storm two blocks to the studio and give my teacher hell for making me cry. Though it was fun to imagine the look on Nina Morable's face when Keith burst in the door to give her a piece of his mind, I knew I could never let him do it. Still, I gained some satisfaction, imagining Nina as terrorized as she'd made me feel.

"The whole lesson was horrible and awful and degrading." I looked into Keith's eyes and added fiercely, "And I can't wait to go back."

"What?" he asked, astonished.

"This isn't supposed to be easy, Keith. I admit, I didn't expect the first lesson to be this awful, but I always knew I had a long journey ahead of me." I paused for a moment, my body still shaking and hiccupping a bit from crying so hard. I felt shaken to the core, but saying aloud that I had every intention of going back made me stronger.

"Having Nina yell at me and mock me was heartbreaking and scary, but it didn't break me. It *won't* break me."

Keith's sexy mouth turned up in a hint of a smile as he listened to me. Deep pride radiated from his sexy blue eyes.

"Today, I know a lot more than I did yesterday. And the next time I'll learn even more. It was weird. By the end of the lesson, I could actually hear the difference in my voice. She taught me how to sing from my diaphragm and, well, first she made fun of me for not already knowing how to sing from my diaphragm …"

Keith's eyes narrowed a bit. It felt good to know he had my back. I knew he would be right by my side through this whole crazy journey.

"But then she taught me how to breathe properly, to sing properly, and I could really hear the difference. And I can hold notes longer now."

Keith smiled and nodded. "Well, that's something, I guess."

"And I learned how to take care of my voice better. I'm not supposed to clear my throat. It damages your voice, apparently. And I'm supposed to drink as much water as humanly possible, so I want to get a water bottle I can carry with me all the time. And I need to drink tea but without caffeine. And I'm supposed to gargle with hydrogen peroxide."

Saying out loud all the things I had learned made me feel stronger still. If I could just somehow tune out Nina's mean-spirited attitude and remarks while retaining the lessons she taught, I could make this work.

"Okay, baby," Keith said, tenderly stroking my throat. "We can stop at the store right now and get everything you need. It's important to take care of your lovely voice."

"Thank you," I said, putting my arms around him and kissing him.

"You know, we could always try another teacher. One who's not a total bitch." The steely blue glare was back.

"No. I want to stick with this one. I think this is something I need to do. This is part of paying my dues, Keith. At least now I'm actually *doing* something instead of just dreaming about it, you know? I feel like that's what separates real artists from the ones who just fantasize."

Keith cupped my face in his hands. "Crista, I am so goddamn proud of you."

"Thank you, Keith. For everything." I pressed my lips against his and he wrapped his loving arms around me.

Chapter 18

A few weeks later, Elyse and I met in the conference room to discuss the electronic health records project I'd been working so hard on lately. We'd spent the last two hours hashing out the details of the sales presentation I was going to give to several hospitals here in New York. If those went well, there were plans to branch out across the United States, and even to different countries. It was a cool project, and I was excited to be in charge of it.

"Okay, so you think you can organize all these notes we made and have a presentation ready in a couple of days?" Elyse asked.

"I'll have it to you tomorrow."

"Even better," she said with a smile. I always did my best to over-deliver on anything she or the higher-up executives asked me to do. Like Elyse, I was highly ambitious. I figured she would inevitably get promoted again and when that happened, I wanted the job she was in now.

Elyse glanced at the clock. It was nearly 5:30—quitting time. Not enough time to start working on anything else. "So, how are things with Crista?"

My face broke into a goofy smile, like it always did when someone mentioned the love of my life. "Great. Things are great. Except …"

"Except what?"

"I just worry about Crista dealing with that bitch of a teacher she has for voice lessons. I know Crista's new, and she has a lot to learn, but does that woman have to be so mean to her?"

"Yeah, that sucks. I'm sure it helps that you're so supportive of her."

"I do what I can. I just can't stand seeing her cry."

Elyse grimaced. "Oh, that's awful. Her teacher really makes her cry?"

"Yeah. Not all the time. Not as much as in the beginning, but still … I don't know. I guess it's toughening her up, and she seems excited about everything she's learning."

"You guys are so great together," Elyse said with a sweet smile.

"Yeah, we are." I felt warm all over, just thinking about Crista. There was no better feeling than when she wrapped her arms around me and kissed me. I didn't have to be jealous anymore when I saw Elyse and Luke acting all lovey-dovey together. "It's funny. It's hard to imagine I actually thought you were, you know, The One for me."

Elyse laughed softly. "Yeah. It is kinda funny. We should be perfect for each other. We have so much in common, it's ridiculous."

I shook my head. "Luke and Crista are so completely different from us. And yet …" I smiled my goofy smile again, making Elyse laugh.

"I know. Well, at least we work really well together. Not many co-workers who've seen each other naked could still work together like nothing happened."

I laughed, nodding as I got up to gather my belongings. "Well, I gotta go. I've got to get Crista to her voice lesson."

"Okay. Try not to strangle her teacher."

"No promises," I grumbled as I headed out the door.

Chapter 19

Not many co-workers who've seen each other naked could still work together like nothing happened.

I replayed the words over and over in my mind, trying to make sense of them. My heart seized in my chest when I overheard Elyse's words. I'd frozen for a few seconds and barely had time to dash down the hallway before Keith saw me.

I hadn't meant to listen in on their conversation, but I'd heard Keith's voice from outside the conference room. It was nearly time to leave for the day, so I thought I'd wait a minute or two in the hallway until they finished their meeting. Elyse and Keith had been spending a lot of time together working on the medical project Keith was so excited about.

But they weren't discussing work. Keith had said he'd once thought Elyse was the right woman for him, then Elyse joked about how they had seen each other naked. I figured Keith had probably dated a lot of women before he met me. But how could he not have told me Elyse was one of them? And why hadn't Elyse ever told me? I thought she was my friend.

Elyse was right: she and Keith were perfect for each other. They were both wealthy, and probably came from similar backgrounds.

And she was so smart. I couldn't even understand most of what Keith was talking about when he explained his technology projects to me. Did he think I was dumb? After all, I only had a high school education. Elyse was an expert in computer science.

Suddenly, all my insecurities came flooding back. Why *was* a guy like Keith doing with a woman like me? We had absolutely nothing in common. Maybe Elyse had dumped him, and I was the rebound woman. A consolation prize. He couldn't have Elyse, who was beautiful and dynamic and glamorous. And *smart.* So he'd had to settle for me.

I'd worked so hard to trust Keith. How could he have kept something like this a secret from me? That his boss—the woman he worked closely with every single day—was his ex-girlfriend?

"Hey, baby, ready to go?" Keith called to me when he found me leaning against the wall for support. He walked over to me, his face suddenly filled with concern at my expression. "Hey, are you okay?"

"Yes, I'm fine. Just a little nervous about my voice lesson, but what else is new?" I said lightly. Keith always knew when I was upset, so I had to work extra hard to hide my emotions. I wanted to be a performer; hiding my anguish would be good practice for me. "Yep, I'm ready to go."

I slipped my arm around his waist and we walked together to his car.

Usually a nervous wreck before my voice lesson, I was so distraught over Keith, I didn't have time to worry about what Morable the Horrible had in store for me tonight. Nina couldn't possibly inflict anywhere near as much pain on me as Keith had by keeping secrets from me. What else had he been hiding all this time?

*****

"Concentrate!" Nina snapped during my lesson when my mind began to wander. "I can tell something is wrong with you tonight."

Inwardly, I prayed she wouldn't ask what was wrong. It wasn't like she would care. She'd probably use my heartache as ammunition against me.

"Whatever your problem is, get over it. *Focus*. On Broadway, you'd be doing eight shows a week. You can't do that if you get all tied up in knots anytime you got a problem."

"You're right," I said, standing up straighter, getting angry with Keith for stealing my focus. I tried not to think about the fact that if it weren't for him, I wouldn't be taking voice lessons at all. Forcing myself to focus on the lesson, I nailed the line Nina had been trying to teach me to sing properly.

"Mmm hmm," she said with a nod. That "mmm hmm" of hers was the only compliment she gave when I got something right. I'd come to crave any scrap of acknowledgment. "Again."

I sang the line again, and Nina nodded. "Okay, let's move on."

Grabbing my water bottle, I took a big swig and saw the hint of approval in Nina's eyes. I'd take any bit of encouragement I could get right now.

If nothing else, my ability to concentrate on my lesson helped bolster my shaken confidence. It was good to get my mind off my doubts and, for once, I wasn't particularly relieved when the lesson ended.

"You okay?" Keith asked when he came to pick me up. He looked worried, but I was usually a bit rattled after my voice lesson.

"Yes, I'm okay." I felt the distance between us widening and I hated it. Keith usually took me in his arms after my lesson, giving me much-needed warmth after I'd been yelled at for an hour. He hesitated now. Yes. He'd already picked up on the fact that something else was going on.

He drove me back to my apartment in silence.

*****

On nights when I didn't have my voice lesson, I often met up with Rosemary at The Creel Foundation. The place was so big, that we always had plenty of room to rehearse somewhere in the building, even when the main auditorium was in use. Evenings were busy at the foundation with all the classes going on. Susie frequently taught dance lessons, and Luke helped out when he could, when he wasn't onstage himself. His show, *Pirated*, was enjoying a pretty successful off-Broadway run.

Being surrounded by performers was exciting, and I felt at home when I was at the foundation. Rosemary was an incredible mentor, and I was honored to help her prepare for her upcoming auditions.

Rosemary and I were practicing tonight in one of the little theater rooms. It had a stage and a few hundred seats, and was used for smaller performances.

"You know, you're doing great with your audition songs," Rosemary told me. She'd been a huge help in selecting songs that showed off my range. "I think it might be a good idea for you to practice them in front of an audience. What do you think about scheduling a little private show? With me, Johnny, Susie and Luke and everybody. And Keith, of course. That way, you could practice the first time with an encouraging audience."

"Sounds like a good idea. I'd love to actually be able to sing in front of a group. Besides you, the only person I get to sing for is Morable the Horrible."

"Ugh. I regret the day I ever gave you the list with her name on it," Rosemary said. "I had no idea how awful she was."

I'd told Rosemary all about Nina's teaching methods, and she did not approve. She'd had tough teachers at NYU, sure, but nothing like Morable.

"You get used to the abuse after a while," I said with a laugh. It was true. I had certainly learned how to weather criticism in that class.

"Oh, hey, Susie suggested another song for your audition book."

"Yeah?"

"She thinks you would sound great doing 'Where Did the Rock Go?'"

My eyes lit up. It was a great song, and I agreed it might work well for me. "Oh, I never thought of that one!"

"Yeah, Susie and Luke did *School of Rock* a little while ago with all the kids."

"I remember Luke talking about it at work. Sounds like he had a lot of fun with it." Luke had played Dewey, the character played by Jack Black in the movie version.

Rosemary laughed. "Oh, he pretty much has fun whatever he does."

"True," I said with a smile. *Was he aware Elyse and Keith were an item once?*

It must have happened before Luke and Elyse got together, but I wondered if it bothered Luke. Keith was a very attractive man. Didn't it worry Luke that his girlfriend spent so much time working with him?

"Hey, are you all right?" Rosemary asked, eying me with concern.

I briefly considered asking Rosemary what she knew about Luke and Elyse. She'd known them both a lot longer than I had. For all I knew, she and Johnny used to double date with them. I suddenly felt stupid and naive. Like everybody in my friends' group knew about this but me. What didn't somebody—*anybody*—tell me? Didn't I have the right to know, especially considering the fact that Keith and Elyse worked together all day every day?

"Yeah, I'm fine," I said.

"Okay," she said gently. "Well, if you ever want to talk about it, I'm here for you. Okay?"

Then why didn't you tell me the truth?

I supposed Rosemary had just been trying to protect my feelings by keeping the truth from me, but I was still hurt.

"Why don't I try practicing the song now?" I suggested, walking to the middle of the stage. Singing was always such a comfort to me. It helped me release some of the mixed emotions I was feeling. "Where Did the Rock Go?" wasn't a love song, thank God, but it was a wistful song nonetheless. Sung by the straight-laced principal of the private school, she wonders what had happened to the rock-and-roll free spirit she used to be.

I took a deep breath and sang the song without any musical accompaniment. I didn't want to wait to find the song on the sound system. I simply wanted to sing.

I infused it with all of my emotion and turmoil. It was a terrific song, full of passion, regret, and hope all mixed up together. There were parts I could really belt out to show my range, then it ended on a quiet note of hopefulness.

"That was beautiful, Crista," Rosemary said softly when it was over. "Simply beautiful."

Chapter 20

Keith and I went out to dinner on Friday night. Our conversation was strained, as it had been the last few nights. I asked him a lot about the medical project he'd been working on. I really did want to know how it was going because I knew how much it meant to him, but I also wanted to know exactly how much time he was spending with Elyse. How I hated feeling so jealous! A rotten, useless emotion that was poisoning my relationship with Keith. I'd replayed what I'd heard over and over in my mind. Keith had made it clear he had once really believed Elyse might be The One for him, the true love of his life. So, what had changed? They had obviously dated … and then what?

Maybe Elyse met Luke and fell in love with him. Maybe that was the only reason Keith wasn't with her. For all I knew, he was still in love with her.

I knew I should simply ask Keith what the hell happened between the two of them rather than keep driving myself slowly insane with all these unanswered questions. But I was scared to death to do it.

Part of me was terrified he would confirm my worst fears. That he was madly in love with Elyse, and he was still pining for her. The other part was terrified that Keith might lie right to my face. He might deny there had ever been anything between them. If he did that, I'd never be able to trust him again.

I wasn't sure which scenario was worse.

Once we got back to his place after dinner, we sat together on the couch and Keith started kissing me. He must have expected me to be intimate with him again, but I just couldn't right now. Not with so many questions hanging over my head. I was more scared than ever of getting hurt. I'd already surrendered my virginity to him; having sex with him again would only make it hurt more if I found out he was still in love with Elyse. My God, what if he thought of her when he was making love to me? The thought made me sick to my stomach.

Keith broke off the kiss. "What's wrong, Crista?"

He sounded irritated and frustrated. He'd worked so hard to get me in bed the first time, and he must have felt like he was starting all over again.

"Nothing."

"Don't tell me nothing when there's obviously something wrong." He looked worried but there was also anger in his voice.

I swallowed hard, looking down to avoid his gaze.

"I'm getting tired of these games, Crista," Keith said, running his hand through his hair.

"What are you talking about?"

"You're shutting down again. Pushing me away, and I have no idea why. What did I do wrong this time?" he asked sharply.

"Please don't be mad at me," I said, my voice shaking. Between Nina's constant fury and my heartache over Keith, I was at my emotional limit. I couldn't bear having him yell at me.

"I'm not mad," Keith said more gently. "I'm just confused. Just when I thought you trusted me, it seems like you don't any more. I can't fix what's wrong if you don't talk to me."

"I know," I said, looking into his eyes.

"What's wrong, baby?" Keith asked, gently stroking my face. "Please tell me, so I can try to make it better."

"You … well, you spend a lot of time working with Elyse, right?"

Keith's brow furrowed with confusion. "Yeah. Kind of. I mean, she's my boss, and she's been helping me with the hospital tech project and all. Does it bother you that I work with her a lot?"

"She's so glamorous. She's beautiful and smart. She's so much like you. I can't help but think you guys are lot more suited to be together than we are."

"Oh, honey," Keith said tenderly, his eyes full of concern instead of anger. "You have nothing to be worried about. It's funny, Elyse and I were just talking the other day about how she and Luke are so different, and you and I are so different, but our relationships work anyway."

I nodded slowly. At least that part was true. I'd heard Keith say as much to Elyse. I was still desperate to know the details of the fling they'd had. How long were they together? Was it serious? Had Keith ended things with her? Was it mutual? *Did he wish he was still with her instead of me?*

"Elyse is a cool boss and a good friend, Crista. That's it. You're the one I love," he reassured me.

"Did you ever … were you ever … Did you ever date her?"

Keith's eyes opened wide. "No. Of course not. There's never been anything between us."

His lie tore my heart apart. I wasn't sure how ready I was to hear the truth about his relationship with Elyse, but I needed him to be honest with me about it. Instinctively, I hugged my arms around my chest to protect myself. My heart.

"You were never … with her?"

"As in, did I sleep with her? No, of course I didn't!"

Of course you didn't. You've seen each other naked, but you didn't sleep together. Yeah, because that's how life works.

I closed my eyes as a sickeningly familiar wave of devastation and humiliation washed over me. It was the same feeling of shock and dread I'd felt when I glanced out the restaurant window and saw a bunch of college boys laughing at me.

No. It wasn't the same feeling. This was much, much worse. I wasn't in love with the horrible frat boy. I had thought I was, but I didn't know what love was until I met Keith. And I'd never known true heartbreak until this moment.

"I'm tired. I want to go home," I said, standing up and forcing myself to walk on shaky legs toward the door. Keith rushed toward me and put a hand on my shoulder. He had a wild look of confusion and fear on his face. I guess he thought I was naive enough to believe his lies.

"Crista! Talk to me. Why are you so upset?"

"I'm okay. I'm okay," I told him. It was more like I was trying to reassure myself that I was okay. That I would survive this nightmare somehow. "I'll take the subway home."

"Crista!" He managed to grab ahold of my arm before I could get away. His eyes open wide, he said, "I'm telling you, there is nothing going on between Elyse and me, and there never has been. You do believe me, right?"

His eyes bored into mine, imploring me to believe him. He seemed so earnest, I almost believed him, but there was absolutely no mistaking the conversation I had overheard. I refused to be taken advantage of by a man. Not again. I was nobody's goddamned victim anymore.

"I have to go," I said, pulling my arm away and running out the door.

*****

What in the hell just happened here?

I paced back and forth across the floor of my apartment, trying to figure out what in God's name had upset Crista so much. I wanted to chase after her, but I figured I should leave her alone if that's what she wanted. She obviously thought I had something going with Elyse, but I couldn't for the life of me understand why. Maybe there was some kind of rumor going around the office about the two of us, and Crista had caught wind of it.

My heart ached for her. I knew how difficult it had been for her to trust me, and I knew she must be torturing herself with thoughts of me cheating on her with Elyse. Crista had been under so much stress with her evil teacher, and this was the last thing she needed.

I wasn't angry with Crista anymore, but I was frustrated and running out of ideas of how to make this relationship work. She and I were meant to be together. I was sure of it. But we couldn't have love without trust. I had never, ever given her a reason to mistrust me, and I never would. What else could I do to prove I would never lie or hurt her?

I texted her several times and got no response. Finally, I sent her a text begging her to at least tell me she got home safely. I hated the idea of her taking the subway at this hour.

My cell phone rang, and my heart jumped in my chest when I saw it was Crista.

"Are you home? Are you okay?" was how I answered the phone.

"Yes, I'm home. I'm okay. I'm sorry, Keith. I shouldn't have run out on you like that."

I closed my eyes, breathing out a sigh of relief and drinking in the sound of her voice.

"Crista baby, *what* is going *on?*"

"I'm just tired. I need some rest. I need some time to think."

Time to think. Good God, was that code for I'm planning on dumping you?

"I love you, Keith," she said quietly. It sounded like she was close to tears.

"I love you too, Crista. More than you could possibly know."

"I'll see you tomorrow night, okay?"

"Yes," I said, wanting to keep her on the phone but not knowing what to say. Tomorrow night she was performing for all of us at The Creel Foundation. "I can't wait to hear you sing, sweetheart."

"Thanks. Good night."

"Good night." I put down the cell phone and put my head in my hands.

If I didn't figure this out soon, I would lose her forever.

*****

The next day, I considered talking to Elyse to see if she had any idea what was going on with Crista, but then I thought better of it. At this point, I was afraid to be seen with her at work. I didn't want to risk upsetting Crista any more than she already was, and if there was some kind of rumor going around about me hooking up with Elyse, I didn't want to add any more fuel to the fire.

Instead, I decided to call Rosemary.

"Hey, Keith," she said cheerfully when she answered the phone. "What's up?"

Understandably, she sounded surprised to hear from me. I'd never called her before.

"Sorry to bother you, but I wanted to ask you about Crista. She was really upset last night and I'm not sure what's going on with her. She tends to shut down sometimes and not talk to me, so I don't know what to do. Do you have any idea what's wrong with her?"

Rosemary sighed. "I know what you mean. There's definitely something that's been upsetting her lately, but unfortunately she won't tell me what it is, either."

"She has a really tough time trusting me. Believe me, she has her reasons."

"What do you mean?" Rosemary asked, a suspicious edge to her voice.

"No, no. I don't mean she has reasons not to trust *me*. I just mean, well, she got hurt pretty badly in the past. It's, you know, personal stuff she confided in me that I won't repeat."

"I understand," she responded, the softness returning to her voice. Yes, contacting Rosemary had definitely been the right call. She was a good friend to Crista and very protective of her.

"I swear to God, Rosemary, I would die before I hurt her. She just doesn't know it. Just when she starts to trust me, she pulls away again. I'm afraid I'm really going to lose her this time." My voice hitched with emotion when I said that last part.

"Oh, Keith, that's not gonna happen," Rosemary said with compassion in her voice for both me and for Crista.

"I'll try to talk to her and see if I can get her to open up to me a little. I should probably wait until after her performance tonight. She's bound to be nervous, and I don't want to upset her before she goes onstage."

"Good thinking." I felt a bit better that at least we had a plan in place.

"It'll be okay, Keith. Try not to worry. Crista loves you so much. There's no question about that."

"Thanks, Rosemary. I'm not letting her go without a hell of a fight, that's for sure."

"That's the spirit," she said. I heard the smile in her voice.

Chapter 21

My performance at The Creel Foundation tonight was shaping up to be one of the biggest challenges of my life. Not only was I performing solo for the first time in front of people, I was coping with the prospect of losing Keith. If he was capable of lying to me, what kind of future could I possibly have with him? Knowing Keith and Elyse had once been an item would have been hard to cope with under the best of circumstances, but I'd have dealt with it and moved on if that was all there was to it. I'd been terribly insecure from the beginning, as Keith was painfully aware. I could understand, to a degree, why he might not have told me he and his boss used to be lovers. But to deny the truth when I point-blank asked him about it? No matter how much I loved him, I couldn't stay with a man I couldn't trust.

Drinking from my water bottle backstage, I focused on the task at hand. This was my first opportunity to perform before an audience, and I was not about to blow it. Miraculously, I'd managed to focus during my voice lessons, despite the turmoil in my personal life and Nina yelling at me. That gave me the confidence to go out there and give it everything I had tonight. I recalled Morable the Horrible's words of wisdom: "On Broadway, you'd be doing eight shows a week. You can't do that if you get all tied up in knots anytime you got a problem."

It hadn't occurred to me until later, but Nina probably wouldn't have said it, if she didn't think I had a shot. She was mean. She was tough. But I had the feeling she wouldn't waste her time with me if she didn't think I had a chance.

"How are you feeling? Are you nervous?" Rosemary asked, rubbing my shoulders supportively.

"I'm absolutely terrified. But I'm also really excited. And I'm *ready.*"

Rosemary's pretty, green eyes sparkled with happiness. "I know you are, Crista. I know you are. Break a leg, baby."

"Thank you!" I said, throwing my arms around her and hugging her warmly. *Break a leg.* It was a showbiz term I'd heard all my life, but no one had ever said it to me before. I felt I was truly a part of the theater tradition.

"I'll be down there, front and center, cheering you on!"

Rosemary left me alone so she could go take her seat with the others. Johnny was here. Susie was here with David. And Luke was here with Elyse. Naturally, seeing Elyse in the audience would make this all the more difficult, but I was determined not to let it throw me. And of course, Keith was here. Now was not the time to try to sort out my messy romantic life. Now was the time to focus on my burgeoning professional life.

I closed my eyes and took a few deep, calming breaths. I was a jumble of nerves.

I walked out onto the stage, and my audience of seven stood up and applauded. Somehow, it made me more nervous. I hadn't done anything to earn their applause. Yet.

"Thank you all so much for coming out tonight," I began in a voice that was much too quiet for the auditorium. For an official performance with a full house, I would have used the microphone, but Rosemary and I thought a mic wouldn't be needed for a small group. In a much louder voice, I said, "It means a lot to me that you're all here to support me."

The sound of my booming voice, combined with the friendly, smiling faces, bolstered my confidence. I walked over to the sound system and started up the music. Strutting back to center stage with as much confidence as I could muster, I began to sing my first song: "Let Me Be Your Star" from the television show *Smash*. A short-lived drama about putting on a Broadway show, it hadn't lasted long on the air, but many of the songs had become standards in the theater world. The song was Rosemary's idea, and it was the perfect choice for me to start with. The lyrics spoke about hungering for fame and craving the life onstage. It started out slowly, then built to an exciting crescendo.

As I'd hoped, singing out loud and strong was incredibly healing for me. It felt so damned good to pour out my emotions up on the stage. I had learned a lot from Nina, and I could really hear the difference in my voice. It was cathartic to sing as loud as I wanted, and singing before an audience was exhilarating.

I finished my first song with a flourish and earned a healthy round of applause. Johnny whistled his approval, and Keith shouted "Brava!" I tried to keep my professional performance face, but I couldn't hide my smile. These were my friends. They would support me no matter what, but I thought I'd genuinely earned their approval.

My next song was "Where Did the Rock Go?" I loved singing that one with all its sweetness and passion. My heart and soul felt soothed with every note I sang. I felt like I was releasing a lifetime of pent-up emotions. How on earth had I made it this long without theater in my life?

I got applause again, but the reaction was more subdued. It was somehow better than the loud clapping. My performance had touched the hearts of my audience with the second, more powerful song. How beautiful it was to be an artist! To have the power to reach people was such a tremendous gift.

The next song would be the most difficult one of my entire set. It was "Think of Me," chosen especially for Keith. I just had to take the song one line at a time. And try not to cry. Though I had practiced it many times, I'd never realized how bittersweet the lyrics were. It was really about the aftermath of love. How, when it's over, you still think of the one you loved, and how impossible it is to purge him from your mind. I tried to look at the whole audience as I sang, but I ended up looking into Keith's eyes most of the time. I couldn't help myself. He gazed at me with love and pride tinged with tremendous sorrow. He was as unsure of our future as I was.

Would he still think of me when he was gone?

I fought hard to nail those high notes at the end without letting my voice betray my breaking heart. Somehow, I managed to do it. But I couldn't look at Keith when the song ended. It was all too much for me.

*****

My heart squeezed in my chest as I agonized over her performance. It almost seemed as if she was saying goodbye to me through song. "Think of Me" was a beautiful song, and the way Crista sang it was so heartbreaking I could hardly bear it. I pondered the meaning of the song now, given everything that was going on between us.

Johnny nudged me and grinned. "You know that last one was for you, right?"

Crista had made it crystal clear. I forced a smile. "Yep. I think so."

Luke put his hand dramatically over his heart. "Oh! I thought that song was for me." His look of mock devastation actually got a small laugh out of me.

"In your dreams," I said, making him pout further.

You already stole one woman out from under me.

As I turned back to watch Crista onstage, it occurred to me how much she and Luke had in common. They were both passionate about theater, and they worked together at their day jobs. Luke was a good-looking guy, and probably the most charismatic man I'd ever met. I imagined how painful it would be if I'd thought for one moment Luke and Crista had ever hooked up. I understood how much Crista must be hurting to think Elyse and I had once been an item. I wished I knew where she got the idea there had ever been something between us, and I wished like hell I could get Crista to believe me.

Crista began her next song. I wasn't familiar with this one, but it featured some insanely high notes which she managed to hit perfectly every time.

"Wow," I said as I watched her.

"I know," Rosemary said with a smile. "She's incredible."

"I wish I had a program or something, so I would know what she's singing," I said.

"Oh, I can tell you," Rosemary said. "This one is 'Glitter and Be Gay' from *Candide*."

I nodded, watching Crista with fascination. This particular selection sounded almost like opera, and I was amazed at how well she sang it. Rosemary had worked hard with her to come up with a list of songs that could really show off Crista's range of talents, and I could see why they had chosen this one.

"Wish I could hit high notes like that," Susie mused as she watched Crista.

"Right?" Rosemary agreed. "I mean … *wow.*"

"Oh, please," Luke said. "I could totally sing that high."

We all chuckled.

When Crista finished the song with yet another impressive set of high notes at the end, we all stood and applauded. She deserved a standing ovation for her performance. She bowed her head modestly and smiled.

"'Breathe,'" Rosemary said as Crista began her next song and we took our seats.

"What?" I asked.

She smiled. "'Breathe.' It's from *In the Heights.*"

"Oh," I said. "I don't know that one."

"Oh, it's a great show. From the creator of *Hamilton.* Has lots of Hispanic elements."

I nodded. "Breathe" turned out to be a passionate song about trying hard to make it and feeling like you weren't good enough.

"It's about a girl coming home after dropping out of college," Rosemary explained, softly. "She tried to make it through school while working several jobs, and it was too much."

I stared at Crista as she sang about having to go back home and tell everyone she couldn't make it.

"Did you pick this one?"

"No, she did," Rosemary said.

A deep sensation of sorrow swept through me like a swirling storm, destroying everything in its path. She wanted so badly to go to school. Why was it so hard for Crista to let me love her? To let me take care of her?

I drew in a deep breath just as Crista sang the final line of the song, saying, "Just Breathe."

Thankfully, her next song provided a bit of comic relief. No doubt it was chosen to show off her lighter side.

"'Spanish Rose,'" I said.

"Yes." Rosemary's eyes lit up with approval that I knew the song.

"She sang it to me in the elevator."

"Nice," she said with a laugh.

Soon we were all laughing as Crista showed off her considerable comedic talent. She strutted across the stage, deliberately over-the-top with her exaggerated Hispanic attributes, which were designed to annoy her future-mother-in-law in the show. I marveled at how funny and sexy she was at the same time, especially when she mimed doing the tango.

As she had in the elevator, she narrowed her eyes at me when she got to the line warning the "Americano" not to mess with her. That elicited another laugh from us. She finished the song with a flourish, and we applauded and whistled loudly.

The next song started out very slow and menacing. Crista walked slowly, methodically across the stage as she sang words threatening revenge.

"What show is this from?" I asked, astonished to see how mean-looking Crista could be.

Rosemary's eyes flashed mischievously. "*Mean Girls*."

"Oh, wow," I said as I watched Crista's performance. The song got louder as she sang about wanting to watch the world burn. The transformation was incredible. There wasn't a trace of my sweet, gentle Crista Rivera up onstage. She was suddenly vicious and cruel. For a few seconds, I forgot it was Crista, the woman I loved, up there. She was *that good*.

Rosemary grinned as she watched my reaction. "And she hasn't even had acting lessons yet."

The song ended with a fierce and fiery crescendo as Crista sang the final powerful line about relishing having the world crash and burn around her. We all went nuts when she finished, clapping and whistling like crazy. Crista laughed softly, and I could see how much fun she was having. It felt good to see her so happy.

"You guys have been a truly wonderful audience. Just one more song left," Crista told us. We all said, "Awwwww," at the same time, making her laugh.

"For the last one, I told her she should just pick any song she really loved," Rosemary explained.

Crista started to sing "In My Own Little Corner" from *Cinderella*.

"Perfect," I whispered, and it really was. I loved hearing her sing that one.

I just hoped to God I was still her prince in this scenario.

Rosemary reached over and squeezed my hand. "I'll talk to her after the show, Keith. Everything's going to be okay. You'll see."

I closed my eyes and listened to Crista's lovely voice.

Breathe. Just breathe.

Chapter 22

Keith was the first to greet me when I walked down the steps from the stage. Nobody else was aware there was anything wrong between us, and we both knew now was not the time to discuss it. He wrapped his arms around me, and I breathed in the familiar scent of his cologne. What I wouldn't give to go back to the time when I felt safe in his arms, both physically and emotionally. Now, I tensed up at his touch.

"Crista, that was beautiful. I knew you were good, but even *I* didn't know you were *that* good," he said.

"Thank you," I whispered, letting him hold me for just a second longer. Thankfully, there was no time for awkwardness as my friends descended upon me.

"Girl, you were terrific," Susie exclaimed, hugging me warmly.

"You're so sweet," I said.

"I mean it! You were phenomenal! You're gonna slay 'em at auditions with that material."

I smiled, grateful to have a few moments to revel in the success of my first public performance. *I did it! And I didn't fall flat on my face.*

"And hey, when you're ready to tackle the dance portion of your auditions, you let me know," Susie said.

"I might just take you up on that."

"Please do," Susie said excitedly. She was an amazing dancer, currently in rehearsals for an off-Broadway show that would premiere soon. She taught high school back in Washington, D.C., and I was sure she was a much nicer teacher than Morable the Horrible.

Elyse walked up to me and opened her arms. "Crista, you were incredible!"

I hugged her, doing my best to relax my muscles. Elyse was the last person I wanted to see right now, but I knew I had to be gracious. She had always been a good friend to me. Or so I thought. Technically, she hadn't lied to me about dating Keith, because I hadn't asked her about it. Still, wasn't that the kind of thing you were supposed to be up front about? By the way, I used to date your boyfriend?

"Thanks," I said, feeling a fresh wave of sadness. I had always been fond of Elyse, and she'd seemed so excited when Keith and I got together. I already missed the friendship I thought I'd had with her. I hugged her for as long as I felt was appropriate.

Luke grinned at me, which lifted my spirits. He was the nicest boss anybody could ask for, and we frequently talked about theater stuff at work. It involved lots of mutual whining about having to work a day job when all we wanted to do was go to the theater.

"Crista, that was so amazing. You crushed it, girl. Way to go!"

"Thanks, Luke," I said, hugging him with genuine enthusiasm.

"Look at this!" Johnny exclaimed, looking at all our friends gathered around me. "You got a ton of fans mobbing you already."

I laughed. It was hard to imagine being one of the Broadway stars who had fans waiting outside their dressing room after a show. It was fun to think about, though.

"Johnny, would you mind terribly waiting around for just a little while? I need to talk to Crista," Rosemary said.

Her words made me nervous. I wondered if she wanted to give me notes on my performance. I hoped I hadn't screwed up somehow.

"Sure," Johnny responded. "Everything okay?"

"Yeah, everything's fine," she assured him.

"I've got a better plan," David chimed in. "Joey can take Susannah and me home, and then he can come back and take you ladies home."

"In the limo?" I asked incredulously. "Oh, you really don't have to do that."

"You're a *star*, Crista," David said sternly. There was gentle kindness behind his eyes that betrayed his gruff manner. "Stars ride in limos."

I laughed. "That's so sweet of you, David. Thank you so much."

"It's my pleasure, believe me." David graced me with his half-smile. "You gave a lovely performance."

"Thank you," I said with a smile.

As the little crowd began to disperse, Keith said, "I'll see you later, Crista. Get home safely."

"I will," I said softly. God, it hurt to look at him.

I suddenly felt so lost, like I had no idea what to do or where to turn. Why, why, why did Keith have to lie to me? That was the one thing I couldn't forgive in a relationship. Even if Keith had slept with *all* of my friends before he met me, I probably could have gotten past it. But lying to my face about it was inexcusable. Lately, I'd been somewhat preoccupied with preparing for my performance, so I'd managed to suppress my agony over Keith. Now it came rushing back, along with the certainty that I had to decide what to do. My choices were limited. And horrible. I could talk myself into staying with Keith, knowing I could never really trust him, and spend the rest of my life terrified he would hurt me again. Or I could end things and suffer a breakup so painful, my heart might never recover.

I snapped out of my morose vision of my future to find Rosemary looking at me with a grim expression.

Oh God, was my performance that bad?

She was probably trying to think of a nice way to tell me I just didn't have what it took to make it in the theater world. I couldn't bear the suspense any longer.

"What did you want to talk to me about? Was my performance that terrible?"

Her green eyes flew open. "No! No, of course not, Crista. You did a beautiful job. You blew everyone away!"

I let out a deep breath of relief.

"I'm so sorry," Rosemary said, putting a hand on my shoulder. "I didn't mean to scare you. You did a lovely job, but that's not what I wanted to talk to you about. Here, come sit with me."

She walked to the edge of the stage and sat with her feet dangling over the front. I watched as she took a quick glance around the auditorium and back at the stage, a small smile on her lips. Rosemary clearly loved being on the stage, *any* stage. I admired—and shared— her passion for the theater.

"Are you okay?" I asked, taking a seat beside her. "What did you need to talk about?"

"Oh, I'm fine. I wanted to talk to you about Keith," Rosemary said gently.

"Oh."

"I know you've been really upset about something lately, and I want you to know it's safe to confide in me."

I nodded. I wanted to believe her, but right now it didn't seem safe to trust anyone. Elyse and Keith had kept the truth from me. I supposed Luke had known about their past, too, but he never told me.

Rosemary waited for me to say something, but I didn't. "Keith called me."

"He did? Why?"

"Because he's worried about you," Rosemary told me. "He knows you're really upset about something, and he doesn't know what to do. He also said he was gonna fight for you, no matter what it takes."

"Did he also tell you he had an affair with Elyse?" I blurted out angrily.

Rosemary's eyes opened wide. "He *what?*"

"Well, no. I mean, affair isn't the right word because it happened before he met me. At least I'm pretty sure it happened before he met me."

"You're saying Keith and Elyse used to be a couple?" Rosemary asked with astonishment. "That can't be right … can it?"

She seemed utterly confused. *Welcome to my world.*

"You really never knew?" I asked, and she shook her head. Scared as I was to trust anybody, I believed Rosemary. It made me feel better that at least *she* hadn't been keeping this secret from me.

"I met Elyse through Luke, so I didn't know her before she was with him." Her brow furrowed, and I could see she still couldn't quite believe what I was telling her. "What makes you think they used to be an item?"

"I overheard them talking about it."

Rosemary nodded sadly.

"Keith was talking about how crazy it was that he used to think Elyse was The One for him. As in, you know, the love of his life." My voice cracked as I spoke. Though it felt good to get this off my chest, it was painful to say the words out loud.

Rosemary put her arm around my shoulder and squeezed me in a quick hug. Thank God I had her to lean on. Literally.

"Okay, well," Rosemary began thoughtfully. "Just because Keith had a thing for Elyse at some point doesn't mean he acted on it."

"Then they joked about how good it was that they could work

together after having seen each other naked," I said dryly.

"Oh."

"Yeah," I said with a bitter laugh. "The worst part is when I asked Keith about it, he denied it."

"Wow, that's really surprising." Rosemary sounded disappointed in Keith.

"I know."

"Maybe he was just trying to protect you," she said. "He still works with Elyse, and maybe he thought it would be too hard for you to know they'd been together in the past."

I sighed. "I guess that's possible."

"I know it's hard to think of Keith being with Elyse—or with anyone else, for that matter—before you. Trust me, I know what you're going through. Johnny certainly had a past before me, and it was a past that *everybody* knows about."

I nodded. Johnny had been a notorious playboy before he met Rosemary, and his hard-partying ways with booze and women had been in the tabloids constantly.

"That must have been really hard for you."

She nodded. "It was at first. It was hard to believe he could go from being with lots of woman to being with just me."

"He loves you so much."

Rosemary's sweet smile lit up her whole face. "And I love him. I can't wait to marry him." She paused for a moment before continuing. "Sorry. That's not what you need to hear right now."

"I don't mind. I'm so happy for you both. Really." I was genuinely thrilled for them. I hadn't known Johnny during his spoiled rich-kid phase. The Johnny I knew was funny and warm and generous to a fault. They made a wonderful couple.

"I remember this one time when we were first dating. Johnny took me out to this beautiful, fancy restaurant. It was his favorite place to go for a drink or for a meal. He took me there for a romantic dinner and there was this table full of women sitting near us. Crista, Johnny had slept with *all of them.*"

"Wow," I said sadly. "That sounds awful."

She nodded. "Yeah, it kind of was. Of course, I'd known all about his past, but seeing the actual girls he was with … It hurt. It hurt a lot. But I was able to get past it because Johnny and I love each other so much. You can't change the past, but I know Johnny's always been faithful to me. That's all that really matters."

"But Johnny was honest about his past right? He told you the truth about sleeping around."

"Well, yes. Yes, he did." Rosemary sighed. "I get why you're upset, Crista. I really do. I was well aware of Johnny's past and, though I don't go out of my way to press him for details, when I do ask him about it I expect him to be honest."

"Exactly. I hate the idea of Keith having slept with his boss, but like you said, you can't change the past. If he'd been honest, it would still hurt for me to think of them together, but I'd get over it. Ugh, why did he have to lie about it? That's what scares the hell out of me. If he lied about this, what else is he not telling me?"

"It's just so hard to believe Keith would lie. It seems so unlike him," Rosemary said. She shook her head, still trying to make sense of the whole mess. "I've always had such a good feeling about him. When you told me he was being patient about waiting, you know, to be intimate, I thought, he's one of the good ones!"

"I know. I don't understand it either, but I'm not stupid. I know what I heard."

"So you heard them say Keith once had a thing for her. But then they were joking about how crazy it seems now, right? Like he can't believe he ever felt that way about Elyse, now that he has you. That's a good thing, right?"

"Yeah, I guess so. That's all well and good, but then they were laughing about how weird it was that they'd seen each other naked and now they work together like nothing happened." I winced just thinking about it. My handsome Keith with beautiful, glamorous Elyse.

"Wait a minute ..." Rosemary said cautiously. "Think really carefully here. Is that all you heard?"

"What do you mean, is that all I heard? What else is there? I might not be as educated and sophisticated and worldly as the two of them," I said bitterly, "but I'm not stupid and naive."

"Crista," she said sternly. "*Did you hear them say anything else? Anything at all?*"

I blinked, taken aback by the look in Rosemary's eyes. "No, that was it."

She put her hand over her mouth for a second.

"What? What already?" I asked.

"Oh my God, Crista. I know exactly what they were talking about, and it's not at all what you think. I can't believe I didn't figure this out sooner!"

My heart hammered against my ribcage. Rosemary was handing me a lifeline, and I was scared to death to take it. I couldn't bear to get my hopes up only to have them dashed again.

"Wh— What do you mean?"

"If Keith says nothing happened between him and Elyse, then *nothing happened.* I believe him, Crista," she said, her green eyes lit up with joy.

"Why?" I whispered.

"Because—" Her face fell. My heart sank. This emotional roller coaster was killing me.

"What? What is it?"

"I can't tell you," she said softly.

"*What do you mean you can't tell me?*" I practically shrieked.

Rosemary grabbed my hand and squeezed it as she looked into my eyes. "Crista, something happened with Elyse a while back. Something very personal, and I can't tell you about it without betraying her trust. I know what you overheard sounded awful, but there *is* an explanation for it and it's not what you think. Maybe Keith did have a crush on her a long time ago, but they were never a couple and they certainly never slept together."

"But—"

"I need you to promise me something," Rosemary said, imploring me with wide eyes. "Promise me when you go into work tomorrow you'll talk to Elyse. Tell her exactly what you overheard, and she'll probably explain the whole thing to you. I wish so much I could clear this all up for you now, but it's just not my story to tell. Do you understand?"

"Yes," I reassured her. I knew she desperately wanted to tell me the truth now. "I understand that you're wonderful and loyal, and anybody would be lucky to have you as a friend. I know I am."

Rosemary threw her arms around me and hugged me tight. "I knew it. I *knew* Keith would never lie to you!"

She seemed so sure about it. I wished I was.

Chapter 23

I had a horrible, sexually explicit dream about Keith and Elyse. They were having sex on the conference room table in every position imaginable. I hadn't even considered how Elyse was probably a lot more experienced and sexually adventurous than I was. Leave it to my subconscious to dredge it up for me.

Rosemary had seemed so sure she knew the explanation for what I'd overheard, and that Keith hadn't lied to me after all. All I knew was I couldn't go on like this. I couldn't stay with him if he'd lied to me, so everything hinged on what Elyse had to say.

Waiting to get to work to talk with her was agonizing. All morning I obsessed over what she might say. I alternated between the hope that somehow she'd have a rational explanation for all this, and despair that she would tell me she had been with Keith. As awful as the confession that they'd been a couple would feel, it wasn't even the worst-case scenario: what if she didn't tell me her secret? I'd be left drifting in limbo with no resolution to this mess.

Riding the subway to work, my mind conjured a lot more ways this could go wrong. What if Elyse was tied up in meetings all day and I couldn't talk to her? What if she was in meetings with *Keith* all day?

I rushed in to work so fast, I had to take a few moments to catch my breath before I approached Elyse's office. Peering in, I saw her at her desk.

Oh, thank God.

This might be one of the worst conversations I'd ever had in my life, but at least it would be over with soon. I stood at her glass door until she noticed me. She looked up from her computer and smiled when she saw me, motioning for me to come in.

"Good morning! How's life?" she asked cheerfully.

Now that was a loaded question.

"Uh … Can I, uh, talk to you for a minute?"

"Of course you can," she said gently, her voice full of concern. "Shut the door."

I did, then shakily sat down in front of her desk.

"Are you okay?" Elyse asked, looking worried. She slid a little ways away from her computer and leaned forward so she could give me her undivided attention.

"Not really. I have something I need to talk to you about. A— and I'm not sure how to—" *How to finish my sentence without crying?*

"Hey, you can talk to me about anything," she reassured me. "Just tell me what's on your mind."

"Did you have … Were you and Keith ever … together?" I asked, forcing myself to look her in the eye.

Elyse seemed stunned. "As in, have we ever *slept* together?"

I swallowed hard and nodded.

"No. No, of course I didn't sleep with Keith. Why on earth would you think that?"

"I don't mean now, like, since I've been dating him. I mean before. Did you ever date Keith?"

"No, I never dated Keith. Honey, if I had, I would have told you. I wouldn't have kept something like that a secret from you."

Elyse seemed genuinely shocked by my question, which made me feel a little better. She certainly wasn't acting like she had anything to hide.

"Crista, what makes you think I had something going with Keith?" She asked the question without a trace of anger, and I realized how much I wanted to trust her, too. Elyse had always been a good friend to me, and I hated having to avoid her.

"I overheard you guys talking," I said, still studying her reaction. She looked confused, which was another good sign.

"Well, we couldn't have been talking about us dating, because we never did. Exactly what did you hear us say?"

"Keith was talking about how he had a thing for you. He used to think you might be The One."

"Oh," Elyse said gently. "That is true, Crista. A long time ago, he had a crush on me. He asked me out a few times, but I was secretly dating Luke. You know how career-oriented I am. I was working really hard to get my promotion, and I didn't want my boss thinking I was distracted, especially since I was dating someone at work. Keith didn't know I had a boyfriend, but when he casually asked me out a couple of times, I turned him down. That's it, Crista. All there is to it."

I let out a deep breath. That explained a little of what I'd heard, and at least Elyse didn't lie about that part.

"We always say how funny it is that Keith thought I was the right one for him. Since he met you, he realizes how wrong he was." She laughed. "I tease him about dumping me for the hot Mexican chick."

I couldn't resist smiling.

"But the truth is nobody dumped anybody because we never dated. Does that help explain things?"

"A little."

"What else?" Her voice was still gentle and kind.

"You guys … You guys were talking about … Well, you two were saying how funny it was that you had seen each other naked and that you still work together like nothing happened."

Elyse's eyes grew wide and she gasped.

"And when I asked Keith if you two were ever together, he denied it." I started to cry. I just couldn't hold back anymore. Grabbing a tissue from the box on her desk, I dabbed at my eyes. "It's okay if you guys used to date, but for him to lie about it—"

"But he didn't lie! Oh, Crista, I'm so sorry about all this. Oh, honey, no wonder you're so upset." Elyse drew in a deep breath and let it out. "Okay, this is going to take a bit of explaining, but I want to make one thing perfectly clear."

She waited until I'd finished dabbing my eyes with the tissue before she went on. Elyse looked me in the eye and said, "Keith and I never dated, and we certainly never had sex, you understand?"

I gazed hopefully into her eyes as I listened. She didn't sound defensive or angry at my accusation. Every word she spoke sounded kind and loving, like she was doing her best to put my broken heart back together.

"Keith and I have never been more than co-workers and very good friends," Elyse said, her voice filled with affection when she spoke about him. "Okay?"

I nodded. I couldn't help but believe her words: they sounded so genuine.

"We did see each other naked, and I'm so sorry you had to hear about it out of context. I know how I would feel if I overheard Luke saying something like that. Okay, where do I begin? All right, well, I told you how I was working really hard to get this promotion and kept my relationship with Luke a secret."

"Yeah."

"Well, I was working way too hard, as always, and Luke was really worried about me. He came to work late at night to talk me into going home and getting some rest." Elyse laughed. "And I know it's so silly, but I always had this, you know, sexual fantasy about Luke …"

My eyes grew wide as I listened. Not only was I curious, but it was an immense relief to talk about her having sex with someone other than Keith. Hopefully, it would help rid me of those terrible images from my nightmare.

"I'll tell you one thing, Crista. Dating a theater performer is *so hot*. There's just something about a man who's a great actor and can be anybody you want them to be. Anyway, when we first started dating, Luke showed me these pictures from a show he did off-Broadway."

"*Bloody Bloody Andrew Jackson?*" I asked. I knew Luke had played the starring role in the successful off-Broadway run.

"Yes! Have you *seen* the pictures from the show?"

I nodded, understanding exactly what she was saying. "Yes. Luke looked incredibly handsome, all dressed up as a rock star."

"Exactly," Elyse said, her blue eyes flashing with desire. "Those tight leather pants and the black eyeliner he wore, oh my God, I've never seen anything so hot in my life!"

We shared a laugh together over that.

"I don't know what it is about those photos from the show, but I just couldn't get the image of Luke as a rock star out of my head. So, I told him about this fantasy I had about him, all dressed up in that outfit, and him just fu— Um, sorry. I mean, you know, him just taking me up against the wall with only his pants unzipped."

"Wow," was all I could say. Yes, Elyse was definitely more sexually adventurous than me. To be fair, I'd had sex exactly once. Someday, I would love to try more stuff in bed, but I needed time to work up to it. I couldn't help but giggle as I pondered Elyse's tale. "Dude, that's my *boss*."

Elyse laughed heartily, and I did too.

"So anyway, Luke shows up to my office at 2am dressed like emo punk-rock Andrew Jackson from the show."

"He what?"

Elyse laughed again. "I know. It was crazy. Sure as hell got my attention, though. He did it to try to get me to come home with him, so we could, you know …"

"Live out your fantasy."

"Yes. Exactly." She let out a sadder sigh this time. "I swear, we hadn't planned on it, but we kinda got carried away and ended up fulfilling my fantasy … *in the office.*"

I stared at her, eyes wide and speechless.

"Yeah. And it was in my old office, which is Keith's now," she said with a chuckle. "Anyway, it was wonderful and exciting and everything I wanted it to be. Luke's an incredible actor. It's so crazy how one minute he can be this hot rock star who had his way with me, and then turn back into my sweet boyfriend who held me in his arms afterward."

"Luke is pretty special," I said. It helped to know how much in love they were. Still, I couldn't begin to fathom what on earth this had to do with seeing my boyfriend naked.

"Yes, he sure is. And he, you know, um, well, 'made love to me' isn't really the right phrase for that particular experience …"

"It's okay, Elyse. You don't have to make it PG-rated."

"Okay, well, Luke fucked me exactly the way I had described my fantasy to him. He stripped me completely naked while he stayed totally clothed and in character. Then when I came into work on Monday morning, everybody was acting weird around me."

I nodded slowly, worried about where Elyse's story was headed.

"I was sure we were alone in the building that night. I'd been working by myself for hours, and I knew nobody was around." Elyse looked at me somberly and said softly, "What I hadn't thought about was the security camera right outside my office."

I gasped loudly. "Oh my God."

"Yeah," Elyse said, laughing bitterly. "When the security guy saw the video, he started sharing it with all the guys in the office. All that time I'd been so worried about my boss and everybody finding out I was dating someone in the building. Oh, they found out all right. After they got to watch me having sex with Luke."

I could see this was a painful memory for Elyse to have to dredge up. "Oh, how awful."

"It was. Oh God, it was. I didn't think I could ever recover from that kind of public humiliation." Her eyes lit up as she recalled something. "Oh hey, remember the day you found me vomiting in the ladies' room?"

"Yes," I whispered. That had been horrible. I didn't really know Elyse at the time, but I clearly remembered the day she ran into the restroom and violently threw up. I'll never forget the way she'd looked when she came out of the stall. I knew right away her sickness wasn't pregnancy or the stomach flu. Something horrible had happened to her. She was crying and shaking all over. It was a terrible sight to see, and I had wished to God there'd been something I could do to help her.

"That was right after I found out there was a video of me completely naked and having sex with Luke, and my boss and all my co-workers had seen it."

I put my hand over my heart, at a loss for words. What a nightmare it must have been for her.

Elyse smiled at me. "Somebody showed the video to Keith."

"So *that's* how he saw you naked."

"Yes. Keith's a gentleman, and he would never have asked to see the video of me, but someone showed it to him without telling him what it was. This was back when he still had a thing for me," Elyse said sadly. "Believe me, Crista, it really was just a harmless crush, but you know how crushes can be. Even if it's just simple infatuation with somebody, it still hurts. It was a hell of a way for Keith to find out I was dating somebody else. I've always felt bad about that. I should have told him from the beginning that I had a boyfriend."

Strange as it was, my heart ached for Keith. There he was, pining for Elyse, only to be shown a graphic video of her having sex with someone else. And Keith had to work in the same building with both of them.

"It gets weirder," Elyse warned.

"How can that be?"

Elyse laughed, and I was grateful to see her smile again. "Even though it wasn't his fault, Luke felt terrible about what happened. I was a complete mess after it all went down. I figured my professional reputation was shot, and I'd never get the promotion I'd worked so hard for. I love my job, and it was like all the joy had gone out if it. I wondered how I could work with all these people like nothing happened. Keith felt terrible, too. And even though we were up for the same promotion, he wouldn't want to get it just because the video destroyed my chances."

"No, he wouldn't," I said, picturing Keith's kind eyes and gentle demeanor.

"So Luke came up with this insane idea to make me feel better. To make things even." Elyse stopped for a moment, watching me carefully. My body tensed as I tried to prepare myself for whatever might be coming next.

"Okay ..."

"He got all the guys from the office who saw the video to get together and perform a strip tease for me. You know, to even the score. That way, I wouldn't have to be so embarrassed that they saw me naked because I would have seen them, too. So they all hatched the plan, told me to go to a strip club for what was supposedly Rosemary's bachelorette party, and when I got there … They all did a surprise strip tease number right there onstage. And I mean, they went the *full Monty*."

Elyse eyed me nervously for my reaction. I just sat there, stunned, trying to take in all this information.

"So, you're saying my boyfriend … Keith … *Keith Foster* … got totally naked onstage at some strip joint?"

"Yes," Elyse said cautiously.

I stared at Elyse for a full ten seconds, then I burst into laughter.

"I can't … I *cannot* believe Keith did a striptease! In public? Like with an audience and everything?"

Elyse laughed happily, looking quite relieved that I wasn't angry. "Oh, yeah. There was a full house, women screaming …"

That made me laugh harder, and I found myself wiping tears.

"And we got the whole thing on video," she added.

"Are you serious?"

"Oh yeah. That was the idea. They wouldn't show my video to anyone else if I didn't show theirs. I was so afraid every new person who worked here would see it, and this was Luke's way of making sure that never happened. I guess it worked, because I never really heard any more about it. And you, apparently, weren't aware of it."

"No, I had no idea. Never heard a word about it."

"So there you have it," she told me. "Keith saw me naked in the video, I saw him naked when he stripped onstage, and the whole thing was so damned insane that we still laugh about it. And that's what you overheard."

I lay back in the chair, feeling happy, relieved, but also emotionally drained. I sat up suddenly.

"Can I see it?" I asked.

"See what? The video?" Elyse asked, taken aback.

"Not your video. The *strip* video!"

"Oh," she said with a laugh. "Well I don't see why no— Wait. I'd have to make sure I get permission from all the guys involved. We had a deal, and it wouldn't be right to show it without their consent."

"You're right. Of course."

"Luke won't care. He's such an exhibitionist anyway," she said, chuckling.

"Luke stripped, too?"

"Yup. Crista, I'm so sorry for all the heartache this has caused you. Oh," Elyse said thoughtfully. "You two have been fighting. That's why Keith's been so sad lately."

"I thought he lied to me," I said, remembering with regret how sad and confused Keith was when I ran out of his apartment after accusing him of being with Elyse. "I should have known I could trust him. From the start, I just couldn't believe a guy like him could really have feelings for me. I guess I just keep waiting for the other shoe to drop."

"I know you have a hard time trusting him. I remember how hard it was to convince you to go out with him in the first place. Keith is the real deal, Crista. It's safe to trust him. He's not gonna hurt you. He loves you so much."

"I love him too. Thank you so much for clearing this up, Elyse. I talked to Rosemary yesterday about what I overheard. She said she knew the story behind it all, but she couldn't tell me. She told me to come straight to you."

Elyse smiled. "True blue Rosemary."

"Yeah," I said, enjoying the renewed faith I felt in all of my friends. None of them had lied to me after all. "Poor Keith. I can't believe what I've put him through." I jumped out of my chair. "I have to go see him right now!"

"He's not here, hon," Elyse said sadly. "He's got that meeting with the hospital today."

"Oh, that's right." If I was any kind of girlfriend, I would have remembered that today Keith had his big medical presentation. *I should have been there for him this morning, cheering him on and kissing him for luck.*

"It's okay, Crista. Go surprise him at home tonight. Talk it all out with him, and then have fabulous make-up sex."

I giggled. "That sounds *wonderful.*"

Chapter 24

My day had been busy, providing a welcome distraction to the loneliness and despair I felt without Crista around. I'd been hoping to get a report from Rosemary about their talk last night, but I hadn't heard anything from her. I took it as a bad sign. Maybe Crista had decided not to trust me and was planning to break up with me. Even if that was the case, I'd meant what I said to Rosemary. I was not about to let Crista go without a fight.

A knock at the door startled me. People rarely visited me in the evening, and I'd been too depressed to even order dinner. I opened the door and was shocked to find Crista standing there.

She was *giggling*. For a second, I thought she might be drunk.

"You …" she began, still trying to stifle her laughter. "You actually *stripped* on*stage*?"

I felt my face get hot and I put my hand on my neck. Laughing nervously, I said, "Ah, well, yeah. Yeah, I did."

"Oh, Keith," she said, her pretty, brown eyes suddenly full of sorrow. "I'm not a challenge. I'm *impossible*."

My heart clutched in my chest. She didn't seem angry or hurt anymore. I was afraid to hope everything might be okay between us.

Crista closed the door behind her and turned to face me. "I am such an idiot!"

"Sweetie, don't say that," I said. "What's going on?"

"I know you've been wondering why I've been pulling away from you again lately."

I nodded sadly.

"Oh, you poor sweet man," she said, tenderly stroking my face with the back of her hand. God, how I missed her soft touch. "At work one day I heard you and Elyse talking. Keith, I swear I wasn't trying to listen in on your conversation. I was just waiting for you to come out of the conference room. Anyway, I heard you talking about how you used to have a thing for Elyse."

I nodded slowly, imagining how tough it must have been for Crista to hear.

"Well, yeah. I did have a thing for her once. But it was a long time ago. I got over it, even before I met you."

Crista smiled, looking relieved. "Thank you for being honest with me about it."

"I didn't tell you before because it really didn't matter, and it would have just upset you."

"I understand," she said, still stroking my cheek. "I also heard the two of you laughing about how crazy it was that you had seen each other naked, and you still worked well together."

"Oh my God," I said, eyes wide. So that's why Crista thought I had been with Elyse. After hearing something like that, of course she would jump to that conclusion. "Crista, it's not what you th—"

"I know," she said. "I talked to Rosemary last night and she told me she understood exactly what you two were talking about. She couldn't explain without breaking her promise to Elyse, but she said if I went to Elyse and asked her, she'd probably tell me. And she did, Keith. She explained everything. About the video of her and Luke and about what you did to help her get over what happened. Oh Keith, I'm so sorry."

Crista wrapped her arms around me and I held her close, breathing in her sweet, feminine scent and reveling in her touch.

"It's okay, baby. It's okay."

"I thought you guys had dated, and the worst part was I thought you were lying to me when you denied it."

I stroked her back, trying my best to soothe her. It all made sense now. Why she had been so hurt and angry all of a sudden. She rested her head on my shoulder, and I just held her for a while.

Eventually, she lifted her head and said, "I'm so sorry I doubted you, Keith."

"You don't have to be sorry, Crista. Anybody would have misunderstood the conversation. You couldn't possibly have guessed the truth about what happened. I know you keep looking for a reason not to trust me because you're afraid you'll find one, but I promise you won't. I know you're worried I have some secret double life, but I assure you, I'm not that interesting."

Crista laughed, and it was a beautiful sound.

"Face it, Crista. I'm a boring, vanilla kind of guy." Sometimes I worried I was *too* boring. Sure, I was sensible and dependable, but that wasn't very exciting.

"You are not boring. You're creative and clever and smart, and not to mention incredibly patient. I'm so sorry for all this drama."

"Hey, you're a theater actress. Comes with the territory."

Her face lit up in a pretty smile like it always did when I referred to her as an actress or a star. I loved saying things like that to her.

"Well, I'm glad you know about everything now," I told her. "Performing at the strip club was the wildest, most insane thing I've ever done in my life, and you have no idea how badly I wanted to tell you about it. But I couldn't."

"Not without betraying Elyse. I understand. You did the right thing by not telling me."

"Sweetheart, if there's ever anything you're upset about, all you have to do is talk to me about it. Just tell me what's going on and we can work it out. Don't ever make yourself crazy like this again."

"I'm sorry I put us both through this torture."

"It was torture thinking I might lose you." I gazed into her eyes, then kissed her softly. "I understand sometimes you need extra reassurance about my love for you, and that's okay. All you have to do is ask, all right?"

"I need reassurance right now," she told me with a smile. "I want you to take me into the bedroom and show me how much you love me."

My cock grew rigid at Crista's sensual suggestion, but I was a little worried she was still feeling vulnerable. I wanted more than anything to take her to bed, but not if she was just trying to appease me after having been so distant.

I pressed my lips against hers and she eagerly kissed me back. "Oh Keith. I've missed you so much."

Desire filled her voice and there was no trace of tension in her body as she pressed against me. She moaned softly, and her hard nipples brushed against my chest. Yes. She wanted this as much as I did.

"Baby, I'll give you all the reassurance you can handle," I said, scooping her into my arms and carrying her into the bedroom.

I lay her down on the bed and quickly went to work on relieving her of her clothes. I took off my tie and let her take care of the rest for me. It took mere seconds for us to get completely naked. I could hardly wait to be inside her again; to prove to her in every way possible she was the only woman I needed.

As much as I wanted to plunge inside her, I entered her carefully to make sure I didn't hurt her. This was only her second time, after all.

Crista let out a long, sensual moan as I slipped into her.

"Feel better than last time?" I asked as I began to thrust a bit more.

Her response was an even louder moan. "Yes, oh yes. You feel so good, Keith."

Hell yeah. It would be *a lot* more fun for her this time around.

"I know I don't have anything to compare it to," she said. "But you feel so *big.*"

My ego soared at her compliment.

"And you," I said as I kissed her. "Are a *goddess.* I love you, Crista. I love you so much."

"I love you too," she said as she kissed me passionately.

I planted my hands on the mattress to pound her harder. I wanted her to physically feel how much I loved and desired her.

"Keith!" she cried out as she dug her nails into my back. Being with her was so exciting. Crista was beautiful, and everything was so new to her. I'd had to be so gentle with her the first time, but now she was ready to experience how pleasurable sex could be. And it was an honor to be the one to show her.

I rammed into her over and over until I found myself getting close to orgasm. I had no intention of gratifying my own needs before taking care of hers, so I pulled out of her. I covered her protests by kissing her. First her lips, then I let my mouth travel down her beautiful body.

Crista let out a soft gasp as she realized what I was about to do to her. I hesitated for a brief moment as I positioned my mouth between her legs. She seemed to enjoy having me take the lead during sex, but I didn't want to do anything she was uncomfortable with. I grinned when she opened her legs wider, when I reached her most intimate spot.

I teased her by flicking my tongue close to her clit but not touching it at first.

"Keith," she begged. "*Please.*"

I tortured her for a few seconds more, then I began stroking her clit with my tongue. She moaned and writhed as I pleasured her, throwing her head back on the pillow, and crying out my name, over and over. Her cries grew louder as she drew close to climax. I flicked my tongue faster and faster until she screamed with release.

Crista lay back on the pillow, panting. I crawled up next to her so I could look at her. Her eyes were hooded, filled with an unmistakable look of sheer sexual satisfaction. "Oh, I never knew anything could feel so *good.*"

"God, you sound sexy when you come," I said, and she laughed softly.

"Come back to me." She glanced at my rock-hard cock and opened her legs. I knew she wanted to make sure I was taken care of, too.

"Want to try something different?" I asked. She nodded.

I grabbed ahold of her shoulders and pulled her on top of me. "Ride me, baby."

Crista bit her lip, her eyes filled with excitement. She straddled me, and I helped lift her up so she could lower herself onto me. I moaned when she had me securely back inside her.

"Move anyway you want," I told her. "Do whatever feels good to you."

Crista leaned forward, putting her hands on the mattress to get good traction. She began rocking back and forth, sending ripples of pleasure through my cock.

"That's good. That's so good, Crista," I said as I looked up into her eyes. She smiled, looking proud of herself. She should be proud. Stage work wasn't the only thing that came naturally to her. She was a fast learner in the bedroom. She listened carefully to the sounds I made and watched for my reaction. Pretty soon she found the perfect rhythm to maximize my pleasure.

"Crista. Oh God, baby you're gonna make me come …"

"I certainly hope so," she said in a sensual voice that only brought me closer to climax.

"I'm not …" I said breathlessly. "I'm not done with you yet. Want to try one more thing?"

"Sure," she said, climbing off me, leaving me agonizingly close to orgasm. I drew in a few deep breaths to force myself back from the brink.

"Okay," I said, sitting up on the bed. "Just, you know, tell me if anything we're doing makes you uncomfortable. It's always okay to say no or stop. Okay?"

Crista nodded. "I trust you, Keith."

Now *that* was music to my ears, and I knew it was the truth. She was relaxed and happy with me. I could feel it in her touch.

"Get on your hands and knees."

Her eyes opened wide, then she obeyed. I came up behind her and pressed my cock against the outside of her vagina. "Is this okay?"

"Yes," she said in a husky voice. "Do it."

This time, I rammed into her as hard as I could. She grabbed two fistfuls of sheet as she held on for dear life. I pounded her hard, thrusting in and out of her and making the bed slam into the wall. I was about to ask if she was okay when she answered the question for me.

"Keith," she said, gasping. "Oh God, I think I'm gonna come again."

I'd been dangerously close to climax myself, but now my top priority was giving my woman another orgasm. Her pre-orgasmic *oh, oh, oh,* sounds made it nearly impossible to hold on. Hearing her pleasured cries was so exciting, I nearly exploded. Gritting my teeth, I forced myself to keep slamming into her and hitting the spot that seemed to give her so much pleasure. Just when I thought I would lose it, Crista let out the most delicious cry of sheer sexual ecstasy.

Seconds later, I followed with a decidedly less sexy, animal-like growl as I came so hard, I thought I might have burst through the condom. It was the most intense and satisfying orgasm I'd ever had, and Crista was the most exciting woman I'd ever shared a bed with.

I pulled out of her and collapsed onto the bed. She snuggled up close to me as we caught our breath.

"You are *amazing*," she told me.

"So are you, Crista. So are you."

She snorted softly, clearly not believing me. "Yeah, right. I'm just a rookie."

"Baby," I said, turning to look at her, "you don't have to be experienced to be good in bed. You just have to be passionate."

"I'm very passionate about you," Crista said.

"I'm telling you, that was, without question, the best sex I've ever had in my life. I wouldn't lie to you."

"No," Crista said, gazing lovingly into my eyes. "No, you wouldn't."

Chapter 25

I fell asleep on Keith's chest, listening to his heartbeat. It was my absolute favorite place to be. I drifted into a restful sleep, being both exhausted and utterly sexually satisfied. Keith was a terrific lover and I was one lucky woman. I slept peacefully for a while, but I woke up with a sudden, awful realization.

I didn't ask Keith how his presentation went.

The medical technology presentation he'd spent months preparing for. The one he hoped would help take his career to the next level. That project was incredibly important to him, and I had forgotten all about it.

I glanced over to see Keith lying there, sleeping like an angel. Guilt surged through me. What did I do to deserve this dear man? I'd spent so much time and energy making sure he was being honest and treating me right, but I hadn't been such a great girlfriend to him. When I thought about all the support he had given me at every turn when it came to my theater stuff, I felt awful that I hadn't done the same.

I resolved to try to be the girlfriend he deserved, starting as soon as we woke up tomorrow.

Naturally, I slept in far longer than Keith. By the time I made it down to the kitchen, he'd already made breakfast for me.

I groaned inwardly as a renewed surge of guilt rippled through my body.

"I don't deserve you," I said as I watched him pour my coffee.

"Oh, stop it," he said with a smile.

"I mean it." I rushed toward him. "I can't believe I never asked you how the hospital presentation went. I am so, so sorry!"

"Oh, that," Keith said. "Don't worry about it." He kissed me and nuzzled my neck. "We were a little busy last night."

Keith's sensual kisses on my throat had me thinking of all the wonderful things he had done to me last night, and how I wanted him to take me, here and now, on the kitchen floor.

No. *Focus, girl!*

"So how did it go? Were they happy with your presentation?" I asked, desperately hoping he had good news to share.

"Yeah, yeah they did," Keith said, his eyes flashing with excitement. "They liked it a lot. They had a couple of good suggestions on how to tweak the technology for their purposes, including a couple of things I'm kicking myself for not thinking of first. But overall, yeah. They seemed really pleased with what we can do. I'll talk to Elyse and Hunter on Monday about the changes they want, but it looks like it's a go for the hospital."

"That's wonderful!" I said, kissing him with enthusiasm. "I'm so proud of you."

"Thanks. That means a lot to me. Come on, have some breakfast with me."

We sat down at the breakfast table. We ate for a couple of minutes, and Keith looked at me.

"I could get used to this," he said.

"What?"

"This," he said, gesturing to the breakfast and then at me. "Me and you. For the rest of my life."

"I know what you mean." I took his hand and gazed at my future husband.

*****

"Sorry I'm abandoning you on a Saturday night," I told Keith later as he drove me over to Rosemary and Johnny's place in Chelsea.

"It's okay, baby. You deserve a girl's night out," he said with a grin.

"Thanks. I'm really excited about it." Rosemary, Susie, Elyse, and I were all getting together to hang out for the evening, and I'd been looking forward to it ever since Rosemary had suggested it. "It's hard to make new friends when you're an adult."

"I know what you mean," Keith said. "I don't have much in common with my old drinking buddies. I don't know. I've outgrown them, I guess."

I nodded sadly, remembering what Keith had told me a while back about being lonely. "Maybe you should try hanging out with Johnny, David, and Luke sometime. They get together a lot."

"Yeah. Maybe I will. So, what are you guys up to tonight?" There was a hint of mischief in Keith's voice.

"Just hanging out and drinking. Nina drilled into my head that I'm not supposed to have alcohol, so it's been a while since I've had a drink. Won't take much to get me tipsy."

"Hmmm. Get drunk so I can take advantage of you when you get home."

I laughed. "I'll probably just pass out once I get home."

"True. Okay, just don't get so drunk that you get a hangover. I want to make love to you in the morning."

"That sounds wonderful," I said, stroking his shoulders. Keith shifted uncomfortably in his seat, and I couldn't help smiling. I loved that I could turn him on with a simple touch.

"You're sure you've got a ride back home?"

Home. He meant his apartment, but he referred to it as if it was my place, too. The thought gave me a calm, peaceful feeling in my heart.

"Yeah. David's letting us have the limo, so Joey will drive everybody back."

"Good."

"What are you gonna be up to all night?" I asked.

"I'm looking forward to a quiet evening at home. Work has been so nuts lately, that all I really want to do is sit and read in my library."

"Sounds good," I said. "Have fun."

Keith pulled up outside Rosemary and Johnny's apartment building and whistled. "Wow, nice place."

"Thanks for the ride," I said, turning toward him.

He cupped my face and kissed me. "Have a good time tonight."

I heard him chuckle just before I shut the door behind me.

Rosemary lived with Johnny in a penthouse apartment at the top of the building. It probably was a good thing Keith wasn't with me—it would have been really tough to climb all the stairs to get to the top. He forced himself to use the elevator in his apartment building, but he avoided unfamiliar elevators whenever possible.

Rosemary greeted me at the door, wineglass in hand. "Hey, girl!" she said, a bit louder than normal.

I giggled. "Been pregaming, have we?"

"You know it. Come on, grab a drink. You need to get where we are now." She gestured to Susie, who was also drinking wine, and Elyse, who held a tall glass of beer.

"Believe me, it won't take long for me to catch up. I'm such a lightweight. So … it's really okay to drink alcohol? Morable the Horrible says—"

"Oh, her," Rosemary said, waving her wineglass and spilling a little. "Is alcohol good for your voice? No. That doesn't mean you can't ever have it. Stay hydrated with water and don't drink every night, and you'll be fine."

"Cool."

"What's your pleasure?" Rosemary asked.

"Sangria if you have it."

"Oh, she has it," Elyse said. "She's got anything you want. Can I show her the booze room?"

Rosemary laughed. "Sure."

For the first time since I stepped into the apartment, I took a good look around. My heart soared as I gazed out at the panoramic nighttime view of New York City that the huge bank of windows offered. Oh, how I loved this city, and hanging out with theater performers made me feel like I was a real part of the theater scene.

"Rosemary, this place is beautiful. And I thought Keith's place was big!"

"Isn't it ridiculous?" she said, looking around in wonder. "I still can't really wrap my mind around the fact that I live here."

We looked at each other, sharing a knowing smile. We both knew what it felt like to be poor, and people like us knew never to take anything for granted.

"Okay, what's this booze room now?" I asked. Elyse giggled and grabbed my arm. We walked across the enormous living room and Elyse flung open a door off to the side.

I followed her inside, then gasped. It was like walking into a full-sized bar in a restaurant. There was a long wooden bar complete with barstools, and several sets of high-top tables and chairs.

"My God, you almost expect a waitress to come by."

"I know, right?" Elyse said. "My name is Elyse, and I'll be your server tonight. May I get you a sangria?"

"Please," I said.

Elyse went behind the bar. She poured a glass and handed it to me. "Might as well take the bottle out there with you. And I need a refill too." She grabbed a fresh glass and filled it from one of the beer taps on the bar. "We need to make sure we have lots of alcohol to drink for the main event."

"The main event?" I asked.

Elyse giggled. "Yup. Come on."

She rushed back to the living room and I followed her, feeling a little nervous. I couldn't begin to imagine what Elyse was talking about.

"Are we ready?" Elyse asked.

"Yep," Rosemary said.

Susie, Elyse, and Rosemary were all looking at me.

"What?" I asked, getting more anxious by the second.

"Crista, we invited you here tonight not only for the pleasure of your company, but we have a very special screening for you," Rosemary announced.

"Screening?"

Rosemary picked up a small remote control and pointed it toward the window. A large flat-screen television slid down from the ceiling. It took me a moment to figure out what was going on, but I finally did.

"Oh my God. Is this …?"

"Yep," Elyse said excitedly. "I told all the guys that since you were dating Keith, you'd get a huge kick out of seeing it."

"That's all you told them?"

"Yeah. There was no need to tell them anything else," she said with a smile.

I was relieved she'd left out the part where I'd had a ridiculous fit of jealousy.

"They were really good sports about it," she said. "They loved the idea of you seeing Keith strutting his stuff."

"Keith knew about this, didn't he? I knew he was up to something," I said.

The women giggled. "Oh yeah. He knew."

"Let me see! Let me see!" I exclaimed.

"Okay, here we go," Rosemary said, pressing play.

It started with an empty stage. A ripple of excitement and nervousness tingled in my stomach as I saw there had been a full house that night. Keith must have been terrified! He was a pretty low-key guy who tended to keep to himself, and I realized how brave he'd been to do this.

The music started, and I recognized the song immediately. "Oh, that is so funny! So that's why Luke calls you 'Uptown Girl'!"

"Well, he always called me that, but that's why he picked the song."

I watched in fascination as I saw Luke prance out onstage, followed by four other men. I could feel Rosemary, Susie, and Elyse watching for my reaction.

"Is that Roger? And Manny?"

"Yup," Rosemary said.

Roger and Manny worked on the maintenance crew with me and Luke.

"And Hunter? How did you get Hunter to do this? He seems so stuck up," I said.

"Oh, he is. He's a total snob," Elyse said. "He's also the one who showed the video to all my co-workers, including my boss."

"Bastard," I said. The sangria was already loosening my tongue. I rather liked it.

"Yeah. Luke said he was the only real holdout, but he talked him into it. Told him it was a good way to suck up to his new boss," Elyse said, hoisting her beer.

"Oh my God, oh my God," I kept saying as I watched my co-workers dance onstage, tearing off their clothes.

Cackling together, we had a grand old time watching the strip club video. We all hooted and hollered each time another article of clothing got tossed aside.

I laughed so hard as I watched Keith dance onstage. "Oh, my poor sweet Keith. He's the most uncoordinated one out there."

"I know," Elyse said, wiping tears of laughter from her eyes.

"It's so cute, though," Rosemary said, and I nodded.

He was so bad at dancing but was up there giving it his all anyway. It made me love him even more.

I watched Luke come down from the stage and strut right over to the table where Rosemary, Susie, and Elyse were sitting. Luke wrapped his tie around Elyse's neck as we all shrieked with delight.

"Awww, that is so sweet," I said, watching Luke serenade Elyse.

"It really was." I could hear the joy in her voice.

Luke sang the part about being her downtown man, and I watched Elyse as she gazed up at the screen, reliving the special moment. Luke went back up to the stage, to join the other men and finish the dance.

"Oh my gosh, is that Terry?" I asked as I watched an attractive African-American woman get up from the table and rush toward the stage.

"Yup," Rosemary said with a giggle.

Terry was Roger's wife. I watched as she stuffed a dollar bill down her husband's pants. We laughed uproariously.

"What a cool wife," I said.

"Oh, she thought the whole thing was hilarious," Susie said.

The camera panned back to the table when Terry returned to her seat, and I saw another familiar face.

"Johnny was there?"

"Oh, yeah. He thought it was a riot," Rosemary said. "He's the one who really made it all happen. Since he's a Creel, Johnny had the clout to let his friends strip onstage."

"Where was David during all this?" I asked, and my question sent the women into hysterics.

"Susie," Rosemary said, trying to contain her laughter. "Susie, tell her what David was doing."

"He was … He was …" Susie said through her laughter. "David was the one who recorded the whole thing. So, he was standing in the back like this."

Susie mimed holding a cell phone camera and turning her head, averting her eyes from what it was recording. That sent us into another fit of raucous laughter.

"Okay, okay, here comes the best part!" Rosemary shouted.

We all turned our attention to the television screen. "No way," I said. "No way … I can't believe they did this."

"I know," Elyse shrieked. "But they did!"

They were down to their underwear.

"Wow, Crista," Susie said with admiration. "You are one lucky girl."

Keith had a terrific body, and I felt proud to see him show it off. He might be a clumsy dancer, but he looked like an underwear model standing there onstage, showing off his muscular chest.

"Yes, yes I am," I said.

At last, the five men ripped off their tearaway underwear and showed everything they had.

"Damn. *Elyse* is one lucky girl!" I shouted as we got a good look at each guy's package before the screen went dark. I'd never realized what a terrific body Luke had.

We hooted and howled with laughter at the finale. It was the most fun I'd had in my entire life.

Rosemary turned off the television, and I went over to embrace her. "Thank you so much, Rosemary."

"Oh, you're welcome, sweetie. We've been dying to show this to you!"

I hugged Susie next, and gave an extra-affectionate hug to Elyse.

"Thank you so much for everything," I said.

"You're welcome, Crista. I'm just so happy you two found each other," she whispered in my ear.

"Me too," I said, tearing up. Too much alcohol plus hanging out with my dearest friends was making me overly emotional, but it was a wonderful feeling.

"You guys are the best," I told them, lifting my glass.

We all clinked glasses and toasted one another.

Collapsing into chairs, we wiped tears of laughter.

After we'd calmed down, I said, "I can't believe I just saw my boss naked." That set us off all over again. "Not to mention Roger and Manny. I'll never be able to look them in the eye again!"

"Oh, I know," Elyse said. "It's weird and then it's not weird, you know? Like we have this inside joke we're all in on."

"Helped you feel better, didn't it?" I asked.

"Yes," she said, letting out a deep sigh. "It helped me get over what happened and finally move on, you know?"

"That's great." I looked at the women surrounding me. "I'm not trying to get all sappy here, but I love you guys."

I expected them to laugh, but they didn't.

"We love you too, Crista," Rosemary said warmly.

"I never could have gotten this far with my theater stuff without you, Rosemary. I mean it."

"Well, you've done a beautiful job with it. You've come a long way in such a short time," she said.

"That's true," Susie said. "We're not just being nice by saying that. You sounded amazing the other night."

"Keith says your teacher's a bitch," Elyse said. "Makes him so mad. He's ready to take out a hit on her."

I smiled at Keith's protectiveness.

"She told me if I could picture myself doing anything other than being a singer, I should," I confessed, my voice cracking.

Rosemary and Susie burst into laughter. Elyse and I looked at each other, not seeing the humor in Nina's hateful words.

"Oh, honey," Rosemary said. "Every singer in the history of theater has heard that line. *Every* teacher says that. It's a test. A rite of passage. And it hurt like hell when she said that, right?"

I nodded.

"And you know what you did?" Rosemary asked. "You went back."

Rosemary lifted her glass to toast me, and Susie and Elyse did the same.

"Oh, you guys," I said, wiping tears. My friends laughed, but it was a gentle laughter.

"Okay, okay, since all you ladies got to see my boyfriend's junk," Elyse said bluntly, sending us into fits of drunken giggles again. "There's something I have *got* to ask. Rosemary …"

"Uh-oh," Rosemary said.

"There's something about Johnny I have always, *always* wanted to ask."

"Oh God, I think I know where this is going," Rosemary said, blushing as she covered her mouth.

"The tabloids about him always said …" Elyse started to say.

Susie, Rosemary, and I started cackling. Oh yes, we had all heard the rumors back in Johnny's playboy days.

"That Johnny Creel is seriously well-endowed," Elyse finished her thought. "Is it true?"

Rosemary blushed and covered her face for a moment, stifling a giggle. Finally, she said, "Yes."

We all laughed and applauded.

"I mean, it's not like I'd been with a ton of guys before Johnny, but yes. He is by far the biggest," Rosemary said with a smile.

"Nice!" Elyse said, toasting her.

"Too bad he didn't strip," I added.

"I know!" Elyse shouted. "You're a lucky girl, Rosemary, but so am I. Luke's a tiger in the sack."

"Good to know," Susie said with a wink.

"Hell, your man's no slouch," Elyse said to Susie.

"Really?" I said out loud before I could stop myself. David Groff was undeniably gorgeous, well-built, and always dressed to kill, but he seemed so reserved, it was hard to imagine him as a red-hot lover.

"I know, I know, he looks cold sometimes," Susie said.

"Oh, I'm sorry. I—I didn't mean …"

"No, no don't apologize. I thought he was a cold fish when I first met him," Susie said with a laugh. "But believe me, he knows what he's doing in the bedroom."

"Tell her about that time in his office," Elyse prompted.

"Mmm, that was a hell of a night," Susie said. "Well, you know David's a fashion designer, right?"

I nodded, eager to hear the rest of Susie's story.

"One time we did some role-playing in his office. That's the fun part of being an actress," Susie said, her blue eyes full of mischief. "You can be anything you want in bed."

"Tell me about it," Elyse said in a husky voice. "Luke fucks me in character all the time."

We laughed heartily. I admired Elyse's bluntness, but I couldn't imagine ever being that brazen myself.

"Well, one night in his office I was his secretary and he was my boss. He tied me up with the neckties he designed," Susie said with a wicked smile.

"Wow. I have to say, I didn't think David had it in him," I said.

"Susie brings out the best in him," Rosemary said. "They're good for each other."

"Yeah," Susie said with a soft smile.

"What about Keith?" Elyse asked me point-blank. I hesitated a moment, her question having caught me off guard.

"It's okay, Crista. You don't have to kiss and tell just because we did," Rosemary said in a gentle voice as she reached over to pour me some more sangria from the nearly empty bottle.

"It's okay. I don't mind," I said. I'd always felt left out of conversations like this. For the first time in my life, I could contribute to a conversation about sex. "Keith's amazing in bed. I mean, he's incredible. He was … well, he was my first."

A chorus of "Awwwws" came from the girls. I was relieved that they didn't seem shocked at my confession.

Rosemary put her hand over her heart. "Oh, Keith is *such* a romantic. I bet he made your first time really special."

"Yeah, yeah he did. He was worth waiting for. I'm glad I waited. Back when I used to work at a college, I almost slept with this frat guy I'd been dating for a while. Turned out he was just using me as a frat-boy joke. They all thought it would be funny if the hottest guy on campus could sleep with the cleaning lady."

My voice cracked as I blurted out the painful story. I hadn't meant to confess what happened, but I was drunk. Besides, deep in my heart I knew it was safe to tell my friends what had happened.

The room went silent.

"Jesus," Elyse said finally.

"Crista, oh my God," Rosemary said. "I'm so sorry that happened to you." She reached over and lovingly took my hand in hers.

"Thanks," I said, my eyes spilling over with tears. "I was so devastated, I quit my job at the college. Those jobs are hard to get because you get tuition remission, and I threw it all away for some jerk. I just thank God I figured out what was going on before I slept with him."

"Yes, that's something, I guess," Susie said. "Oh Crista, that's awful. I'm so sorry."

"Thanks," I said quietly, suddenly glad I'd told my story. "Until now, Keith was the only one I ever told about that." I turned to Elyse and struggled to express my feelings to her without crying. "And that's … That's why I had such a hard time believing Keith cared for me. Keith is a rich executive. He's wealthy and handsome, and it felt like it was the frat guy chasing the cleaning lady all over again."

I started to cry, and Elyse pulled me into her arms. "Crista, honey, I'm so sorry. I had no idea what you were going through. No wonder it scared you to death when you overheard Keith and I talking."

I nodded as I pulled away from her to grab a tissue.

"I hope you understand now how much Keith loves you," she told me. "He'd never do anything to hurt you."

"Yeah," I said, smiling through my tears. "I know now."

"Good," she said firmly.

"I'm sorry. I didn't mean to put a damper on things," I said.

"Not at all. That's what girls' nights are for. Dishing about sex and telling secrets," Rosemary said with a smile.

"Right," Elyse said. "So back to the important matter at hand." She folded her hands neatly in her lap and turned to Rosemary. "Tell me more about Johnny's dick."

Chapter 26

"I love you," I told Crista as I stopped the car to drop her off at her voice lesson.

"I love you too," she said, tenderly touching my hand.

"Don't take any crap from her," I said sternly. Crista was happy with everything she had learned during her lessons, but she still seemed beaten down when I came to pick her up afterward.

She smiled and kissed me. "See you soon."

I watched as she got safely inside the building, then I stepped on the gas and hightailed it out of there. I usually parked the car and wandered around for a while. Fortunately there was a quaint little bookstore a few blocks away that I frequented while Crista was at the studio. The staff knew me by name and enjoyed seeing me; I'd spent a fair amount of money there over the last few months.

Tonight, I had more important things to do. I fought traffic for the next few blocks and left my car with the valet outside Patinkin's Pub, where I was meeting up with the whole gang for drinks.

"Hey!" Johnny said, greeting me loudly when I walked in. He was seated with Rosemary, Susie, David, Elyse, and Luke at a large table near the bar.

I could tell they'd been here drinking for quite a while. Everybody seemed to be in a good mood. I just hoped they weren't too drunk to help me with my problem.

"Thanks so much for meeting with me, guys. I don't have long because I have to be back to pick Crista up in an hour."

Johnny signaled the waiter for me, and the young guy walked over.

"Um, just a beer. Elyse, you pick out something good. You're the beer expert," I said. Elyse knew everything there was to know about microbrews.

"Give him the Tiger Eyes Hazelnut Brown Ale," she said.

The waiter nodded and left to get my beer.

"Okay, I got you all together because I need your help with the next step of Crista's theater career," I said, looking around at everyone at the table.

"Damn," Elyse said. "I was hoping you wanted our help in proposing to her."

Rosemary giggled and nodded.

"Ah. Sorry, I should have been more specific." All I'd said to Rosemary was I needed everybody's help to do something for Crista, and she agreed to get everyone together. I couldn't blame them for misunderstanding. "First thing's first."

"She'd make a great wife, you know," Elyse said.

"Yes," I said with a grin. "I am well aware."

"She's crazy about you," she continued. "And she says you're great in the sack."

My face went hot immediately. Not that I wasn't pleased with the compliment. I was proud Crista had told her friends I was a good lover.

"Elyse!" Rosemary admonished with a laugh. She looked over at me and rolled her eyes. "You know how Elyse is. She doesn't have much of a filter anyway, and it's worse when she's been drinking."

"You know it," Elyse said, hoisting her beer.

The waiter arrived with my beer, and I took a huge gulp.

"I hope you told them I'm great in the sack," Luke said, pretending to sound miffed.

"She did," said Rosemary and Susie at the same time, making us laugh.

"Okay, back to business," Rosemary said. "Keith, what do you need and how can we help?"

"Crista's first set of voice lessons are almost over."

"Good," Susie said, an edge to her voice. I looked at her questioningly. "Don't get me wrong. I can tell she's learned a lot, and she sounds amazing, but I just don't think it's necessary for her teacher to be so cruel."

Rosemary and Elyse both nodded.

"I can't argue with you there," I said. "The problem is what's next for Crista. She wants to get her theater degree so badly, and nothing in this world would make me happier than to pay for her education, but she won't let me. I'm doing my best to respect her decision, but I can't really understand why she won't let me help her."

"Sound familiar, baby?" Johnny asked Rosemary, his gray eyes full of affection for his bride-to-be.

"Sure does," Rosemary said with a smile. "Crista mentioned your generous offer a while back and we talked about it. She told me she was uncomfortable with the idea of taking your money, and I told her how that's how I used to feel, but I changed my mind. I don't know, I guess in some ways it still feels weird to be surrounded by such wealth. I'm so spoiled all the time and now I'm getting ready to marry a billionaire." There was weariness tinged with worry in her voice.

"No," Johnny said. "You're not marrying a billionaire. You're marrying *me.*"

Johnny took her hand in his and gazed into her eyes.

"Yeah, I am," Rosemary said softly, and I could see the calming effect Johnny had on her. It was obvious she loved him with all her heart. "That's what's important."

"You're a lucky man, Jonathan Creel," David said, tipping his scotch glass at him.

"Don't I know it," Johnny said with a grin.

Rosemary turned to me. "I told Crista there was no two ways about it. If it wasn't for Johnny, I never would have been able to go to NYU. I would have spent most of my time working to scratch out a living, and it would have been really tough for me to prepare for auditions. I worked like hell to get where I am today, but I really needed a leg up to get there."

I nodded. "Yeah, that's what I tried to tell her. I just want to pay her tuition, but she'd be the one doing all the work. She told me the whole idea of me paying her way makes her feel uncomfortable. Like it puts our relationship on a parent-child kind of level."

"I guess I can kind of understand that," Susie said. "David's really wealthy, too, and it's hard to say how I would feel if he had to pay for my college. But my parents paid for mine. Isn't that sort of the same thing?"

"Yes," I said grimly. "So, we're back to the parent-child thing. I respect her feelings on the subject, but she wants this so badly, and I can't bear to have her lose the momentum she's gained from these voice lessons."

"Who paid for those?" David asked.

"I did, but it took an awful lot of convincing. Not only that, but part of the deal was I made a vow that I wouldn't bring up the college thing ever again. I told her all she had to do was say the word, but it had to be Crista who brought it up next." I looked over at Rosemary and said quietly, "She cried after your graduation."

"Oh," Rosemary said, putting her hand over her heart.

"Yeah. I mean, don't get me wrong. She was thrilled for you. You're one of her best friends, and she thinks the world of you, but it hurt. She couldn't help it. Crista … well, she had a chance once to go to school and it fell through. It was pretty awful."

"She told us what happened, Keith," Rosemary said gently. The women were all nodding with sympathy. Clearly, Crista had confided in her friends about that horrible frat boy.

After taking another big swig of beer, I said, "I don't know what to do or how to help her. How can I convince her to let me pay her tuition if I'm not even allowed to talk about it? I can't let her walk away from her theater dreams now. Not when she's doing so well."

"I hear ya, man," Luke said with uncharacteristic somberness. "Crista's good. Like, *really* good. I agree we can't let her talent go to waste."

I nodded, grateful for Luke's support.

"So how can I—"

"I think I have an idea," Susie said suddenly. She turned to Rosemary and Luke, the only other theater performers in our little group. "Crista's doing great in her voice lessons, despite her horrible teacher, and she blew us all away when she performed for us at The Creel Foundation. What's the one thing she *hasn't* done yet?"

"Been in a show!" Rosemary said excitedly.

"Bingo," Susie responded.

"Keith," Rosemary said. "Believe me, if you're truly meant to be a performer, there is nothing in the world like being in a real live show with an energetic audience. It's the high every performer craves, and once you get a taste of it, you'll crave that high more and more."

Rosemary's eyes were aflame with passion as she spoke about the theater. Susie and Luke nodded with knowing enthusiasm.

"She's right, dude," Luke said. "Performing in front of a crowd is what theater life is all about. Once Crista gets a taste of it, there'll be no going back for her."

"Right," Susie said, her blue eyes bright and happy just like Rosemary's. Out of the corner of my eye, I caught David watching her with admiration. He cracked a half-smile, which was a huge display of emotion coming from him. "So I say we get her to star in a musical at The Creel Foundation, and that's when you hit her with the college thing. When she's still high on performing, and she'll do anything to make her dreams come true."

"Wow," I said, liking this idea more and more. Crista would be excited to star in a show of her own. Maybe her friends were right. "You think she would go for it? Like, she won't be suspicious if we suddenly tell her she's starring in a show?"

"No, I don't think so," Luke chimed in. "We'll just tell her we're helping her get her feet wet, and a show at The Creel Foundation would be a great place to start."

"Better yet, we'll tell her it's a fundraiser for The Creel Foundation," Rosemary said.

"Well, I don't want to lie to her," I said.

"No, no. I mean, it *will* be a fundraiser for the foundation. We can do that, right Johnny?" Rosemary asked, punching her fiancé in the shoulder.

"Owwww," he whined. "Careful, you're gonna cut me with that enormous diamond ring." Rosemary giggled, and he grinned at her. "Yeah, I think it's a great idea. Susie and I can get the word out and do some publicity."

"Definitely!" Susie said happily. She worked at The Creel Foundation on the business side for a few hours during the day. She used to teach at night, but right now she was in rehearsals for an off-Broadway show most nights. "So what show should we do?"

Rosemary and I looked at each other and said at the same time, "*Cinderella.*"

Susie clapped with excitement. "Perfect! I can be in it too, if it helps. I'd *love* to play a wicked stepsister. I assume this is a one-night-only gig, right? If so, I should be able to squeeze it in."

"Yes," Rosemary said. "I think that's best. Give her a taste of stardom, but if she wants more, she'll have to go to school."

"Agreed," Susie said.

"I played the prince in *Cinderella* in high school," Luke said. "Made me a huge hit with the *lay-duzzz.*"

"Really?" Elyse asked.

Luke frowned. "No, not really. Mostly they just thought I was gay."

Elyse cackled. "Well, I think you would make a handsome prince." Then she murmured in his ear, "You know, I've never gone to bed with a prince before."

"Crista has," I couldn't resist saying. Everyone burst into laughter and I blushed a bit.

"Nice," Johnny said, fist-bumping me. David tipped his scotch at me.

"Thanks, guys. Thanks so much for all your help. This might just work."

"It will, Keith," Rosemary said, squeezing my hand. "You'll see."

Chapter 27

Rosemary called me the day before Crista was to go on as Cinderella.

"I'm an idiot," she said the moment I said hello. Her voice was upbeat.

"Don't say that. What's up?"

"I just came up with the perfect solution to Crista's problem. I don't know *why* it didn't occur to me sooner!"

"I'm listening …"

Rosemary wasn't kidding. It really was the perfect solution. I just hoped to God Crista would go for it. Everything hinged on how Crista's performance went at The Creel Foundation. If Rosemary, Susie, and Luke were right, Crista would get her first taste of what it was like to perform in front of an audience, then spend the rest of her life pursuing that high. No matter what happened in her career, I knew she'd be happy to spend her life in the theater, whether she made it all the way to Broadway or not.

The day of the big show finally arrived. On shaky legs, I made my way to my seat in the auditorium. Though I was sure Crista would do beautifully, I was still a nervous wreck. I remembered Johnny had said he'd thrown up before Rosemary's Broadway debut, and I understood exactly how he felt. I wished Rosemary was here. She had a way of keeping me calm. She was in the show, so at least she was backstage with Crista, probably keeping *her* calm.

"She's gonna be fine, Keith," Elyse reassured me in a calming voice. "Believe me, I know what you're going through."

"Yeah, I guess you do," I said with a nod. "Crista's wanted to do this for so long. I just hope it goes well."

"It will. Wait 'til you see her after the show when she's got that performance glow," Elyse said with a smile. "I love when Luke looks like that. Theater is where he belongs, and it's such a joy to watch him in his element. Crista did wonderfully when she did her solo show here for us, and believe me, performers really feed off the energy of the crowd. She's gonna have the time of her life up there. You'll see."

"Thank you," I said. Maybe having Elyse by my side was even better than having Rosemary here, because she understood what it felt like to be on this side of the stage.

My nerves calmed a bit, until the overture started, then I began to wring my hands. If I was this nervous watching the show, I wondered how Crista must be feeling.

Please, please, please let this go well.

*****

Waiting backstage to go on was terrifying, much more so than I had imagined. Everything up to this point—practicing at home, going to voice lessons, performing in front of my friends—seemed like playing make-believe until it suddenly turned into reality. There was a real live audience out there. A packed house waiting to see this show, and I was the star. For one panicked moment I didn't think I could do it.

Then it was time to make my first entrance onstage. I drew in a deep, cleansing breath. I had survived Morable the Horrible. I'd spent weeks preparing for this show. No. I'd been preparing for this moment my entire life.

Hell yes, I can do this.

I stepped out on the stage and began to sing. It was jarring to see all those people in the seats, but knowing Keith was out there helped. He was probably more nervous than I was.

The first part was relatively easy. In the Prologue, I only had to sing a few lines. It was a bit unnerving that I didn't get any applause when I was done, but it was a brief song: there really wasn't time.

Luke was up next, singing "Me, Who Am I?" to introduce himself as the prince. He got applause, as well he should, because he sounded fabulous. The prince in this show was a somewhat comic character, so Luke was the perfect choice. I knew all the little girls in the audience would fall in love with him by the end of the show.

Next, I got to sing my favorite song, "In My Own Little Corner." As soon as I began singing, I was transported. Sweeping across the stage, I sang about my wildest dreams, imagining I could be anything I desired. I got lost in my performance. I *was* Cinderella.

The only thing that snapped me out of my reverie was the wild applause when I finished my song. I kept my composure and remained Cinderella on the outside, but I was bursting with joy on the inside. I heard Johnny's familiar whistle of approval and Keith's shouts of "Brava!"

Keith was right. I *belonged* on the stage. This show was only the beginning of a lifelong love affair with the theater.

*****

"She's doing great, Keith," Elyse said happily.

"Goddamn right she is," I said proudly. This was the first time I had seen her in character for an extended time, and she made it so easy to believe she was Cinderella. Maybe I was blinded by my love for her, but I was sure the audience agreed with my assessment. Johnny had paid to have lots of inner-city children bused in to the theater, and the kids seemed mesmerized by the show. The adults seemed pleased as well, giving Crista lots of applause after every song.

Rosemary and Susie were hilarious as the wicked stepsisters. Both funny and cruel at the same time, the girls had the audience eating out of their hands. Johnny and David beamed with pride as they watched their women perform.

It was strange to say the least to watch Luke as Crista's prince onstage. They looked so much in love it was scary. I did my best to squelch my petty jealousy, but it was tough. There was Crista singing "Ten Minutes Ago"—the song we had danced to on our first date—to Luke instead of me.

Then came the time for Luke to kiss her. I tortured myself, wondering how many times they'd had to practice that in rehearsal. Suddenly, I was struck with the totally irrational yet very real feeling that Luke would take Crista away from me the way he had taken Elyse.

I felt an arm wrap around my shoulder, and Elyse gave me a quick squeeze.

"I know it's weird," she whispered softly, and I realized this wasn't easy for her to watch, either. "It never stops being weird. But the truth is she loves you and he loves me, and they're just two damn fine actors."

"I know," I said, feeling a lot better. It was nice to have Elyse to empathize with.

"The first time I met Susie, she was making out with Luke onstage."

"Oh shit."

Elyse giggled and nodded. It was a good thing Elyse and Crista were such good friends. I liked the idea of having Elyse in the audience with me whenever Crista was onstage. She understood the unique stresses of loving an actor.

As I watched the rest of the show, I knew in my heart that Crista and Luke were no more in love than Rosemary and Susie were bitchy women in real life. They were acting, and that was all there was to it.

At the end, I watched Luke propose marriage to my future wife. It was still unsettling to watch, but my pride in Crista's performance far superseded my petty insecurities. She *crushed* it tonight.

We all stood and roared our approval when the performers came out to take their final bows. One of the stagehands gave Crista a bouquet of flowers, and I had never seen her look happier. Watching the woman I loved fulfill her lifelong dream was the most beautiful moment I'd ever experienced.

I wiped tears from my eyes as Crista reveled in the moment she'd spent a lifetime working toward. Johnny reached behind Elyse and clapped me on the back. He laughed as he watched me get all emotional.

"I get it, man. Believe me. I cried like a baby when Rosemary got the part on Broadway," he admitted.

It was a little embarrassing to be caught crying. It was so unlike me. But then again, Crista always brought out the emotional side in me.

Crista's debut performance had been a smashing success. Now was the time to see if Crista would go for Rosemary's ingenious solution to her schooling dilemma.

*****

Keith rushed up to me the moment I stepped down from the stage. He didn't have to tell me how proud he was. I could see it in his eyes. Rosemary took my bouquet of roses from me so I could embrace him.

He hugged me so hard he lifted me off my feet. When he set me back down, I noticed his eyes were red.

"Have you been crying?" I teased.

"Yeah, maybe. What can I say? Your performance was so beautiful, it brought me to tears." He tenderly pushed the hair out of my face. "Was it everything you hoped it would be?"

"Yes!" I cried out, finally able to release the pent-up exuberance I'd had to hide while in character. "Everything I wanted and more!"

"That's wonderful," Keith said happily. "Rosemary, you're up."

"What?" I asked.

"Crista, you did an amazing job up there. I couldn't be more proud of you," Rosemary told me. She set my roses down on the stage and hugged me warmly. When she let go, she said, "You really know for sure this is what you want to do for the rest of your life, don't you?"

"Yes!" I said, feeling more alive than I ever had before. "Yes. This is my purpose. What I'm meant to do."

"I know," Keith said softly, gazing at me lovingly with those impossible-to-resist blue eyes.

"Then you really need to continue with your theater education," Rosemary said. "Now, I know you're not comfortable taking Keith's money ..."

My heart sank. No, I still wasn't comfortable with having Keith pay my way. I wished with all my heart that I felt differently.

"I have a proposition for you," Rosemary said, and I heard Keith draw in a breath. "As you know, Johnny's family is very wealthy."

"But I don't want—"

"Hush!" Rosemary said, putting a finger against my lips. "Girl, you're gonna listen to what I have to say!"

My eyes grew wide and I nodded. Keith laughed. Rosemary dropped her finger from my mouth.

"My future father-in-law, Walter Creel, is insanely wealthy. I don't even know how much money he donated to NYU when I graduated, but it was a hell of a lot. If you'll just let him pull a few strings, he can easily get you a job at NYU. A good job. There's nothing wrong with being on the maintenance crew, but you don't have to clean anymore if you don't want to. You're so smart, Crista. Plus, you're bilingual. There are tons of great jobs you can do if you only accept a little help in using my connections to get one."

Keith walked over and stood next to Rosemary, presenting a united front with her.

"So, you could have a good job with pretty good pay," Rosemary continued. "And, since it's NYU, they have—"

I gasped, suddenly understanding what she was saying. "Tuition remission!"

"Yes," she said with a smile. "If you work at the college, you get to attend for free. So, *you* would be the one working a full-time job and *you* would be the one putting yourself through college. But first, you have to accept a little help in getting the job to begin with. Can you do that?"

Keith and Rosemary stood there, waiting for my answer.

"Nobody makes it completely on their own, Crista. Everybody needs a leg up somehow. And when you're well established and you're high up on the theater ladder, I know you'll reach down and pull up the ones underneath you. Right now, you need just the tiniest bit of help to get started. Will you let Walter Creel get you a job so you can go to college?"

I covered my mouth as my eyes filled with tears. Finally, I whispered, "Yes."

"Yes!" Keith shouted, punching the air triumphantly. It occurred to me that Rosemary must have discussed her idea with him earlier, and that he'd been in on this all along. As always, Keith never gave up on me.

"Oh, Rosemary, thank you so much!" I cried, flinging my arms around her. "Forget wicked stepsister. You're like my fairy godmother, you know that?"

Rosemary laughed and hugged me. My tears kept flowing.

"Stop it!" Rosemary said, wiping my face as her own tears began to spill. Dear, sweet, heart-of-gold Rosemary.

I turned to Keith. "And you," I said, putting my arms around him and kissing him. "I never, ever would have been able to pursue my dreams without your love and support."

Keith kissed me and held me in his arms for a few moments.

"I'm so happy for you, Crista. Even if I don't get the privilege of paying for your education, I'm just glad you're going to college."

"You have an important job to do, too, Keith," Rosemary said softly. "It's your job to provide encouragement and be by her side through it all. To support her. Love her. Be there when her heart is broken, and when she doubts she has what it takes to make it in this business. Believe in her on those days when she stops believing in herself. Will you do that?"

"I will," Keith said as solemnly as if he were taking a marriage vow.

"I know you will," Rosemary said, wiping another tear. She grabbed Keith and hugged him, and he chuckled and returned her hug.

"Thanks for being such a great friend to her," Keith said. "And to me."

Keith gazed at me and smiled.

I was going to NYU to get a theater degree. I had wonderful, loyal friends. Keith Foster loved me.

Talk about a fairy tale ending.

Chapter 28

"I'm gonna miss you around here," Elyse said, hugging me as I stood in the hallway on my last day on the job.

"I know. I'm gonna miss all of you," I said, looking at all the friends who had gathered around to wish me well. Luke was there, as were Roger and Manny and several others.

"Good luck with everything, girl," Roger said. "I can't wait to see you onstage."

"It's only fair," I murmured in his ear as he hugged me goodbye. "After all, I've seen you onstage."

Roger cackled and punched me lightly in the shoulder. I hugged Manny, as well as several other women who worked on the cleaning crew.

"Do the honors," Elyse said, pointing at the elevator button. "One last time."

I smiled as I pressed the elevator button. I'd been a cleaning woman for so long, it was hard to imagine doing anything else, but I was certainly looking forward to the challenge. The elevator dinged, and the doors slid open.

And there was Keith in the elevator car, down on one knee, holding an open ring box.

"Oh my God!" I cried out, and I heard laughter and murmurs of excitement from all my co-workers, who had clearly all been in on this little surprise.

"Crista," Keith said on bended knee. "If getting back into this elevator doesn't prove how much I love you, nothing will. Will you marry me?"

He held up the box, which contained a beautiful, shiny diamond engagement ring.

I'd always known I would marry Keith, but I didn't think it would be this soon. The truth was, I would marry him today if he wanted.

"Yes!" I cried. "Now get out of there."

I reached out my hand to him. Keith stood and pulled the ring from its velvet casing, handing the empty box to Elyse to hold for him. He slipped the ring onto my finger and pulled me in for a kiss. My co-workers all erupted into applause.

"Oh, Keith, you were so brave to get back into that elevator," I murmured in his ear.

"Well, I thought it was appropriate. After all, that's where I was when I first fell for you, my sweet princess."

He wrapped me in his strong arms and held me close.

"And they lived happily ever after," I whispered as he held me.

Keith had gotten it right from the very early days of our relationship.

I belonged on the stage. And I belonged with him.

*****

A few weeks after we got engaged, Keith came to pick me up at The Creel Foundation. Elyse had just shown up to pick up Luke, and we all decided to go out to dinner together.

Luke's off-Broadway show, *Pirated,* had been on hiatus for a bit while they worked on some rewrites, so Luke had come back to teach a few classes at the foundation.

"He's not in the classroom," Elyse told me as she and Keith and I walked together down the hall.

"He's probably in the main auditorium," I told her. "You know him. He usually tries to squeeze in a little stage time after class."

"You're probably right."

We walked to the auditorium and Elyse quietly opened the door. Our friends and family members were always respectful of our theater space and did their best not to disturb us if we were in the middle of working on a scene or something.

Luke was there all right. He was sitting in the middle of the stage, head in his hands. He was very still.

"What's wrong with him?" I asked, feeling alarmed.

"I don't know," Elyse said, looking worried. "I better go check."

Keith and I exchanged worried glances as Elyse approached the stage.

"Luke?" she called out. Luke looked up and saw Elyse. Slowly, he got to his feet. She went over to him, and Luke said something to her. Standing in the back of the auditorium, we couldn't hear what he said.

Keith slipped his arm around my waist as we watched and waited. Elyse wrapped her arms around Luke as they held each other for a moment. I was afraid that perhaps someone close to Luke had died or something.

Oh, Luke. Whatever it is, we're all here for you.

Elyse let go of Luke and took a small step back.

Standing in the middle of the stage, Luke threw open his arms and shouted, *"I'm going to Broadway!!"*

Beloved Reader,

I hope you enjoyed seeing Keith get his well-deserved happy ending, as well as seeing Crista get her second chance in love and in her career.

This brings us to the final chapter of the Wall Street to Broadway Series. The fifth book will bring you the star-studded, celebrity wedding of Johnny Creel and his beautiful bride, Rosemary Sutton. You'll also see Luke achieve his life-long dream of performing on Broadway. Luke's not the only one performing in *Pirated*; another familiar face you've come to know and love also gets a starring role in the Broadway show.

Also joining the cast is world-famous movie star Therese Andrews. Stage Manager Roman Pinza can hardly believe the news when he hears Therese has joined the show. He's adored her for over a decade, the image of her sexy movie poster burned into his memory from his teen years.

Roman's so nervous around her that he can barely speak. Soon, he finds himself falling in love with the real woman instead of his teen fantasy version.

Therese is weary of being used by men who are in lust with her movie characters. Can Roman convince her that he loves Tessa, the woman, rather that Therese, the movie star?

I hope you'll join me for the final performance in the Wall Street to Broadway series.

TIRED OF JOINING AUTHOR EMAIL LISTS?

Ugh. Email overload. I hear ya.

I'd LOVE to have you on my email list (join at http://lindafausnet.com/)!! Even so, I understand if you've already got too much in your inbox.

To stay updated on my latest releases without being on my email list, here are some alternatives:

Click the FOLLOW button under my author bio in Amazon

FOLLOW me on Bookbub

Join my Author Reader's Group on Facebook
https://www.facebook.com/groups/1231597956891811

ARE YOU ADDICTED TO ROMANCE NOVELS?

Join Romance Novel Addicts Anonymous (RNAA) on Facebook, Twitter, Instagram, and/or Pinterest and feed your addiction…

RNAA is a fun, judgment-free fan club for all things romance. Hope to see you there!

www.ingramcontent.com/pod-product-compliance
Lightning Source LLC
Chambersburg PA
CBHW050508190726
48284CB00003B/728